EXIT
STRATEGY

EXIT
STRATEGY

JEN J. DANNA

KENSINGTON BOOKS
www.kensingtonbooks.com

KENSINGTON BOOKS are published by

Kensington Publishing Corp.
119 West 40th Street
New York, NY 10018

All Kensington titles, imprints and distributed lines are available at special quantity discounts for bulk purchases for sales promotion, premiums, fund-raising, educational or institutional use. Special book excerpts or customized printings can also be created to fit specific needs. For details, write or phone the office of the Kensington Special Sales Manager: Kensington Publishing Corp., 119 West 40th Street, New York, NY 10018. Attn. Special Sales Department. Phone: 1-800-221-2647.

Kensington and the K logo Reg. U.S. Pat. & TM Off.

Library of Congress Control Number: 2020931333

ISBN-13: 978-1-4967-2788-6
ISBN-10: 1-4967-2788-6
First Kensington Hardcover Edition: August 2020

ISBN-13: 978-1-4967-2790-9 (e-book)
ISBN-10: 1-4967-2790-8 (e-book)

10 9 8 7 6 5 4 3 2 1

Printed in the United States of America

For Rick
For years you've put up with my crazy schedule, my
tendency to discuss plot at any moment, and all the time
I spend hunched over my laptop, ignoring everything around me.
Your support and patience with my quest to "go big or go home"
has been unending.
This one's for you . . .

CHAPTER 1

"*H*ow's your mom?"

"I swear she's worse almost every time I see her."

Gemma Capello studied her best friend with concern. She loved Frankie like a sister, and watching her mother's illness eat away at her tore Gemma apart. "Did she know you?"

"She doesn't know any of us anymore. She held on to Dad the longest—now he's a stranger too. It's killing him. It's killing all of us, but mostly him."

Gemma reached across the restaurant table to squeeze Frankie's hand. "He's a good man and they've been married for nearly forty years. His life as he knew it is over. It was already changing while she was in the house, but now she's in hospice. . . ."

"He's mourning her while she's still alive because the inevitable is coming. He can't stand to rattle around the apartment alone, so if he's not with her at the hospice, he's in the bakery working himself into the ground. I get tired just watching him."

"And I get tired just watching *you*. Like father, like daughter."

"I'm hardly doing that mu—"

"Francesca Russo, don't give me that. Every time I've been in the bakery lately, it's the two of you, shoulder to shoulder. You work just as many hours as he does, possibly more. You let him slip away to visit your mom knowing the bakery's in good hands. You *are* doing that much. Now, tell me about your latest visit with her, so I'm up to speed when I stop by this week."

"She's slipping downhill. I think back to the days a few months ago when she was aggressive with the nurses because she was scared when she didn't recognize people and places. Then she had life. Now she's . . . not there."

"Alzheimer's is always hardest on loved ones. At this point, she's probably unaware of her decline. Maybe that's a blessing."

"We've brought stuff in for her—her favorite perfume and blanket, a portable CD player and stacks of CDs, photos of the family—so her room feels like home." Frankie's voice caught on the last word. Bracing her elbows on the table and weaving her fingers together, she dropped her forehead onto her knuckles, her long blond hair falling forward to shade her face.

Gemma gave Frankie a moment to gather herself. Friends for as long as she could remember, they'd grown up together in the Little Italy neighborhood of Lower Manhattan, running in and out of each other's kitchens on weekends with a familiarity that spoke of kinship. Both taking after their mothers, Gemma's Sicilian brown eyes, olive complexion, and curly hair so unruly it never looked the same two days running complemented Frankie's classic northern Italian fair skin, blue eyes, and blond waves. But sisters didn't have to look alike to be two parts of a whole. They didn't even need to belong to the same bloodline.

Frankie tipped her face up. "I'm such a killjoy. This is supposed to be a fun Saturday night out on the town at a swanky restaurant, and here I am bringing down the mood."

"You're not bringing down the mood. And I want to know everything. She's my mother too, you know."

Frankie's mouth tightened, and she blinked furiously. "She always loved you like a daughter. Especially after . . ." Frankie pulled in a deep breath and shakily released it. Then she forced a laugh, brushing away moisture from the corner of her eye. "Okay, no more sadness. We're going to have fun tonight, eat too much, splurge on dessert, and maybe even get a little tipsy."

Gemma grinned at her. "That sounds perfect."

Frankie picked up her menu, opened it with a flourish, and studied it intently.

Gemma opened her own menu and quickly decided on her meal. She let her gaze idly scan the tables around them. She loved the Fireball's rooftop patio—original to the 1919 landmark building. An arcade of paired Corinthian columns and brick arches surrounded it, opening the seating area to the sky as the towers of the city rose around them in glowing spears. The walls and pediments of original warm brick stood tall with fairy lights suspended between them, twinkling over the rows of tables below. The space between the heavy Corinthian columns was open, and only a short wrought iron fence topping a truncated brick wall separated diners from a lethal drop.

It had always amazed her that city inspectors allowed the design of the patio, but sometimes historical buildings found all the right loopholes in modern construction codes. To be honest, the open-air design was one of her favorite aspects of the restaurant's atmosphere. Seventeen stories down, the permeating noise of the city—from cars honking to the wail of sirens—was a muted echo of the street-level cacophony. High above it all, there was music piped through hidden speakers, the clink of glassware and dishes, the warm waft of summer's breeze, and the buzz of conversation. Perfect after a long week with even longer days on the horizon.

With a contented sigh, Gemma took another sip of her wine and relaxed against the woven seat back.

A baby's unhappy whimper caught at her, the sound jarring in the light babble of the surrounding crowd.

Near the entrance, a young woman stood with a tiny baby wrapped in a sling against her chest.

Tired. Pale. Dull eyes.

She remembered Rachel, her sister-in-law, in those first weeks following Nate's birth. No sleep, breast-feeding struggles, jaundice, and touches of postpartum depression. Even with the support of her family around her, she'd been a wreck.

This woman looked worse.

What is she doing in a late-night hot spot with a newborn?

Frankie closed her menu with a snap. "That was tough. Too many great choices, but I think I've decided. What about you?"

The woman started to weave through the tables.

Something is very wrong.

Her eyes stared almost sightlessly ahead.

Not just dull. Hopeless.

Instincts honed during fourteen years in the NYPD, with the last two in hostage negotiation, snapped the puzzle pieces into place, and Gemma's gaze swung to follow the woman's trajectory. She stood abruptly, her chair jerking back with a screech of legs scraping across the floor.

"Gem? Gem, what's wrong?" Her hands braced on the tabletop, Frankie half rose out of her chair in alarm.

Gemma didn't take her eyes off the young woman. "Call 911."

"What? Why?"

"Tell them there's a murder-suicide attempt in progress." Gemma's voice was absolutely controlled. "Tell them a detective is on scene, but needs assistance." She didn't wait for Frankie to respond, but moved, pushing between the tables, trying to catch the woman who was still easily twenty-five feet away.

And only ten feet from one of the gaping archways. The brick base of the opening was three feet tall, but had a bench seat running along its length. The low wrought iron fence capping the brick was perhaps only eighteen inches high.

Step onto the bench seat, onto the bricks, over the fence. And fly.

"Ma'am? Ma'am, excuse me." Gemma's attempt to catch her attention was met with silence, so she raised her voice. "Ma'am. NYPD. I need you to stop."

It was like the woman was sleepwalking. She didn't pause; she didn't even slow down. She didn't turn to look. She had one goal, one intention.

The baby's whimpers morphed into a full cry.

The woman stepped up onto the bench seat, drawing the startled looks of diners around her and a few cries of "Hey! What are you doing?" Then she climbed over both brick and iron to stand on the small ledge on the far side, the warm summer breeze blowing the ragged skeins of hair that escaped her ponytail around her face.

A man at the table directly behind her twisted around and clamped his hands around the young woman's ankle. She immediately struggled with him, pitching from side to side as she tried to break free.

"No, *stop!*" Gemma had her badge out of her pocket, extended to show her detective shield as she sprinted between the tables. "Sir, let her go!"

The man jerked back and the woman wrapped her hands around the pillar at her back. The baby let out a full-throated wail, its face turning beet red. A tiny fist pumped its way out of the sling.

The woman made no move to comfort her child, but stared straight ahead, as if scared to look down.

Seventeen stories. I'd be scared too.

But the woman's white-knuckled stranglehold on the pillar hinted at indecision.

Gemma still had a chance.

"Dannazione." The Italian curse slid out under Gemma's breath. No help for it. She had to get up there. Not out on the ledge, but up closer to her. Close enough to make eye contact.

She jammed her shield in her pocket as she met the startled gaze of the man who had tried to stop the young mother. "Give me your hand."

He reflexively held it out.

She slapped her right hand into his and clamped down with a death grip. "Do *not* let go under any circumstances. Get help if need be. There's no time to bring in a safety harness." She braced one foot on the bench beside his hip as understanding dawned in his eyes. He gave a single sharp nod and gripped her hand tighter. On the far side, a woman grasped his arm as if to add her own weight as ballast.

Gemma stepped up onto the bench seat and then up another level to balance on the bricks just inside the wrought iron fence.

Only mere feet higher, the wind was stronger, blowing her hair into a mad tangle about her face. She didn't spare a glance for the deadly drop below, but turned to the desperate woman just out of reach. "Ma'am, I'm Detective Capello of the NYPD. Please don't go any farther."

Tired blue eyes flicked in her direction before moving away.

The baby continued to wail, the screams rising to an eardrum-vibrating pitch.

Gemma raised her voice to be heard clearly while still keeping her tone calm and soothing. "Ma'am, I'd like to talk to you. To help you. But we can't do it here. Please give me your hand and let's step down. Any problem you're having, we can work it out."

"There's no point."

The successful tactics of crisis negotiation were so ingrained, repeating the question to reinforce to the woman that she was being heard was an instantaneous response. " 'There's no point'? Why do you think that?"

For the first time, the woman looked down. Gemma followed her gaze, down over vertical lines of windows, and what felt like miles of brick, concrete, and steel, to the dimness of light and sound below.

She was running out of time to make a connection. Normally, the longer a negotiation went, the more time was on the side of the negotiating team. But that didn't count when you were balanced on a ledge only a handful of inches wide above a seventeen-story death drop. She had only minutes, at most. "Ma'am, let's start with your name. Can you tell me that?"

"Joanna."

"Joanna, I can see you're at the end of your rope, but what you're doing is very dangerous. For you and your baby." Out of sight, Gemma gripped the man's hand harder and felt the answering hold in response. Her lieutenant would have her head for taking such a chance, but there was no time and no other way to get the woman back inside. Taking a deep breath, she extended her free hand. "I can help you, or I can find someone who can. Take my hand. Come back in, talk to me about what's upset you."

"What's upset me?" Joanna's head whipped toward Gemma, even that small, isolated movement causing her to wobble slightly on the ledge.

But the life in her eyes gave Gemma hope. Joanna had just opened the door to a conversation that could save two lives. "Tell me about it." When the woman's lips folded into a tight white line, Gemma pushed on. "I'm a great listener. I might even know a little bit about what you're feeling."

"You have children?"

"No, but I'm an aunt several times over, and I've watched my sisters-in-law with their newborns. Those are tough days. I know you must be feeling stretched to the breaking point. How old is your baby?"

"Four weeks tomorrow." She took one hand off the pillar and slapped it over her ear. "And she won't stop screaming. I need her to stop screaming. I can't do anything to help her."

Gemma eyed the infant, trying to evaluate if there was any way to free her from the sling. *Wrapped too tight.* "That must be very distressing for you. You must feel useless, but it's not your fault."

"I'm her mother. If I can't help her, who can? Her father works shifts and can't be home all the time. I. Just. Need. To. Make. It. *Stop.*"

Her expression never changed, but Gemma's heart rate spiked at the slightly hysterical edge in Joanna's tone. This wasn't working. *Time to try a different tack.* "Haven't you thought about life with her? Watching her first steps? Dropping her off at her first day of kindergarten? Helping her find her feet in life with your guidance? A daughter needs her mother for that."

A scene streaked through her mind at her own words: *Huddled bodies, terrified eyes, screaming, a gunshot. Feeling utterly alone in the middle of the chaos.*

She pushed it away. *Focus.*

As if hearing Gemma's words, the infant's wail dissolved into a weak whimper punctuated by squeaky, gasping hiccups.

Joanna's hand dropped from her ear to reach behind her and scrabble for the pillar.

Gemma reached out farther, leaning far enough over the wrought iron railing to make her mouth go desert dry. "You feel alone and overwhelmed. Like nothing you do is right, and you're going to mess her up. Like some days you can hardly get out of bed. But this isn't the way. Don't you love your daughter?"

Joanna's eyes slid closed and a single tear broke from her lashes to trail down her pale cheek.

"Help me save her life. You brought her into this world, now keep her safe in it. You're not alone. There are many people who want to help you. Who *will* help you. You just have to reach out your hand. Trust me, Joanna. You both have so much to live for."

Joanna took a shaky breath and opened her eyes. Then she reached out with her left hand.

Gemma caught it in hers, feeling the tremor that wracked it.

How lost would you have to be to not only feel the need to take your own life, but that of your child as well?

Gemma prayed she'd never experience it.

"That's it, step slowly to your left. Slow. Careful. That's it. Just about there."

When Joanna stepped up to the railing, hands appeared from all around, closing over arms and clothing, coaxing her over the railing, and the two women in and back down to safety.

The young mother's knees buckled and Gemma went down to the floor with her, wrapping her arms around both woman and child as Joanna broke into sobs.

Gemma rubbed a hand up and down her back soothingly. "It's going to be all right. You're going to make it."

A hand squeezed her shoulder and Gemma looked up to find Frankie standing behind her.

"You're amazing," Frankie said, grinning. "My mother would be so proud of you."

The laugh that bubbled up was part joy, part overflowing nervous energy. Now that she was down and safe, Gemma shivered with a delayed adrenaline reaction.

The baby between them made a small noise and Gemma pulled back far enough to run a hand over the warm, downy head.

Two lives saved and a family brought back from the brink of devastation.

Not bad for a Saturday night out on the town.

CHAPTER 2

*G*emma crowded the last golden ball into the layer of tomato sauce pooled on the platter. "Rachel, the *arancini* is ready," she said, turning to face her sister-in-law. "Can you carry it out?"

The slender blonde shifted to reveal the baby balanced on her hip. His toothless gums gnawed at the tiny hand jammed into his mouth as a long line of drool slid slowly down his chin. "I would, but I'd need two hands for it, and . . ." Rachel indicated the teething baby with a cocked head and raised eyebrow.

"I thought Teo was taking him outside."

"He was going to, but then Dad grabbed him to help set up the tables."

"Well, I'll swap you this"—Gemma tapped the edge of a large white platter loaded with deep-fried risotto balls—"for him, if you can send the boys back in to help carry everything out. You can nail them with the mom eye and they'll do your bidding."

"I think you're overestimating the power of the mom eye. Plus, you'll get soaked."

"I'll love every minute of it. Hand him over. Come on, Nate, my man. You can be my plus one at lunch." She accepted the baby from Rachel and settled him on her hip. "Now go. I'm not over-estimating your power. The men will be back in here inside of three minutes, you just watch."

Gemma's only overestimation was in how long it would take to corral the men back inside. In under two minutes, the kitchen was filled with three rowdy brothers jockeying for who got to take which favorite family dish outside. Just as Gemma was about to pull out a whip and a chair, her fourth brother, Alessandro—Alex—her closest sibling in both age and personality, arrived.

"Hey, look who's here!" Joe called out as Alex stepped into the room. "Find any pizza in the subway today?"

Alex sent him a slitted, sideways glare and flipped him the bird.

Gemma rolled her eyes hard enough she could have cataloged the spice rack behind her. Three of the four men were NYPD cops; the third brother, Matteo, broke with family tradition to join the FDNY. The cops in the family, especially Joe, the eldest, could be merciless to their youngest sibling. Alex was a member of the Internal Affairs Bureau, or the Rat Squad, as New York's finest sneeringly labeled it. Thus, the pizza rat smear.

"Sei tutto idiota." All eyes swiveled to the sole woman in the room. She might be the only female sibling, but Gemma knew how to manage her brothers. "Enough with the rat gags." She laid one hand on the top of a covered cake stand. "Or I'm taking my *torta setteveli* and my cannoli home without you getting even a single taste." Gemma knew the power of desserts in this family, and her seven-layer, sky-high, chocolate-and-hazelnut seven-veils cake was legendary. No other leverage was needed.

Groans of dissent were followed by some good-natured grumbling, but they mostly laid off Alex and even helped him with the plates he carried. As they went out the door, she heard Teo ragging on his little brother that Alex's Hawaiian shirt—jet black with green palm trees and brilliant red-and-blue parrots in flight—was louder than their father's favorite plaid golf pants.

They're such children. They can pick on their little brother, but God help anyone else who does.

She organized the men and got the food to the picnic tables set up outside. All the traditional Sicilian family favorites were there: *pasta alla Norma,* with fresh tomatoes and eggplant; *scaccia ragusana*—a rolled pizza filled with various toppings; stuffed artichokes; stuffed swordfish rolls; the fried risotto balls; and Gemma's father's favorite, *parmigiana di melanzane*—eggplant parmigiana. And, of course, overflowing baskets of fresh Italian breads.

Cradling a loaded platter of antipasto in her free arm, Gemma stepped from the coolness of the house into the blazing sunshine of her father's narrow, grassy backyard. It was bedlam around tables loaded with food as Joe's two boys—holy smokes, had they both grown two inches since she's seen them last?—chased their grandfather's dog in circles, and as the men relaxed with beers in hands, or tossed a Frisbee to Mark's daughters. Already seated at the head of the table, her father directed Rachel to rearrange certain plates, and for Joe to get his kids to the table before he ate it all without them.

With thumb and pinkie tucked between his lips, Joe gave a piercing whistle that immediately brought his boys bolting for the table, and the girls wandering over at a more sedate pace with their father and Uncle Teo. Rachel relieved Gemma of the antipasto platter so both of her hands were free to settle her nephew into his high chair. After calling their sister-in-law Alyssa over, she and Rachel sat on either side of the wide-eyed baby, leaving the rowdier men and older children clustered together.

Everyone took their seats around the sprawling tables and started passing platters, which gave Gemma a few moments to sit back and soak in the pandemonium, grateful for the opportunity to spend time with her crazy, raucous, headstrong, loving family.

It had been a family tradition for years. As first responders, everyone's schedule was constantly unpredictable. And even with seniority, it was often hard to secure popular American holidays for family get-togethers. So they'd started celebrating August 15, the Sicilian Feast of the Assumption, as a chiseled-in-stone day when they would get together for a midday meal at the Capello homestead in Brooklyn, even when it fell on a weekday, as it did that year. This meant it wasn't a fight for vacation days for those who were scheduled for duty that day. They were lapsed Catholics since the death of Gemma's mother, but *Ferragosto* celebrations were a tradition all the way back to their roots in Siculiana, in the shadow of Mount Etna in Sicily.

Whatever the reason, it worked for them, giving them a day to connect and strengthen roots.

Gemma glanced down at the baby beside her. With the next generation filling out the ranks, that was more important than ever.

Alex nudged her other side and she looked up to find him offering her the platter of swordfish. She grinned at him and helped herself.

"So, Gemma Elena . . ."

Gemma looked down the table to her eldest brother, seated beside their father. "So, Giuseppe Pietro . . ."

"A little birdie tells me you had an interesting night on Saturday. A little off-duty work."

Their father looked up sharply from his plate, his gaze rapidly surveying his daughter before his shoulders relaxed fractionally.

"I may have." Teo held up one of his bottles of homemade red wine and she gave him a nod. "Absolutely. No reason not to enjoy when we're off duty."

"My thoughts exactly." Teo flashed her a saucy grin and filled her wineglass nearly to the brim.

"I said 'enjoy,' not 'get hammered.' " But she picked up her glass, and tapped it carefully first to Rachel's and then Alyssa's before drinking deeply.

"I hear you were seventeen stories up and balanced on a ledge overlooking the street without any safety gear," Joe continued.

"I was never on the ledge."

"I notice you're not denying the lack of safety gear," her father said. "Why am I only hearing about this now?" After forty years on the force, and as the Chief of Special Operations, Tony Capello made a point of staying up to date with his children's careers.

"Because it's not a big deal."

"Apparently, someone thinks it *is* a big deal and wants to put your name up for a commendation." Joe met her eyes from the far end of the table. "I heard the story. You spotted the woman holding her newborn baby before she was even in harm's way. But you couldn't physically get to her in time, so you had to talk her off the ledge. Literally. And at potential risk to yourself. She could have gone over and taken you with her."

"There wasn't any other way to handle it. There were only seconds to get her back."

Joe nodded. "I know." He raised his wineglass to her. "Well done."

She saluted him with her own glass. "Thanks." She met her father's gaze and held it. Then he gave her an approving smile, and she grinned back at him as he turned to Joe to inquire about a current gang squad case.

Alyssa leaned in across the table, her brown eyes wide. "You went out on a ledge to keep a new mother from jumping?" She kept her voice low, as if to spare the children from the story, even though they'd just heard it if they'd been paying attention.

"With her baby?" Rachel inched in closer around the high chair between them.

"I don't think I could have done it without having watched you two excellent mothers."

The sisters-in-law exchanged puzzled glances. "Us?" Rachel asked. "How did we help?"

"You were pretty fresh in my mind. Those first days and weeks with Nate? Alyssa, all those years ago with the Sam and Gabe? How tired and overwhelmed you both were."

Alyssa groaned and rolled her eyes skyward. "Oh yeah. Those were tough days."

"I took one look at her, so incredibly out of place and with a newborn, and knew that was part of the issue. I found out later she'd been suffering from postpartum depression. Her husband just thought she was a little blue, not in serious trouble."

"Men." Rachel cast a dark look toward the far end of the table. "Sometimes they're so clueless." She affectionately considered her infant son. "I need to teach you how to understand women better."

"If the husband didn't understand before, it must be absolutely clear at this point," Alyssa said. "He could have lost everything."

"Let me assure you, he has the full picture now," Gemma said.

"Officers responded and arrived shortly after I got her down, but I stayed with her. I didn't want to leave her until her husband arrived. He was beside himself when he got there."

"Angry?"

"Not at all. Stunned he'd missed the signs, clearly feeling guilty because of it, and ready to do whatever was needed to keep his family together. Then Children's Services showed up, because the responding officers called them."

"Of course, they did." Rachel reached out blindly to stroke a hand over her son's head. "Did they take the baby into custody?"

"I'm not sure. When I left, mom and baby were being taken to Bellevue—mom for a psych evaluation and hold, and baby for an examination to make sure she wasn't harmed in any way. After that, it's in ACS's hands, but the father's in the picture, so I'm hopeful he'll get to keep the baby under their supervision." Gemma took another sip of wine. "But enough about Saturday night. Alyssa, how are Gabe and his Little League team doing?"

The meal passed pleasantly as traditional favorites were enjoyed and the wine flowed freely. When dessert was brought out, there was as much hooting and cheering from the adults as from the children.

The excuse was a meal, but the real reason for the day was the brief oasis that allowed them to reconnect at their leisure after too many months of crazy lives, where phone calls and texts stood as their main forms of contact.

When the insistent peal of a phone ringing from the head of the table broke through the merriment, Tony scowled. The scowl deepened when he glanced at the number. "I told them not to call me today unless the president decided to make a surprise visit. If this isn't a major event, heads are going to roll."

Joe chuckled. "Which guarantees it's going to be a scheduling issue. Take your call. We'll be having seconds of cake. If you're lucky, we'll leave you some."

Gemma watched the exchange with amusement. "Joe, another piece of torta?" she offered loudly, and then laughed when her father jabbed an accusing finger at her as he rose while mouthing "troublemaker." He pressed the phone to his ear and turned his back to the table.

"You bet." Joe passed his plate down the table toward her. "Make it a big one."

Standing, she pulled the cake a little closer and picked up the knife. She was just sliding the knife through layers of chocolate when Mark's phone rang. She froze, her gaze flicking first to Mark and then to Joe. Together, they turned to look at their father.

Tony stood five feet from the table, turned away from his family, his back ramrod straight and his shoulders locked.

Alarm flickered over Gemma's nerve endings. *Something's wrong.*

She studied Mark, who rose to step back from the table. A patrol sergeant with the Fifth Precinct, Marco Capello was experienced, steadfast and capable, and commanded his men with high expectations, but also with compassion and understanding for how hard it was to be a patrol officer in New York City. If anything was going down in his precinct, he'd be looped in immediately.

She met Joe's gaze just as his phone rang. She could hear his mouthed expletive as clearly as if he'd spoken it aloud. Whatever was going on, it had a potential or confirmed gang connection if they were calling Joe.

"Gemma?" Alyssa asked the question from across the table as she stayed focused on her husband. "What's going on?"

Gemma set down the knife. No one was going to be eating cake now. "I don't know. Whatever it is, it's not good. Alex?"

"I'm in the dark, but I agree—something's hit the fan." Alex's gaze darted from brother to brother. "I can call in and find out."

Gemma shook her head. "No need. They'll let us know as soon as they're—"

Her phone rang. She lunged for it and answered the call. "Capello."

"I need you down at City Hall now."

There was no introduction, but she didn't need one to recognize the clipped voice of Lieutenant Tomás Garcia. "Sir, what happened?"

"Intel is sketchy, but we have a hostage situation."

"Do you have any details?"

"Almost nothing. Witness statements report multiple hostages and at least one high-capacity weapon."

Gemma looked at the three other cops around the table, who were all on their feet. "What aren't you telling me, sir?"

"He may have the goddamned mayor of New York City, Capello. And if he does, he's going to be the hostage most at risk of a bullet to the back of the head."

Gemma surged to her own feet and steadied herself with a hand clamped over Alex's shoulder. She met his eyes as her commander snapped out his final command.

"I'm handpicking the team, and I want you. Get down here now."

CHAPTER 3

*O*nce they got past the roadblocks, the streets of Lower Manhattan were eerily deserted.

"This is all wrong." Rachel leaned against the steering wheel, peering out at the deserted sidewalks of Centre Street and the surrounding empty roads. "I've never seen it like this, not even at three in the morning. There's always someone on the streets."

"They had to clear the area, including shutting down both the Brooklyn Bridge subway station and the bridge itself," Tony said from the passenger seat. "There was even a big sustainable energy sit-in already in progress on the front steps of City Hall, with a planned march across the Brooklyn Bridge to follow. Luckily, because it was a scheduled demonstration requiring a city permit, the NYPD had extra officers down here for crowd control, so they used those same officers to clear everyone out. Pull over," he said, pointing at the David N. Dinkins Municipal Building to their right. "We've all got our orders and can get where we need to be on foot from here. Teo will want you out of this area right away, so you need to turn around and head back to Brooklyn."

"I will."

Gemma, Tony, Joe, and Mark had all been called in as news of the hostage taking spread. While they all felt sober after their holiday lunch, none of them wanted to risk being behind the wheel. Rachel—who hadn't been drinking, as she was still breast-feeding Nate—had been roped into driving them into Lower Manhattan.

Once they made it over the Brooklyn Bridge, they'd been stopped by the cop redirecting traffic away from the Civic Center and down to FDR Drive. After a mass showing of badges, he'd stepped back to let them through, with the promise of Rachel's immediate return.

Rachel pulled over to the curb and they all climbed out. Gemma met Rachel's eyes in the rearview mirror and answered her mouthed "Be careful" with a nod. Mark slammed the door shut behind them and rapped his fist twice on the roof of the SUV, sending Rachel on her way. She swung around in a U-turn in the empty street, making her way back to the Brooklyn Bridge and over the East River.

Father, daughter, and sons took a moment together on the curb.

Tony made eye contact with each child in turn. "Be careful, every one of you. I know you're all supposed to be out of harm's way, but you know how these situations can turn on a dime. This one's going to be high profile, and we don't know what kind of splash the hostage taker plans to make. Stay alert and stay safe."

Gemma reached up and lightly kissed her father's cheek. "Same goes for you."

She gave his arm a squeeze, exchanged silent nods with her brothers, and jogged away from them down Centre Street, taking care to keep to the far side in the unlikely case the hostage taker was at a window on the near side of the building. She flashed her shield at the cop standing on Park Row at the top of Beekman Street and he waved her through. Only then did she consider herself far enough away from the building to cross the road to enter City Hall Park. As she jogged past the Jacob Wrey Mould Fountain in the middle of the park, she threw a quick glance to her right. City Hall was visible at the end of the path, three stories of graceful marble French Renaissance architecture, blindingly white in the afternoon sun. At its center, the figure of Justice stood atop the domed tower, holding her scales aloft to pierce the cloudless blue sky.

Somewhere inside, victims are in danger.

She remembered the frozen terror of staring down the barrel of a captor's gun, knowing her life could end instantly at his slightest whim.

Gemma ran faster.

She arrowed toward Broadway on the far side and the address Garcia had provided for their impromptu negotiation head-quarters. As she broke from the park, heading north, she spotted the location across the street. Only months before, it had been a Citibank branch on the corner of Broadway and Murray until the branch moved to bigger quarters; now the deserted space would be perfect for the negotiation team. Close enough to visualize the building, but far enough out of the way that if bullets flew, they'd be safe.

The golden rule in negotiating was that no negotiator ever died while on the phone with a suspect. That was the trick: physically remove yourself from danger to keep that immediate stress at bay, allowing you to maintain the deadly calm essential in every successful negotiator. Leave the bullets to the Apprehension Tactical Team.

Gemma knew the A-Team would already be on-site, and she scanned the tops of buildings as she sprinted across Broadway. She couldn't see anyone, but knew they'd already have their best long-distance sharpshooters in spots with a perfect line of sight on the building, and that positioning would change as they became surer of the hostage taker's location. There were likely even a few of them up the trees close to City Hall if they could find a position with line of sight through summer's dense leaf canopy.

She pushed through the door of the old branch office to find the kind of organized chaos that always occurred at the beginning of a situation. A map of Lower Manhattan was tacked up on the wall at a slight angle, which spoke of a rushed effort. A white board with multicolored scribbles was propped on a chair. Tables were covered with aerial shots of the building and the surrounding park and Civic Center, City Hall blueprints, a list that was likely a roster of departments in the building, and the beginnings of the briefing book—the negotiator's bible during any hostage situation. As the incident wore on, information about the hostage taker and his history, as well as details concerning the victims, would be added. She spotted Garcia's bulky form and salt-and-pepper hair as he bent over the book, pointing something out to a tall man with a military bearing, a high-and-tight haircut, and who was dressed in tactical gear, with his helmet tucked under his arm.

Gemma swallowed a groan. *Great. Sanders.*

The A-Team was high-stakes and high-stress 100 percent of the time, but she always felt this commander pumped it up an extra 10 percent. Sanders was a firm believer that "might makes right," and he was known to jump the gun when negotiations took longer than he'd like. While sometimes that was the right call, it didn't always lead to a positive outcome.

She understood the origin of some of Sanders's logic, even if she didn't always agree with it. Sanders wasn't just a mustache-twirling complication sent in to make their lives even more difficult. She'd heard the story from her father—a hostage situation early on in Sanders's career as a commander that had started as a domestic violence call between an estranged husband and wife, with their three young children caught in the middle. There'd been a handgun involved and the standoff had gone longer than Sanders wanted. He'd argued for going in to remove the children and had men ready to do so. But the primary hostage negotiator had convincingly argued for more time.

By the time Sanders finally followed his gut, overruled the negotiator, and had sent in his teams, the hostage taker and a baby, toddler, and preschooler were all dead. The wife had been shot and ended up surviving her wounds, but only as a shell of the woman she'd been. Sanders had reportedly raked the negotiator over the coals for pushing so hard to keep him and his teams out. But in the end, Sanders recognized the final decision had been his to make. And it was one he clearly never intended to miss again.

So now they'd not only be fighting the suspect and the clock, but possibly the man running the operation, if they couldn't convince Sanders to give them the time they'd need to effectively negotiate. In some ways, it was too bad the serial approach to hostage situations—talk first, then show your tactical abilities when you hit a wall—wasn't nearly as effective as the parallel approach—talk while making a visible tactical show—to get a hostage taker's attention and cooperation. It was always a fine line to walk: a large show of force could make a suspect insecure and desperate, while a small show of force could leave the suspect overconfident and unwilling to work with the negotiators.

Damned if you did, and damned if you didn't.

She spotted two more negotiators at the back of the large room and nodded in approval at Garcia's handpicked choices. Granted, with a high-profile situation like this, he could have any of the over one hundred Hostage Negotiation Team members at his beck and call, even if they were in the middle of their own incidents, which some, no doubt, were. The HNT dealt with hundreds of cases annually, which boiled down to more cases in a month than most NYPD divisions had in a year. With each major incident needing rotating rounds of four negotiators at a time over extended periods, that was a lot of manpower.

Gemma made a beeline toward the two men who stood in the doorway of what had once been the bank vault. The massive door was propped open against the back wall, and cords and cables ran from the main room into the vault. Inside the vault, Gemma caught a glimpse of a familiar setup of two back-to-back tables. One table was large enough for the primary negotiator and the team member acting as coach, someone who listened in and passed notes suggesting alternate courses of action. The second table provided space for all the recording equipment, another team member to act as scribe, noting every aspect of any communication for instant reference, and the last chair was for the coordinator. In this case, the coordinator was the senior negotiator, who not only functioned as the chief adviser with the most experience, but also as the officer who would run interference with any other departments, including the tactical team. And, most important, the coordinator would be the person standing between his negotiating team and the brass, allowing the team to stay focused on their situation, and not on the politics and pressure that might rise up around it.

A clock displaying the time in large, glowing red numbers was set up at the end of the tables where everyone could see it. That clock would rule their lives during negotiations. The hostage taker would want action and to cut the time short. Their job was to stretch out the situation as long as possible, hoping calmness, sanity, and exhaustion would play to their advantage. Several laptops for research or notes completed the setup.

"Hey," Gemma greeted the detectives as she approached. "What do we know?"

"Only minimal details so far."

Elijah Taylor towered above Gemma, as always, dressed to perfection in an impeccably tailored charcoal suit, with a snowy shirt and a burgundy tie that complemented his dark umber skin tone. Taylor was well known as a stickler for details, for his precise notes, and for his calm with a hostage taker when an incident was exploding around him. On the other hand, team members who weren't pulling their weight up to his expectations were easy targets for any simmering frustration with the situation Taylor couldn't show the suspect.

"We're gathering additional details. We need to establish a line of communication to the hostage taker. However, we don't know where he is in the building. We only have scanty witness reports to go on. The fire alarm was activated, emptying the building, but witnesses report seeing a man armed with an assault weapon with an unknown number of people on the first floor."

"We've tapped into the building's security feeds, but this guy is completely out of sight. The corridors are deserted." Fair-haired, freckled, and only about two-thirds Taylor's size in height and weight, Trevor McFarland wore an ill-fitting, smudge brown suit that hung on his bony frame. Gemma couldn't care less that he wasn't a fashion plate because McFarland was a whiz with technology. Communications would be smooth sailing with him on the team once they made contact with the suspect.

Gemma glanced down at her picnic attire—a gauzy, V-necked peasant blouse, white denim capris, and matching mesh summer sneakers—and felt extremely underdressed. But with Garcia's marching orders, there simply hadn't been time to detour home to change into her usual no-nonsense dark suit. She pushed the thought away; they had a job to do, and, at most, the hostage taker would only hear her voice. At least she had both her shield and her Glock 19 in a molded, black clip-on holster on her right hip under her blouse—luckily, her service weapon had been in the lockbox in her car when she was called in, so at least she had some of her normal on-duty trappings.

"It sounds like we're running on very little. The mayor's office is on the first floor. Do we think he has the mayor? And his staff? What about the first deputy mayor?" she asked.

"That's unclear." Taylor cocked his head in the direction of a group of people standing by the front window. "One of the witnesses reported the mayor was inside his offices, but according to his calendar, he was supposed to be off-site at a meeting. The larger issue is that no one can get hold of him. Until we know otherwise, we have to assume the mayor is inside City Hall and does not have access to his phone."

"There's been no communication? No request for money or resources?"

"None."

"Is the A-Team deployed? Do we at least have eyes on the building?"

"You bet," said McFarland. "Sanders is in contact with them. But unless something's popped in the last few minutes, they don't have line of sight on him yet."

Movement out of the corner of her eye drew Gemma's attention as Sanders strode away from Garcia and out the door. Turning left on the sidewalk, Sanders disappeared.

Garcia approached the group, carrying a stack of papers and files. "Communications all set up?"

"Yes, sir." McFarland glanced back into the vault. "Are they patching a call through?"

"No, nothing from inside the building yet. It's been too long with no word, so we're going to try to make contact. We don't have eyes on the situation, so we're going for ears. I've got a directory for the whole building, but we're going to start with the mayor's office, since that lines up with the location noted in the latest witness reports." As he spoke, Garcia headed for the vault. "We're going to do this a little differently than usual. Normally, I'd put you on this call, Taylor, and I'd coordinate. But this one is too high profile, and no one has more field experience and institutional memory on past cases than I do, so I'm going to run it, at least to start. Taylor, you're scribe for now, but be ready to step in when needed." He handed the directory to McFarland. "McFarland, you're communications. Capello, you're coach on the call, no matter who is primary. We'll take turns liaising with the other divisions and keeping the chiefs at bay for whoever is on the call at the time. If Taylor and I switch off, McFarland, you're scribe and I'll coordinate. Now, let's find this bastard and get the mayor and any other hostages out of there."

They settled around the table, everyone taking up their respective posts. Garcia took the farthest chair at the back of the vault, strategically placing himself where he could see through the bank to the front door in case of new arrivals. Gemma sat to his right, with Taylor across the table and McFarland on the far corner, surrounded by equipment. McFarland handed Garcia a headset with a microphone, and then handed regular headsets to the rest of the team before putting on his own. Taylor pulled a yellow legal pad from the top of a short pile and selected a pen. Gemma did the same, so she could make her own notes about the call and suggestions for Garcia.

Garcia scanned his group. "Ready?"

"Yes, sir." Affirmation went around the circle.

"Good. Starting with the mayor's office. McFarland, put the call through."

The call rang through their headsets. Four rings. Five. Six. "You have reached the office of Kevin Rowland, Mayor of the City of New York—"

McFarland disconnected the call, but only lifted his fingers an inch off the buttons. Gemma could practically hear the slow count of ten ringing in his head.

Second attempt.

Wait.

Third attempt.

Wait.

Fourth.

Voices rose outside the vault, and a tall woman dressed in Emergency Services Unit black, with her dark hair pulled back severely, appeared in the doorway. The name tag over her right breast pocket read KALANI and the stripes on her sleeve marked her as a sergeant. "Sir, we have reports of shots fired in the building."

Garcia braced to rise out of his chair. "Without making contact?"

"They don't think he's shooting hostages. They're losing security feeds around the mayor's office on the first floor. Looks like he's taking out the cameras."

"Which confirms the hostage taker is armed, and also tells us he's a decent shot," Gemma said.

Taylor set his pen down on his legal pad. "And he must have a significant supply of ammunition at hand if he feels free to spend that much of it disabling cameras."

"It also confirms his approximate location," said McFarland.

"Only if he's the sole captor, and we don't know that yet." Garcia indicated the phone. "We know at least one suspect is there. Now we keep calling until we get him to answer the phone."

They called, again and again, for five minutes with no response.

"This guy's got nerves of steel," Garcia said. "Assuming they haven't pulled the cord out of the wall, most people would have already picked up the phone and screamed at me to shut it down. They'll be nervous and jumpy and the constant ringing would only make it worse."

"Tells us something about the person at the other end of the line," Gemma said. "That could work both for and against us—a suspect who won't snap and kill hostages because he's on edge, but he'd also be happy to wait for a very long time to get what he wants."

Garcia's smile was calculating. "We can be patient too. We have food, and power, and freedom. At some point, he's going to feel the walls closing in. Dial it again."

One ring.

Two.

"You're very persistent." The voice on the other end of the line was calm and steady.

A familiar frisson of satisfaction shot through Gemma. *Contact, finally. Now we have a chance to make progress.*

"This is Lieutenant Tomás Garcia of the NYPD Hostage Negotiation Team. Who am I speaking with?"

"Look at that. A negotiator who gets right to the point." He laughed. "I'm not going to make it that easy for you, Garcia."

Gemma closed her eyes, concentrating on the single sense that could give a hint of who they were dealing with. It was a male voice, older, and slightly world-weary. He had an accent she quickly pegged as hailing from the Bronx from its flattened *aw* sounds, sharp initial consonants, and dropped final *r*'s. From the well-structured sentences, she deduced he was educated. But, most strikingly, he was deadly calm. The voice didn't have a single waver or hesitation. She quickly jotted down her thoughts on the pad of paper.

"It's not about making it easy for me. It's about what you need. What can we do for you so you feel you can let your hostages go?"

"Oh, there are things I want. But not yet."

Gemma focused her attention past the voice and into the room. The space beyond was so quiet you could hear a pin drop. If he had the hostages with him, he had terrified them into silence, possibly by threat. The room itself sounded small and furnished—there was no echo of high ceilings or bare walls and floors.

"How about what can we do for the people with you?" Garcia continued. "How many are there? Do they need food? Medical attention?"

The laugh that came over the line sent a shiver down Gemma's spine. It was the sound of someone in complete control.

"Your fact-finding mission's a failure, Garcia. I'm not telling you anything about the hostages."

"There must be something you need. Something you want."

"Sure, you can do one thing for me. You can pass on a message to the mayor." The words were suddenly iced, the consonants biting like tiny daggers. "Tell him his first deputy mayor is going to die, and it's all his fault."

The line went dead.

CHAPTER 4

*T*he room erupted with everyone speaking at the same time.

"Goddamn it!"

"This guy's got balls of steel."

"He doesn't know where the mayor is."

"When Sanders hears about this, he'll be difficult to hold back."

As the noise level rose, and it was clear no one else was focusing on what Gemma saw as the salient point, she slapped her hand down onto the tabletop hard enough for the sound to reverberate through the small room. Falling silent, everyone stared at her.

"He doesn't know where the mayor is," she repeated. "He doesn't have him and clearly has no idea where he is or he'd deliver the message himself. So, where is Rowland?"

Garcia pushed his headset down to hang around his neck. "This is ridiculous. We're working with our hands tied. Capello is right. We need to find out where Rowland is. He didn't just evaporate. If he's not in there"—Garcia jabbed a thumb in the direction of City Hall—"then he's somewhere else. I don't care if it's a temp from the typing pool, *someone* has to know where the man running the city is."

"There aren't actually typing pools anymore, Lieutenant."

If looks could kill, McFarland would be lying on the floor in a dismembered pile from the irritation burning in Garcia's eyes. "Thanks for the tech lesson, McFarland. I actually already know that." He swiveled toward the open doorway. "Sergeant Kalani!"

Ten seconds later, Kalani stepped into the doorway. "Lieutenant?"

"Is there any news on Rowland's location?"

"No, sir."

"The perp doesn't have him. In fact, he doesn't know where he is, because he wanted us to pass on a threat to First Deputy Mayor Willan's life. We need to find Rowland and we need to get him in here. He may know this guy."

"Yes, sir."

"And have someone get me Sanders. Either on the phone or in person, but he needs to know about the threat to Charles Willan, and I can't go out and find him myself."

"Yes, sir." Kalani left the vault.

Garcia drew in a slow breath and then huffed it out. "Okay, we don't have much time, so let's regroup. Give me your first impressions."

"It was a short conversation, but he presents as older, so we're not dealing with someone who's twenty-five," Gemma said. "Fully structured, likely first-language sentences, spoken in a Bronx accent. And I don't think he's in the mayor's office, but in one of the side rooms. The space sounded too . . . small. And like there were no bare surfaces."

"Like a window?" McFarland asked. "None of the snipers can see him, so that would make sense if there's no window in the room. Totally internal."

"That type of planning, or at least that kind of strategic placement, is indicative in itself," Taylor said. "Perhaps we're looking at someone who is ex-military. Even with field experience."

"That's a good possibility," said Garcia. "What else?"

"He's one cool customer," said McFarland. "Steely nerves. Some suspects take hostages and are either scared by their own bravado or get high on the power. This guy is neither."

"On the surface, it appears as if he's playing a long game," added Taylor. "I've never experienced a hostage taker like this. Usually, there is something they want, or some revenge scheme they're enacting. This scenario reads more like cat and mouse."

"I think you're right that he's playing a long game." Gemma

looked down at her notes, considering the precious little they knew so far. "He's not young and he's well spoken. There's zero panic in his voice. I know we've hardly talked to him, and he's holding his cards close to his chest, but the one overriding characteristic he's putting out there is control. He has it, and he's not going to want to relinquish it. He dropped a bomb and hung up, just to make that point."

"And we have no idea how much longer we can negotiate with him," McFarland said. "He threatens to kill Willan, but doesn't apply pressure by laying out a timeline or specifying something he wants in exchange for Willan's life."

"He makes it sound like there isn't anything he wants." Gemma tapped her pen beside the single sentence she'd underlined on the notepad. " 'Tell him his first deputy mayor is going to die, and it's all his fault.' " She looked up from her notes. "There's no hesitation, no room for negotiation in that sentence. He's not asking for safe passage in exchange for Willan's life. He's planning to take it, end of discussion."

"But why?" McFarland's gaze was fixed on his screen as he hunched over his laptop, alternately typing and clicking. "I'm not seeing anything political that Willan or Rowland is involved in that might lead to this kind of deadly animosity."

"The same issue that incites motive in one man won't seem important to another. You may not be seeing it in the same light as the suspect."

"Could there be an upcoming issue or event?" Taylor suggested. "Something the suspect thinks he can stop?"

"Or influence," said Garcia. "Look for something Rowland is pushing that needs Willan's support. Maybe if Willan is out of the picture, some process or new law falls apart? It could point us to the hostage taker's ID."

Gemma continued to stare at the last part of the sentence she transcribed: *and it's all his fault.* "Maybe, but that's not playing for me. What if the more important aspect is their relationship?"

McFarland looked up. "You mean as mayor and his administrative right-hand man, the first deputy mayor?"

"No, I mean about their background. They've been friends

since high school. Were in the student union together and ran against each other for class president. Willan won that time around. But then they got into New York City politics and have been friendly rivals ever since." At Garcia's raised eyebrows, Gemma explained, "In the early days, they used to bump into my dad occasionally at his favorite pub, and they'd have a beer together. He's always had an interest in them, because he got to know them personally, not just as politicians. So threatening to take Willan out isn't just a threat to an employee—it's against a lifelong friend. That says personal revenge to me."

"If that's true," Garcia said, "then his reason for the threat is to torture the mayor and to milk his panic for as long as he can."

"The culmination of which could be an actual death." Taylor's gaze dropped to the clock. "In which case, we need to move faster before he crosses any lines."

"Unless we tell him we can't find the mayor." Gemma held up a hand when Garcia started to cut her off. "Hear me out. This could be a test of whether we're on the right track or not. We call him back and tell him we can't find Rowland. If he wants Rowland pressured with the possibility of the death of his friend and colleague, it doesn't work if Rowland's in the dark. We may be able to tell from his reaction if that's his plan. Without any overt message, he'll be telling us more than he'd want us to know."

Garcia nodded slowly. "I like it." He slid his headset back into place. "And if we're lucky, by the time we're off the phone with him, someone will have figured out where the hell Rowland is. Ready?" Everyone nodded and McFarland put the call through again.

One ring.

Two.

Three.

Four.

Just when Gemma was sure the call would go unanswered, a male voice came over the line. "You can talk all you like, but I've already made up my mind."

"Every man has something he wants," Garcia said. "Maybe we can get it for you."

"I have what I want."

"A chance to kill First Deputy Mayor Willan."

"I'm a man of few needs."

"That seems like a big one."

"But the only one."

Gemma closed her eyes, concentrating on the voice on the other end of the line, weighing not just his words, but his tone of voice and attitude. So much of human language wasn't conveyed by words. She always preferred a visual of the suspect to give her more to work with, but in the absence of sight, she'd make use of every clue possible to gain an advantage.

Lives depended on it.

"Why is it Mayor Rowland's fault?" Garcia continued, his tone light and mild. Casual, as if they were discussing last night's Mets game. "He's completely out of touch, so I haven't been able to get ahold of him to ask myself."

There were a few beats of silence, then, "Where is he?"

"Honestly, I don't know. He's been MIA for a while now. We're trying to reach him, but may not be successful for a few more hours."

"Maybe you should try a little harder to locate him. He might have a vested interest in what's going on here."

Gemma's gaze flicked to Garcia. From his slow smile, he'd heard the edge in the suspect's voice as well, and the venom behind the words "vested interest."

"We'll certainly do our best."

"Yeah, you do that."

Then they were listening to a dial tone.

Garcia leaned back in his chair and grinned at Gemma. "That was a good call."

"It was subtle, but you decidedly unsettled him," Taylor said. "He maintained the overwhelming majority of his control, but the frustration and disappointment leached through, if you were listening for it."

"And that buys us a little extra time." Garcia looked up to find Kalani in the doorway. "Got something?"

"Sanders is coming in," she said. "He wants a face-to-face."

"Thought he might." Standing, Garcia took off his headset. In the main room, the door banged open. "That'll be him now. Lieutenant!"

Two men stepped in to fill the vault doorway, Sanders in front and a tall, blond officer behind him. Gemma was surprised to recognize the second officer—Detective Sean Logan, a fellow trainee from her days in the police academy. They'd been rivals from day one, the star cadet and the woman trying to knock him off his throne, a challenge made harder because of her gender. Women had been a part of the NYPD for decades, but they still had to work that little bit harder to be considered equals. And when you were the third Capello in a single generation to go through the academy, it was even harder because every instructor had a story about a brother who was stronger or faster in any given task. But Gemma was smarter, and what anyone might have felt she lacked in strength and male aggression, she made up for in intuition and strategy—valuable tools in her current position.

She'd been a thorn in Logan's side all through the academy, just as he'd been in hers. And the one night they'd blown off some of that competitive steam in his bed was never acknowledged afterward by either of them. She didn't need an entanglement when she was focused on clawing her way to the top of the class, and she imagined he felt the same. Still, more than a decade later, it was a night she'd never quite been able to forget.

Both officers were in full SWAT gear, dressed all in black, carrying their tactical helmets, and sporting bulletproof vests with NYPD ESU emblazoned on them. They cross-carried Colt M4 Commando rifles slung across their chests, the barrel pointed to the floor, each securely holding the rifle with a hand on the pistol grip.

Gemma met Logan's eyes, and he gave her a brief nod.

"I understand a threat has been made against the first deputy mayor." Sanders didn't bother with a greeting, but got right down to business. "We need to get eyes on what's happening in the mayor's office. I have a team ready to go in."

A slight tightening around Garcia's mouth was his only sign of dissent. But just as he started to reply, the outside door banged open again and Mayor Rowland entered. A tall man with a tendency to portliness, his face was an unhealthy mottled pink. He yanked at his tie to loosen it as he stalked toward them. "What is going on? Why are my people still trapped with a madman?"

Gemma exchanged glances with Taylor and McFarland. Someone had obviously updated the mayor, and it was going to be two against one with only Garcia fighting for a calm and patient approach to hostage extraction. Garcia had risen to lead the HNT because he was steady and logical in a crisis, and no hostage taker or senior officer ever saw him lose his cool. But Gemma suspected he was going to need every ounce of restraint to remain calm today in the face of such a high-profile hostage and while under a significant amount of outside pressure from both the city and NYPD brass.

"Mr. Mayor, we're very glad to see you," said Garcia. "When we couldn't get in touch with you, we were afraid you were still inside City Hall."

Rowland popped the top button of his shirt and wiped the sweat from his brow with the back of one hand. "My meeting with the state attorney general started considerably later than planned and then went for more than an hour, so I silenced my phone, knowing someone would come get me if I was needed. I had a new staffer with me, and I told him not to interrupt me for any reason. He actually took me literally. When this situation blew up, he stopped any calls from getting through to me. Finally word leaked through to the AG and I left right away." He scowled. "Make that an ex-staffer. Now, what's going on? Who's still inside? How many people are holding them? When are you going in to get them out?"

"We don't have many details yet, sir. We know there's one suspect, but don't know if he has any accomplices. We don't have visuals, so we don't have a full count of the hostages, but officers are working with your staffers who made it to safety to determine who is unaccounted for. We've been in contact with the suspect and are starting negotiations. I *highly* recommend not moving to a tactical entry at this time due to the nature of the threat."

"Which is?"

"The suspect has not outlined what he wants in exchange for the hostages. He has simply said he has a message for you." Garcia turned to his officers. "Detective Taylor, read back the exact wording."

"Yes, sir. 'Tell him his first deputy mayor is going to die, and it's all his fault.' That was at two thirty-seven p.m."

Rowland reached for the back of Garcia's chair to steady himself. "He has Charles."

"Yes, sir." Garcia pointed to the first-floor blueprint spread out on the table. "A number of security cameras were shot out less than a half hour ago. Based on the location of those cameras, we think he's holed up with the hostages in one of your inner offices. The A-Team has not been able to get visuals through any of the first-floor windows, so it looks like he strategically chose an internal location." He pointed to a conference room and an assistant's office. "Possibly one of these two locations. Both rooms have phones, and both could pick up our incoming calls. He may have chosen the room based on how many people he's taken hostage."

"So, if we go in," Sanders interjected, "we know where we're going and have a limited area to cover."

"If you go in," Garcia countered, "he'll simply follow through with his threat to kill Willan, because what does he have to lose?" Garcia swung back to face Rowland. "Mr. Mayor, we've bought ourselves some time because we told him we have no idea where you are, and he wants you to know what's going on. He wants you to suffer with that knowledge. As long as he thinks you're in the dark about Willan, he's in a holding pattern, at least in the short term. That won't last forever, but, in my opinion, he won't kill anyone during this time. He's going to wait for you to resurface. While we can't see him, he also can't see us, so he won't know you're back in touch, unless he has some other way of getting that information."

"You mean being in contact with someone on the outside?"

"Yes." Garcia turned to Gemma. "And that's a problem. The FCC won't let us shut down the cell towers in the area, but we can certainly isolate the landlines going into the building so we're his only link to the outside world."

"I can set that up," she said.

"That would go a long way to furthering his isolation." Garcia swung back to the A-Team officers. "You need to give us time. We've bought some by throwing him off guard. We don't know who he is or why he's doing this, but he sure as hell already has a plan in place. I bet Plan A was the mayor being in-house so he could deal with him directly. He's now likely moved on to Plan B. But without the mayor, he's left treading water. Let him tread a little longer. A suspect under pressure can be off guard and we may be able to learn more about him, and then use that leverage to steer him down another path. Hostage negotiations aren't about fast resolutions. When they are, history has shown us you tend to get a bloodbath and everyone dies." He met Rowland's eyes. "Including Willan. We need time and you need to give it to us. Step back and let us do our jobs. And be sure to keep a low profile until we tell you otherwise."

From Rowland's furrowed brow to his clenched jaw, indecision was starkly outlined on his face. He was used to calling the shots in his city, and being blocked was evidently unfamiliar and uncomfortable.

Gemma was willing to bet Garcia was happy to use Willan as specific leverage to buy the time they needed.

"Fine." Rowland snapped out the word. "But I want results from this. If not, then you"—he punctuated this with a finger jab at Sanders—"are going in and getting my people out." Elbowing his way past Sanders and Logan, he strode toward the exit.

"You better make this work." Sanders leaned in to Garcia, as if to apply additional pressure by sheer presence. "You're not the last word in the command structure. If the ESU decides we need to go in, then we're doing it, no matter how much time you think you need."

"Understood." Garcia's tone was flat and emotionless, but the fist that tightened over the top of his chair spoke volumes about his frustration with that structure. "We'll get the phone lines isolated, and then work on talking him down."

Prompted by Garcia's words, Gemma bent over her phone to find the number to call the techs.

When she looked up, Sanders and Logan were gone.

CHAPTER 5

Gemma walked back into the vault to find Taylor and McFarland, but not Garcia. "The techs are working on the phone lines now. They need some time because of the number of lines going into City Hall. But they can isolate that one line." She tapped Garcia's empty chair. "Where's the lieutenant?"

"He said he wanted five minutes to walk around the block to clear his head," Taylor said.

"That's what he said, but my money is on punching a wall in the back alley," McFarland said. "Totally called for, to blow off steam, in my opinion. Which he probably needs more than head clearing. Though Sanders usually makes me want to put my head through a wall, not my fist."

"There can be pitfalls in working with the tactical team," Taylor said. "Some of them are overenthusiastic and prefer to shoot first and ask questions later during a high-stress situation."

Gemma thought of Logan, an officer who would not remotely fit that description. She'd rarely seen a cooler head or a steadier hand when everything went to hell around him. It was one reason he'd been so hard to beat.

Garcia came through the doorway carrying a tray of extra-large coffees and a bakery box. He looked around at his officers and shrugged. "I needed a minute and had to walk over a few blocks to find anything open. The caffeine and sugar are also appreciated." He set the box on the table and then pushed the tray of coffees into the center of the table. "We could all use both." He sat down, selected a coffee, and took a long swallow. "Dig in. No contact yet, I assume?"

"Nothing so far," said Taylor.

"I didn't think he would call. It's a good idea at this point to give him time to think and, hopefully, start to worry about how his plans are collapsing. If he's off balance, he'll be more open to compromise." Garcia reached into the box and pulled out a chocolate-glazed donut. He pushed the box toward McFarland, who selected a Boston cream and jammed it into his mouth to take a huge bite.

"When do you want to make contact again?" Taylor asked.

"Now. This has been long enough. I don't want him to forget we're out here." Garcia slid his headset back into place. "Everyone ready?" Affirmatives came from around the table. "Let's get him back on the line."

McFarland dialed the phone, and they sat through it ringing again and again. After six rings and the click over to voice mail, he cut the connection, waited to a count of ten, and tried again. He was unsuccessful for a second time.

They were just about to try again, but Kalani stopped short in the doorway. Her whole stance radiated restrained intensity at needing to speak, but not wanting to interrupt a call.

Garcia gave her a go-ahead wave. "Sergeant?"

"We made contact with someone inside, but it's not one of the hostages. He's on line three. He was in the mayor's office and was on his way out with the fire alarm when the armed suspect came in. He hid in one of the back rooms, listening as the suspect rounded up all the hostages, but the guy doesn't know he's there. He called 911 and they patched him through to us."

"Getting him out without being captured or worse will be tricky." Garcia pointed at McFarland, who punched the lit button for line three. "This is Lieutenant Tomás Garcia of the NYPD. Who is this?"

"Rob Greenfield." The name was just a wisp of sound Gemma had to strain to hear. She quickly jotted down his name and the time of contact.

"Where are you?"

"Under the mail table in the photocopy room."

"Can you see the suspect from where you are?"

"No. He's in the library and conference room next to me."

Garcia pulled the blueprints toward him, picked up a pen, then circled the conference room down the hall from the mayor's office in blue ink. He put an X in the room next door. "He can't see you either, then. Good. Rob, I've got a copy of the building blueprints. That places you near the end of a hallway in a closed room. Is that accurate? Or is there a window or door you could use to get out of the building?"

Gemma leaned over the table to study the blueprints. Completed in 1812, the building was over two hundred years old and a designated historical landmark. There was no chance a new door had been put in recently and wasn't on the blueprints. Still, it was a question Garcia had to ask, just in case.

"No. That's why I'm calling. I don't know what to do. The only way out takes me right past the conference room door."

"You're the first person in communication on-scene, Rob. Can you tell me how many people there are holding the hostages?"

"I think it's just the one guy. He's the only one I've seen, the only one I've heard."

"Okay, let me talk to my tactical team. Now we know you're there, it's a new ball game. If you can't move out unseen, then I'm going to have to ask you to hole up where you are for now. You're safer if the suspect doesn't know you're there. And in the meantime, we'll work on a plan to get you free. Maybe we can get the hostages moved, or can create a distraction just long enough for you to get out of there."

"Thank God." Greenfield's voice wobbled with relief.

"Hang in there, Rob. Give me your phone number in case we get disconnected." Garcia jotted down the number. "Do you want someone to stay on the line with you?"

"Could you?"

"Not me, I'm going to work with a team to get you out, but I'm going to give you to Detective Gemma Capello. She'll stay with you." Garcia made a hand motion to Gemma, indicating for her to go out into the main room to get on the line until they could get another phone set up in the vault for a direct line to Greenfield.

Gemma nodded and rose, starting to slip the headphones off, when Greenfield suddenly cried out.

"No! Get off me!"

There was an earsplitting clatter Gemma guessed was the phone being thrown to the floor.

Gemma froze, half out of her chair, her heart rate spiking and her horrified gaze locked on Garcia, who was on his feet as if he could leap through the phone to join the fray.

Helpless, they listened to the sound of a struggle as furniture crashed and the combatants grunted and strained. Finally there was a cry of pain, followed by a dull, muffled *thump*.

Now, in the background, there was nothing but a low moan. The HNT officers exchanged fatalistic glances. They'd seen situations like this before.

A series of indistinct noises came through the phone; then "Who's this?"

It was the voice they hoped not to hear.

Hands braced on the edge of the table, Garcia hung his head. "Tomás Garcia."

"*Garcia.*" The word came out on a hiss. "Plotting behind my back, were you? Is this one of your guys? Were you thinking you could catch me off guard?" His laugh was dark and joyless. "Well, you failed. He's a lousy cop. I could hear him whispering from outside the door."

"He's not NYPD. He's a staffer who got trapped when you took hostages in the office. He was just trying to do the right thing and get help."

"'The right thing'?" The man's voice rose to a dangerous pitch. "How could he know 'the right thing,' when he doesn't know why I'm here or what I'm fighting for? I'm on the side of the angels."

"He doesn't know that. If you send him out, we'll guarantee you won't be charged for his mistreatment. He wasn't one of your original hostages. You don't need him. And it sounds like he needs medical treatment."

"Not happening. Now he's here, he gets to join the group. Whether I keep him remains to be seen. An extra hostage could be considered disposable." His words dripped acid. "Hopefully, he won't bleed out on the carpet while I decide what to do with him." With a *click*, he was gone.

Garcia ripped off his headset with a vicious curse, then slammed it down on the table hard enough to rattle the equipment.

Unbelievably, the situation had gone from bad to worse.

CHAPTER 6

*G*arcia gave the team thirty seconds to react to the situation, and then held up a hand for quiet. "Everyone take a breath." He took a long sip of coffee and then set the cup down with enough force that it rocked a little before steadying.

The hand he lifted from the cup vibrated slightly, and Gemma realized Garcia, too, had been thrown off balance by Greenfield's attack. To give her lieutenant a moment to steady himself, she took the lead. "McFarland, can you find anything on Rob Greenfield? We don't know who he is, so we don't know if this will exert extra personal pressure on the mayor."

"Sure," McFarland said. "Give me a few minutes to run some searches."

Taylor sat back in his chair, adjusting his tie to loosen it slightly. "There's additional pressure simply because of the increased hostage count, but the less personal pressure applied to the mayor, the better."

"From a first-response perspective, we don't know what happened just now, or how injured Mr. Greenfield might be." Gemma turned to Garcia. "Sir, what would you like to do next?"

"We have to reestablish communication, which is going to be harder now. And we have to do it fast. We bought time saying the mayor was out of touch, but letting him know the mayor has resurfaced may be our only way now to get him to talk. He's holding all the cards. We could have been satisfied with letting the situation drag out, letting him start to feel the walls closing in with no food or fresh air. But now there's an injury that may or may not be life-threatening. Hopefully, he's letting the other hostages help Greenfield, so he's not bleeding out. If we're lucky, we've got at least one person in the group who is willing to stand up and take the lead."

Take the lead. Garcia's words jerked Gemma back to the day that changed her life.

Cold marble under her legs as she sat on the bank floor. The stark white rotunda surrounded by towering columns overhead. Huddling beneath the faces of gods, pressing against her mother. Wanting to cry, but not daring to call attention to herself.

Until her mother took all the attention.

"It's unfortunate we lost a witness who could have assisted with suspect identification." Taylor's voice jolted Gemma back to the present. "It's exponentially harder to make progress in a negotiation when you don't know who you're negotiating with."

"Or what buttons to push," McFarland interjected.

"As I see it, we've only got one button," Gemma said. "The mayor. But even if we got him back, you might not be able to convince him to talk to the guy."

McFarland stopped his search and looked up. "Or worse, what if he insists on going in?"

"Prior to that," said Taylor, "we need the hostage taker to answer our calls. We can't offer a conversation if we can't get through to him."

"I'll go stand under the mayor's window with a bullhorn if he won't pick up," said Garcia. "But I think we can get there without jumping through hoops."

"He said something that's bothering me." Gemma looked down at her notes and then across at Taylor's. It was the last line he'd written as well. "He said he's 'on the side of the angels.' Meaning he's on the moral side of right? Am I reading him correctly?"

"That's how I took it," said Garcia. "And it's the first sign of what's really driving him. This isn't likely going to be 'I'm annoyed by three hundred unpaid parking tickets,' but more likely

something in the neighborhood of 'the homeless are dying because of a lack of social services.' It's going to be something personal, even possibly something not having anything to do with
Rowland's official role as mayor. We definitely need to make contact again. I also want to know what's going on with the other
hostages. Up to the time of Greenfield's arrival, there was only
one hostage who rated a mention, and that was Willan. He considers Greenfield disposable. But what about the other hostages?
We need to find out."

It took them three rounds to finally contact the hostage taker.

"Calling to find out how the new guy is doing?"

Gemma was pleased to hear an underpinning of stress in the
man's voice. The calm wasn't quite as pronounced this time
around.

"Yes," Garcia replied. "I'd also like to know how everyone else is
doing."

"And why would I tell you?"

"Because that's how this works. I scratch your back, and then
you scratch mine. Tell me what you want? I'm listening."

A heavy exhalation came across the line. "I want the mayor."

"You can't have the mayor."

"Why don't you let him make that call."

"Because, for once, he's not in charge, I am, and I don't like
giving him to you. If that's what you need, I want something significant in exchange."

Silence ticked by for a few seconds. "Like?"

"I want proof of life of the hostages. And I want to know the sta-
tus of Rob Greenfield."

"You don't ask for much, do you?" The voice was practically a
growl.

"You give me something, I give you something." Garcia's voice
took on a note of steel. "In that order." He looked over at Gemma
and held her gaze. He was pushing it, but they were at a stalemate
and something had to shift.

"Fine."

Gemma hadn't realized how tight she'd been holding herself

until her muscles relaxed. She gave Garcia a thumbs-up and met McFarland's grin across the table.

"Define 'proof of life,'" the suspect said.

"Each person saying their name clearly so I can hear it, and reporting if they're okay. Then the last hostage reporting on Greenfield as well, if he's unable to speak for himself."

"Hang on, I'm putting you on speaker."

Garcia pointed first at Gemma, and then at Taylor. His message was implicit: Even though the conversation was being recorded, he wanted notes that captured everything, duplicated in case the information came too fast, or was garbled.

The names came one after another, each voice faint and distant, but loud enough to be understood:

"Clara Sutton."

"Angelo Carboni."

"Janina Lee."

"Elizabeth Sharp."

"Charles Willan."

"Jamal Bowen."

"Andy McLaughlin."

"Carlos Rodriguez."

Everyone was physically well; though to Gemma's ear, most of them sounded terrified. Willan's voice, in particular, had a tremor that telegraphed he'd been in the room when the hostage taker had predicted his oncoming death.

They needed to get him out of there, but were torn because of the injured in the room.

"What about Greenfield?" Garcia asked. "Mr. Rodriguez, can you tell me about Mr. Greenfield?"

"He's unconscious. He has a head wound that bled a lot, but is slowing down now."

"Is that his only injury?"

"Yes. He was hit—"

"That's enough for now." The suspect's voice cut off Rodriguez's response. "Now it's time for you to do something for me. Don't screw me over, Garcia."

"We're negotiating in good faith. I'll get back to you when I've talked to the mayor." Garcia ended the call and took off his headset. "Finally some progress, though I'm sure you all noticed he didn't want us finding out the extent of Greenfield's injuries. Now we need to get the mayor back here. We have no choice but to get them talking."

"You aren't actually thinking of sending him in, are you?" Gemma asked.

"Not a chance in hell. He'd never make it out alive. The suspect said he wanted the mayor. So that's what he's going to get, but we're controlling how he's getting him. It's already bad enough we're going to have to hand the phone to someone with no training and a frayed temper. And all we'll be able to do is sit back and pray he doesn't get all the hostages killed."

CHAPTER 7

*T*he mayor returned in a whirlwind of sound and fury, followed by two scurrying aides. He made eye contact with Garcia as soon as he strode into the building and held it as he stalked toward the vault.

"Uh-oh," McFarland muttered sotto voce. "He's pissed."

"Because that's just what we need," Garcia murmured. He pushed back his chair and stood respectfully to face Rowland. "Mr. Mayor."

"I'm not used to being summoned like a schoolboy, Garcia." Rowland's voice whipped like a lash. "I was trying to help my staff get a head count on who's missing."

"We have that information." Garcia pushed his pad of paper across the table toward the mayor. "Right now, you can help us more here."

Rowland picked up the pad of paper and scanned the list. His face darkened as his eyes traveled down the names. "I don't know who Sharp and Rodriguez are, but the rest are definitely mine or Charles's staff."

"Let's confirm who those two are," Gemma said.

"On it." McFarland bent over his keyboard again, his fingers flying.

"What do you need me for?" Rowland demanded.

"The hostage taker wants to talk to you."

Rowland lost some of his ruddy color. "*To me?* Is this part of your theory that he wants me to suffer?"

"Possibly."

"I thought you were trying to convince him you couldn't find me."

"That was before he found Mr. Greenfield hiding in your photocopy room and attacked him. We're not sure how badly he's hurt, but we do know he has a head injury. And we don't want to cross the line of losing the first hostage."

"Of course, we don't want anyone to die." Rowland's tone carried the sting of insult that someone would even consider he might think otherwise.

"True. However, in hostage negotiations, there is a clear line of demarcation before and after the first loss of life," Garcia explained. "Before that happens, the suspect is often more careful, more circumspect, because he has less to lose. He hasn't done anything that serious yet. After a hostage dies, the risk to the other hostages greatly increases, as the suspect knows a long jail sentence awaits him. Or he often feels he personally is an even greater target, so he has nothing to lose in taking other hostages with him. If Greenfield dies, we'll have a very different situation on our hands, so we want to do everything in our power to keep that from happening."

"What do you want me to do?"

"The suspect himself must have something he wants from you or something he feels you need to atone for. First and foremost, you need to focus on listening to him rather than talking yourself. He's fixated on you for some reason, and we need to know why. We also need to know if you can identify him. In most hostage situations, we either know who the suspect is or we know right off the bat what they want. This man is a black box. Any information you can provide us or can coax out of him is valuable."

Rowland pushed past Garcia and stepped toward the table, his hand outstretched, reaching for a headset.

Garcia grabbed his arm, and then pulled back quickly at the mayor's venomous glare. "Sir, slow down. If we rush into this, we'll do irreparable damage. A few more minutes won't make a difference."

"What else do I need? We're wasting time and my staff must be terrified in there. More so, now that they know this guy won't hesitate to hurt them."

"We may only have one shot at this, so I just need to make sure you're going in with the right mind-set. If you project an attitude of control and power, his response will be to push back to show he's in charge, likely to the detriment of the hostages. You need to step back from the persona of mayor for this call. You have to let him think he's in charge, even if he's not. You need to listen to what he needs and show him you understand. That builds a connection and will give you influence over him, though he won't realize it. Be genuine with him, and, most important, no matter what he says, you need to keep your temper under control."

"What do I do if he wants something?"

"The only way he gets something is by giving something in return. From our perspective, we want to discuss releasing the first hostage. And because of his injury, it needs to be Greenfield. If he does that in good faith, then we'll agree to give him something within reason in return."

Garcia glanced at Gemma, who read his tacit order loud and clear. She picked up her notes and pen and stood, offering Rowland her chair. Taking off her headphones and leaving them on the table, she went out into the main room, grabbed a spare chair, and pushed it into the vault, setting up a station for herself at the end of the table between Rowland and Taylor.

Garcia sat down and pulled his pad of paper and pen into position before him. "I'll start the call. I know already we're going to hit a major bump right away because he's going to want to see you in person, and that simply isn't going to happen."

"If Charles's life is at stake—"

"It will be more at stake if you're standing there. If he wants to kill the first deputy mayor to make a point to you, what better way than right in front of you? This is us compromising—putting you in touch with him in a safe manner. He can't harm you over the phone line. Yes, he has hostages, but we won't be adding to the list of victims by sending in anyone but the A-Team. If you don't agree with me, we'll get the chief on the phone, and he'll back me up."

Rowland sat back heavily in the chair, reluctance coming off him in waves. "He would."

"Then let's get this started. Once I get him talking to you, I'll stay on the line and will advise you as we go along. You're not in this alone. We'll all be here. McFarland, pass me a headset with a mic and then connect us to the mayor's office."

"Yes, sir." McFarland handed Garcia a mic'd headset, waiting until he had it in place; then he dialed the call into the mayor's office.

The phone rang twice before it was picked up. "Are you sending him in?"

Garcia held up a hand as Rowland opened his mouth to respond. "I have the mayor here with me. He has agreed to talk to you."

"Then send him in and we'll talk."

Garcia's gaze flicked up to meet Gemma's.

Here we go.

"I have him here on the phone and he's ready to talk to you."

"That's not what we agreed on." The man's words held a combination of fury and suspicion.

"Sure it is." Garcia tapped an index finger beside a line in his notes. "I have it right here. You said, 'I want the mayor.' I found him and have him here for you."

"I meant *in person*. You fucking knew that."

His control is slipping.

But Garcia's mild tone never wavered. "You never said you wanted to see him in person. And you know I can't do that. The brass would never allow it. Getting him on the phone is a compromise."

"I'll give you a compromise."

In the background came the sound of a scuffle, followed by the cry of a woman. "No! Don't! I'll do whatever you want."

The bottom dropped out of Gemma's stomach and she leaned down to hurriedly scratch out a note and then shoved it toward Garcia: *Not Willan. Picked someone disposable. Careful.*

Garcia nodded. "I need you to stand down." His words were

calm and measured, only his clenched fist betraying his tension at the chaos they heard.

Another terrified cry made Gemma scan her notes. Only three women: Clara, Janina, and Elizabeth. Who did he have? Her voice sounded young, but without more details about the hostages, it could be any of the three.

"Why would I do that?" It was a snarl. "I gave you what you wanted and you fucked me over."

Garcia pinned Rowland with a sharp look and pointed first at him and then at the phone.

"No, he didn't." Rowland's voice came out with a slight tremor. "He didn't." This time, his words were steadier. "I'm right here."

"Mayor Rowland?"

"Yes, you asked to speak to me, and I'm here. You have my undivided attention, Mr. . . . ."

Another cry, followed by a *thump,* and the sound of harsh, broken breathing came through the line, followed by a low murmur of voices.

Gemma pictured male hands pushing away a woman's slender form, and her gasp of pain and fear as she overbalanced to tumble to the floor.

"That's not important. I need to talk to you. You need to understand."

"Help me understand. Then we can talk about releasing your hostages."

"Come in here."

"I can't—"

"If you want to save lives, you will." The hard edge was back in his words.

"I'm happy to talk to you like this. Tell me about what has you—"

"No! Garcia, you had a chance, now you're done."

A scream of terror stabbed across the line, making Gemma wince in pain.

Then silence as he cut the connection.

CHAPTER 8

"**G**et him back!" Garcia ordered.

McFarland was already dialing. But the phone simply rang and rang. Voice mail. Again. Voice mail.

After the third attempt, McFarland looked up. "He's not picking up. On purpose. He knows it's us."

"Of course, he does." Garcia pressed his balled fists to his temples. "Goddamn it, we need eyes in there. He could be killing them all and we'd have no idea."

"That won't happen unless Sanders and his team go in," Taylor said, his voice calm.

"Given how the last five minutes have gone down, you know he's going to push hard for that." McFarland punched redial again and they all listened to the ringing again and again.

"We're going to need proof of life again." Garcia's tone was sour.

"But not from you," Gemma said. "Sir, let me talk to him."

Garcia's head snapped up. "You?"

"Yes. Your relationship with him is over. As far as he's concerned, he fulfilled his end of the deal and you hung him out to dry." She held out a hand to forestall his protest. "You know you did what you had to do, and so do I. But he's not going to see it that way. We need to start over with him. Sometimes it's the second negotiator who makes a better connection."

"I agree with you, Capello." Taylor sat forward in his chair, intensity radiating from him. "We need a fresh voice. But it should be me. I have more experience and a stronger voice of authority."

"But that's just it," she argued. "He's having a problem with authority. You need me because I'm a woman."

Garcia started to say something, then caught himself, and considered her thoughtfully while the phone rang futilely in the background of their headsets. "You think he'll see you as weak? A pushover?"

She nodded. "He's older, and I get a vibe from him that says he's old school. Old Testament even, given the 'on the side of the angels' reference. He strikes me as an 'eye for an eye' type of guy. I bet he's also the type whose wife stayed home and raised the kiddies while he brought home the bacon. The type of man who thinks today's women are rising above their own station. Which we all know is BS"—she gave Taylor a side-eyed glance—"but I think that's his take on it. And he'll lump me into that category."

"He's wrong."

"Thank you, sir. But he won't know that until it's too late."

"We'll use his own prejudice against him. I like it. Taylor, we're going to hold you in reserve for now, but if this backfires on us, I want you ready to step in."

With a curt nod, Taylor sat back in his chair, the expression on his face clearly stating he wasn't pleased, but he acquiesced to the decision structure.

Garcia swung around to McFarland. "We need to get through to him."

"Trying, sir," McFarland grated between gritted teeth.

Garcia cleared the chair for Gemma and they switched headsets and places. "Now, if we could only—" Garcia cut off abruptly at the *click* on the other end of the line.

"I'll talk to you when I'm good and ready, Garcia, and not a second be—"

"I'm not Garcia." Gemma purposely kept her voice quiet and nonconfrontational as she pulled her legal pad and pen toward her. Kept her tone light, feminine.

"Who's this?"

"NYPD Detective Gemma Capello."

There were several seconds of silence, broken only by a low background keening; then he said, "Capello."

"Yes, sir."

Gemma imagined the conference room. She saw shelves lined with books and legal decisions surrounding a long conference table. A faceless man stood at the head of the table, his back to the open door. Hostages huddled at the far end of the room, trying to put as much distance between them and their captor as possible.

Her heart racing too fast, so fast her lungs couldn't keep up, and feeling on the edge of hyperventilation. Hostages huddling together, drawing comfort from the stranger beside them who had suddenly become the second most important person in the room. Fear keeping her immobilized, her eyes fixed on the fathomless hole at the end of the gun pointed at them. Her father had taught her respect for firearms and how to handle them safely. But he'd also taught her they were killers in the wrong hands.

Like right now.

"What do you want, Capello?"

"To talk to you."

Another pause. "That's all?"

"I think that's a good place to start. What can I call you?"

His laugh was harsh and derisive. "I'm not telling you my name."

She echoed his laugh with one of her own, one she hoped sounded brainless and bubbly. At McFarland's raised eyebrows, she rolled her eyes. "I didn't ask for your name, I asked what I could call you. 'Hey, you' doesn't seem polite. Surely, there must be something I can call you?"

Rowland stared at her in confusion, but Garcia was nodding because he could see exactly what she was doing. Establish a connection by offering assistance and a friendly ear, get the suspect talking, start to build a bond. Nothing else could proceed without those bedrock steps.

"Henry? James? Bart?" She randomly threw out names. "Darren? Steve? Patrick?"

"That'll do," the man interrupted. "Or you'll be at this for hours."

"Wonderful." Gemma let her smile infuse her tone as she wrote the name down on her pad of paper in block letters and underscored it with a single bold line. "Patrick. Now, you know I have to ask after the hostages. We heard a scream when you hung up. I need to speak to Clara, Janina, and Elizabeth."

"Why would I do that? Garcia asked for that last time and then didn't follow through."

"You're not dealing with Garcia. You're dealing with me." She glanced at Garcia and shrugged her apology. "And he might not have been, but I'll be straight with you. If I say a thing will happen, it will. Talk to me. Tell me what you need. I'm listening."

"That's what you do, isn't it?"

"Of course."

"Tell me, does your daddy approve of your career?" The man's tone implied he was talking to a small child.

There it was, the old-school misogyny. She'd nailed his personality. "He does. Look, Patrick, this isn't about me. It's about you. You're holding all the cards. You're the one who orchestrated this situation perfectly. You're calling the shots. I can provide what you need up to a certain point. But to do that, I need the hostages in one piece. *All* of them." She paused for emphasis, hoping her words would also give Willan some comfort. "If not, there's nothing I can do to help you. So, again, I need to speak to Clara, Janina, and Elizabeth."

"And then what?"

"And then we'll get the mayor back here"—out of the corner of her eye, she saw Rowland jerk in surprise—"and then you can have the conversation you want. That's what started all of this, isn't it? Something bad happened? Something that pushed you to take this kind of step so you could have a conversation with the mayor?"

"I want a face-to-face conversation."

"I promised you honesty, Patrick. I'm not going to hoodwink you. You threatened to kill the first deputy mayor, so there's no way the NYPD will allow Mayor Rowland to set foot into City Hall. I can't promise you a face-to-face meet, but I can arrange a phone conversation. And then we'll go from there. Is that fair? I can tell you right now, you won't get a better offer."

Gemma could practically hear the man grinding his teeth in frustration as he weighed his options. "Fine." The word was clipped.

"Wonderful!" Gemma poured every bit of enthusiasm she had into the single word. "Let me talk to the girls. Then I'll call back in a few minutes, once we get the mayor back in the room."

He didn't say another word, but after a few seconds, she heard the low rumble of the man's voice and a scuffle of movement, followed by a tremulous female voice. "H-hello?"

"This is Detective Gemma Capello of the NYPD Hostage Negotiation Team." All traces of lightness were gone. The hostages needed to hear the strength of the team fighting for them, and Gemma was their voice. "Who's this?"

"Janina Lee."

"Janina, have you been hurt?" Gemma used the familiarity of the woman's first name to build a bond of trust in as few words as possible. "Are you all right?"

"That wasn't me. That was Clara. I'm okay."

"Thank you. Hold on, Janina, we're going to get you out of there. Please pass on the phone."

The next voice was preceded by ragged, watery breaths.

Clara.

"This is Clara. Clara Sutton." The woman's voice was only the thread of a whisper, but it was coherent.

"Clara, this is Detective Gemma Capello of the NYPD Hostage Negotiation Team. Are you hurt?"

A whimper was the only response.

"Can you describe your injuries?"

"Hit me. With his gun. Across my cheek."

Gemma beat back the fury that rose like a wave. *Pistol-whipped. But still talking and coherent, so likely not concussed or with a broken jaw or cheekbone, which is probably better than Greenfield.* "Clara, we're going to get you out of there. Stay strong."

Gemma took the murmured response as an affirmative and then asked that the phone be passed on to Elizabeth.

After assuring herself the last female hostage was okay, Gemma hung up and stared thoughtfully at the phone. That had gone better than she expected.

Suspicion reared its ugly head. *Why* had it gone better than expected?

What had she missed?

CHAPTER 9

"**W**hy didn't you let me talk to him?"

The mayor's question pulled Gemma's thoughts from her contemplation. "I'm giving him the impression he's in charge, when, really, we are—we control when the calls go through and who talks. And I wanted to give him a few minutes to think over that call, and to feel confident in how it went. What he perceives as a weakened position might make him desperate. A position of control may make him more likely to deal with us and consider any offers fairly." She sat back in her chair, pushing her headset down to hang around her neck, and turned to her team. "But there's something . . ."

Garcia looked at her sharply. "What?"

She shook her head slowly. "I'm not sure. Something about that conversation is bothering me. Something I'm picking up, but can't put my finger on yet. Did anyone else get anything from it?"

"Besides his slightly placating attitude that they stuck him with a woman?" McFarland asked. "Not that he 'little lady'd,' you or anything obvious, but it was in his tone. You told him you were a detective, but he may think you're freshly minted."

"In which case, he's not carefully considering the situation," Taylor interjected. "This is likely the most important hostage situation in the city all year. He started with a lieutenant, so we aren't going to follow up with a cadet."

"I don't think that's it," Gemma countered. "He's old school.

Those are the guys who *will* 'little lady' you. And he didn't. But I feel like something important is just out of reach." Gemma turned to Rowland. "Which means you're up, sir."

"Any new instructions?" Rowland asked.

"Lieutenant Garcia laid it out for you before. The only thing I can add is to avoid being the 'voice of authority.' You may run this city, but you don't run this incident. We need you to step back from that. I didn't get the impression from you that you recognized his voice?"

"No."

"Then call him by the first name he's assumed and let him call you by yours. That will put you on a more even playing field in his mind. Otherwise, just listen very closely to everything he says. And we'll be here to advise during the whole call." She pulled her headset back into place and nodded at McFarland. "Put us through."

The suspect picked up on the third ring. "Is the mayor there?"

Gemma motioned to Rowland. *Go ahead.*

"I'm here. Is this Patrick?"

"Yes."

"Hi, Patrick. Please call me Kevin. I understand you wanted to talk to me."

"Yes."

"Before we start, I'd like to talk to First Deputy Mayor Willan."

Gemma's head whipped sideways to face him, but Rowland was staring unblinkingly at the table in front of him.

"That's how you're going to start? With a demand?"

"I'm happy to talk to you. I just need to make sure Charles is okay."

Silent seconds ticked by as Gemma's heart rate picked up. She glanced at Garcia and recognized the lockjawed expression. Her lieutenant wasn't happy. He'd given the mayor instructions, and the mayor had done what he damn well pleased.

"Fine." The man's answer carried a note of suppressed anger. "Wait a second."

The *thump* of the handset being dropped on the desk was followed by mumbled voices. Then there was the sound of something heavy falling and a ragged exhalation, as if the man had pushed Willan into a chair near the phone.

The handset was fumbled; then a new voice came over the line. "Hello?"

The mayor slumped back in his chair, relief etched on his florid face. "Charles, it's Kevin. Are you okay?"

"I haven't been physically harmed." Unsaid was the first deputy mayor's stress level, since he was being held hostage. "You'll talk to him?"

"I will. I'll do everything I can to get you out of there."

And the rest of the hostages, Gemma thought, but the words went unsaid by the mayor.

Rowland continued, "The team I'm working with knows—"

Gemma was reaching to close her fist over Rowland's headset microphone, but McFarland was already ahead of her. He jabbed a button, looked up, and said, "Muted."

Garcia leaned over the table, temper snapping in his eyes. "You're going to risk getting them all killed. Do not give away any information about our operation or any information we specifically know. We don't know if the suspect is listening or if he'll harm Willan to get the information from him." He nodded at McFarland. "Unmute it." He stabbed a finger at Rowland and mouthed, "Go."

Rowland stared blankly at him for a moment. "Uh . . . the team I'm working with is really solid and will treat your guy fairly. Charles, hang tough. I'm going to help them get you all released."

"Kevin, if I don't make it out—"

Rowland cut him off. "I don't want to hear that."

"I know. But if not . . . tell Sonia I love her. And make sure she's taken care of. I wouldn't trust anyone more than you."

"Christ, Charles. Of course, I will." Rowland drew in an uneven, shaky breath and straightened his shoulders as if going into battle. "I'll see you when this is all over and the first round at Carmichael's is on me. Hell, I'll buy one for the whole damn place to celebrate. Now give the phone back to him."

"Rowland?" The suspect was back on the line.

"Patrick, I'd like to avoid any more violence, so please tell me how I can help you."

"And you'll listen? And fix the problem?"

"Tell me what you need and I'll do my best."

"That's not good enough." Anger crept into the suspect's tone.

Gemma could feel the conversation already sliding sideways and hurriedly wrote and passed a note to Rowland: *Don't argue with him. Ask him to explain the problem so you can help.*

Rowland scanned the note and gave her a curt nod. "Let's start with the problem, Patrick. It must be something that has you very upset to feel this is your only option."

The laugh that carried across the line was dark with cynicism. "You might say that."

"Tell me about it. And then we'll see how we can help each other."

The man paused for a moment. The room behind him was silent, as if the hostages were collectively holding their breaths, waiting on his next word. "I want you to reverse the decision on stop-and-frisk."

Rowland's head jerked sideways to stare at Gemma in confusion. "This is all about stop-and-frisk?"

Upheld by a Supreme Court ruling in 1968, stop-and-frisk had been a controversial tactic used by police forces for decades, allowing officers to conduct a "reasonable search" of an individual before a potential arrest if they believed that individual to be dangerous. Police officers said it allowed them to find weapons and to protect both themselves and the community. However, members of the public protested that stop-and-frisk perpetuated racial profiling of blacks and Latinos. It had been such a contentious issue in New York City for decades that part of Rowland's mayoral platform was dedicated to doing away with the practice. After winning the election, city council passed strong legislation against racial profiling and Rowland had worked personally with the NYPD brass to institute a number of new protocols, including de-escalation and bias training, and the use of body cameras by officers.

"We need to talk about the city's stance on it," the suspect continued.

"It's not just the city's stance on it," Rowland protested. "I campaigned on the issue. I was elected on it. It's what the people wanted."

"Not everyone."

Alarm bells were already going off in Gemma's head, but through the building noise, her subconscious gave her a jolt of clarity as her elusive thoughts suddenly coalesced.

"I'm listening," she had said.

"That's what you do, isn't it?" he'd replied.

He wanted to reinstate what many saw as an illegal search and seizure, trampling the personal rights of the public as a means to an end. There was a subset of one group that felt it was an acceptable practice and wanted it back.

His pause when she'd given him her name. Then moments later, he had asked: "Does your daddy approve of your career?"

That wasn't misogyny. That was name recognition. He didn't mean any daddy; he meant Tony Capello.

Her eyes shot wide and she grabbed for her paper and pen, hurriedly scrawling, and then she turned the paper around and pushed it across the table toward Garcia.

He's a cop.

She didn't have time to watch Garcia's reaction because Rowland's conversation was careening straight off a cliff.

"I'm sorry if that's how you feel, because I really want to help you. But on both constitutional and legal grounds, my hands are tied."

Gemma motioned to Rowland to wrap up the call. She could see he was getting emotional and she needed him to end the conversation before he said anything to make the situation worse.

"So that's it. You're not even going to try. I guess First Deputy Mayor Willan's life doesn't mean anything to you."

"No, no! Of course, it does!" Rowland's tone took on an emphasis of stress, as if he was just realizing his single-minded crusade might not be appropriate now. "But this isn't my call. City council is involved, and legal. This isn't something I can change on my own. There must be some other way I can help you. Something else I can do." He cast desperate eyes up toward Gemma. "We can make an exchange. We'll do something for you, and you can send Willan out."

Gemma winced inwardly, trying not to let the expression show on her face. They had injured who needed medical care, but the mayor was really only interested in one person. She needed to get back into this conversation before the hostage taker ended all channels of communication.

"Patrick, it's Gemma again." Keeping her voice cool and soothing, she laid a hand on Rowland's arm and squeezed. *Let me take over.* "Clearly, you have the mayor's attention and he wants to help. I think you need to give us more time. You're asking for a pretty major change."

"It's what I want."

"I understand that."

"I'm not sure you do. How about a little more incentive?" The unmistakable metallic *snick* of the hammer of a gun pulling back sounded, followed by a woman's cry in the background. "What if time isn't something I'm interested in? Let's play this game. You've got fifteen minutes. If I haven't heard from you in that time, I'm going to execute the first hostage."

More cries and a low moan of "No, no, no" in the background.

"And then I'll just keep doing that every fifteen minutes until I hear from you." The suspect's voice rose, getting louder and more insistent with each word. "Will that make you take me seriously?"

There are times in a negotiation when a corner has to be turned or else lives will be lost. Gemma knew this was one of those times.

All pretense of being a submissive female dropped away. "Patrick, stop. Listen to me. We hear you. But you're not asking for ten thousand dollars in small bills and an escort across state lines. You're asking for something that takes time and can't just be the mayor's decision. You have to let us work on this. Or else everything you've done here today will be for nothing. You're doing this for what you consider to be a good reason. Don't throw it all away because you want to rush." She glanced at Garcia, who gave her a nod of encouragement. "Let's make a deal."

"I don't think you're in a position to make deals."

"Actually, I am. Because you need something from us."

"Something you can't give me."

"But what if we can?" Gemma glanced at Rowland, who was looking up at her like she'd lost her mind. "Mayor Rowland just said that city council is involved. You know how politics works—one city council makes a law, the next one changes it. Why can't the same council change its own mind on a law it's already passed? You know, if they come to see the error of their ways."

Silence came through the line, but at least he didn't disagree with her.

"What do you need from me? You know this can't be done quickly—so, what would satisfy you? A commitment from council members to reverse the policy? You know it didn't pass with one hundred percent support, no law ever does. How about we start with that? I'll provide a list of council members who would support your cause as a first step. Better yet, let me see if I can get the council majority and minority leaders in. You can talk to them yourself, get their commitment to your cause. But then you need to do something for me."

"Why?"

"You know how this works, Patrick. We do something for you, you do something for us."

"Like?"

"I want Rob Greenfield. We'll do an exchange. Greenfield for all the information we can compile on that bill and a chance to speak to the council leaders."

Rowland grabbed her wrist and she shook him off with a single hard flick. She already knew where his priorities lay, but she had to get the injured man out and to a medical facility. More than that, her gut told her he'd turn down the suggestion of an exchange for Willan because he felt the first deputy mayor was his main point of leverage. She needed to keep him focused on forward motion, not kill the embryonic compromise before it ever had a chance.

"Patrick? Talk to me. What do you think? Can we work together on this?"

"Maybe." His voice was sullen. "But I'm not willing to wait all day."

"I don't want to wait all day either. I'd like to see Mr. Greenfield getting medical care as soon as possible. I'll call you in thirty minutes with an update and, hopefully, council members for you to talk to. But I need your word the hostages will be safe during that time. I can only get people down here so fast."

Seconds of silence stretched out. Gemma's head bowed and her eyes closed as her hope for the situation wavered. *Come on, come on . . .*

"Fine."

Her head shot upright with a grin of triumph at McFarland across the table. "Thank you." She carefully kept any trace of victory out of her tone. "Thirty minutes, Patrick. You have my word on it. And I have yours the hostages will be untouched?"

"Yes." He hung up without another word.

Gemma sat down heavily and blew out a long breath. "That was close. I wasn't sure we'd pull out of that one."

"You aren't the only one." Garcia drilled an index finger onto the legal pad. "I know we've got to move fast here, but what makes you think he's a cop?"

"In addition to wanting to reverse the decision on stop-and-frisk," Taylor cut in. "As a black man, I understand my brothers' desire for fair treatment. As a cop, I understand why other cops are upset about it, but understanding doesn't mean I agree they should be allowed to trample personal rights. So that earmarked him potentially as a cop for me, but I suspect you heard something I missed."

"It was a couple of things he said. When I told him listening is what I do, he agreed with me in a way that, looking back on it now, felt like someone familiar with our protocols. He *knows* what

HNT does and how we do it. And that's a problem. The other was subtler, but it was his reaction to my name. It caught him, when it shouldn't have. Your name didn't give him pause, sir," she said to Garcia. "He just kept going. But when he heard the name Capello, it stopped him momentarily."

"I didn't catch that," McFarland said. "But put that in with the fact he asked later if your daddy approved of your career as a cop, then that's not the old-fashioned, sexist comment we chalked it up as. It's a comment directly referring to Chief Capello."

"That's how I'm seeing it now. Our hostage taker is not just on the job, he's NYPD."

"That's going to add an extra level of difficulty then," said Taylor. "He will be familiar with every protocol we have in place. He will know what teams we called in, possibly even the individual officers themselves. And he will know we have sharpshooters on every nearby rooftop, severely limiting his chance of escape."

"It also explains his location." Garcia pointed at blueprints in the middle of the table. "Someone who didn't know what they were doing would probably take over the mayor's actual office. There's more room in there, and a comfortable chair he can sit in to feel like he's the one running the city. It would be an ego boost for your average Joe. But it's also a room with large windows and straight shots from several nearby rooftops, even with the surrounding tree cover. But this guy picks a completely internal room so no one has eyes on any of them, and no sniper has line of sight on him specifically. We thought he might be military, but he's law enforcement."

"The other important factor we're in the dark on is what's his trigger?" McFarland asked. "We're not looking at some out-of-control citizen who snapped and is trying to make a point. We're talking about a cop, someone who eats stress for breakfast and keeps on going. What pushed him this far?"

"It has to be a life-changing event," Taylor said. "Whatever it is, he's willing to go to jail because of it."

Gemma sagged back in her chair as the full import of the situation blossomed. "A cop in jail? You know that's a horror show and so will he." She looked from one team member to the next. "He's not just willing to go to jail for it. He's willing to die for it."

"Shit." The worry lines carved into Garcia's face deepened. "If he doesn't care if he makes it out, he's not going to care about the hostages."

"No, he's not," Gemma agreed. She turned to Rowland. "We need to find a way to work with him or it's not just Willan we're going to lose. You're going to lose every staff member in there. We have to find a way to compromise with him."

"Then Charles is a dead man because Patrick's asking for the impossible," Rowland said. "Even if I wanted to change our policy, I don't have that kind of power. Not to mention we had a challenge from the ACLU and a lawsuit from stop-and-frisk. There's no way for me to snap my fingers and make it happen. Is he out of his mind?"

"With rage or grief, yes, he is. Or else we wouldn't be here like this. You're looking at this as a politician, and someone who knows the process. He's simply reacting through emotion. He's a cop and would be thinking this through if there wasn't some other overlying emotion clouding his thinking." She glanced at the clock. "We're wasting time and I have to call him back in twenty-six minutes. Sir, we need your help on this. I need you to get the council majority and minority leaders down here. We can offer a police escort, but we need them *now.*"

Rowland rose from his chair. "I'll call them." He hurried from the vault.

Gemma met McFarland's gaze across the table with trepidation. Her plan was a logical way to play for time, but each additional minute would make Sanders and his A-Team even twitchier. And that could mean a situation even more deadly for the hostages.

They had to move fast.

CHAPTER 10

*G*emma smiled at Carol Baker and Terell Robinson, the majority and minority council members, and checked the clock once again. "We're right on time. Are you both ready?"

Baker glanced nervously at the phone and then at Robinson, who nodded his agreement. "Yes," she said. "We know what to do."

"Then here we go." Gemma nodded at McFarland, who keyed in the phone number.

Mayor Rowland was off with his own people outside HNT headquarters when the council members had arrived only minutes before. After a quick prep talk from Garcia, they had taken their chairs, donned headsets, and sat, tension radiating from their stiff shoulders.

"I'll let you know when to talk, but this round it's going to be quite short. Just enough for him to know you're here."

The call rang in their headsets.

"I commend you on your timeliness," said Patrick.

"I told you I'd be honest with you, Patrick. When I say I'll call, I will." Gemma turned to the two council members, sitting ramrod straight beside her. "As promised, I have Majority Leader Baker and Minority Leader Robinson with me." She pointed at Baker and then at Robinson.

"Hello." Baker frowned at the slight shakiness in her words. "Hello, Patrick, I'm Carol Baker." Her voice was steady now and carried a crisp formalness. "I'd very much like to hear how we can help you today." She laid her hand on Robinson's arm and gave him a go-ahead nod.

"Hello, Patrick, it's Terell Robinson. Councilwoman Baker and I are here to assist you."

"Good." The suspect sounded satisfied. "You can start with—"

But Gemma quickly cut him off. "Patrick, you know that's not how this works. I've done what I promised, and I brought you the council leaders. Now it's time for you to meet me halfway. You need to release Rob Greenfield."

"How do I know you won't screw me over?" Satisfaction had twisted to pure suspicion in his tone.

"Because you have the rest of the hostages. The only way for me to save them is to deal fairly with you. Once I have confirmation that Rob Greenfield has been safely recovered, I'll call you back and we'll start the conversation. I want Greenfield to come out of the building through the main entrance and down the central staircase. Officers will meet him there and escort him off-site."

"What's to stop them from storming City Hall once they're already there? You think you can pull a fast one and get officers in the building without my knowledge?"

"Not at all." Gemma met Garcia's cool stare and made a judgment call. "Do you have access to a television feed?"

He paused before answering. "Several phones here have Internet access."

Gemma noted he didn't say he had a cell phone. *Probably didn't take one in with him. Wants to make sure we don't have any way to track him.*

"Give me fifteen minutes and I'll get a camera crew in here. They'll film the release of Greenfield live, and you'll be able to see the whole thing and be assured no one will enter the building. Does that work for you?"

"Yeah."

"Let me set it up, and I'll call you when you can send Greenfield out. Is he ambulatory?"

"Ambulatory enough." The coldness in the suspect's voice

made it clear he didn't care what happened to his hostage. Once Greeenfield's use as a bargaining chip was fulfilled, he no longer mattered. "Tell your men they can wait for him at the bottom of the steps. I don't want them any closer."

"I'll set it up, then I'll call you back." Gemma motioned to McFarland to cut the connection and pushed her headset off as she locked gazes with Garcia. "Sanders?"

"Yeah, I'll call him and set it up. Call ABC7. When I did that coffee run, I saw their truck only a block from here. They'll get a crew here right away."

Within ten minutes, the camera crew was setting up halfway between City Hall and the Jacob Wrey Mould Fountain, down a footpath with a clear line of sight to the main steps leading up to the front door. Two minutes later, Sanders, Logan, and another officer Gemma didn't recognize were standing in the doorway to the vault.

"Are your men ready?" Garcia asked.

"Affirmative." Sanders looked from one officer to the next. "Logan and Cummings will meet Greenfield at the bottom of the stairs and will escort him to the ambulance waiting outside on Murray. What are our guarantees your guy's not standing at a window ready to pick off my men?"

"There aren't any," Garcia said. "But this guy isn't stupid. If he can see us through a window, we can see him and then he's an easy target. He also knows it will be over for him the moment he goes after one of us. He wants something we can give him, so that's not the way to handle the situation. I think this is going to be a fast in and out." He looked over his shoulder at Gemma.

"Agreed." Gemma met Logan's eyes. "But stay alert. We don't have a confirmed ID, but I suspect he's a cop."

Logan's eyebrows rose in surprise, but he stayed silent, simply giving her a nod of acknowledgment.

"He's going to know our protocols and general game plan," she continued. "Play it clean."

"We don't do it any other way," said Sanders. "Give us a few minutes to get into position." He led his men toward the front door and then out of the bank.

"ABC7 is already broadcasting." McFarland waved his cell phone. "It's streaming live."

Everyone brought up the video feed. Gemma noted their location with satisfaction—close enough for a clear, zoomed view and far enough to avoid collateral damage if the exchange went to hell—and set up her phone so it faced her on an angle so she could keep an eye on it.

She slid her headset back on. "Okay, dial me in." She waited until the hostage taker answered her call. "Patrick, we're all set. Please ask someone to stream ABC7 for you. You'll be able to watch Mr. Greenfield exit the building and meet the two officers we've sent in."

"I don't want them to even set foot on the steps. Nothing that looks like an incursion."

"Incursion." You can't lose the cop lingo, can you?

"That's fine," she agreed. "We'll make sure they know." Out of the corner of her eye, Gemma caught Garcia passing the information along to Sanders. "You can send him out now. I'll stay on the line with you while he goes out. Then you can talk to the council members right away."

Gemma muted her headset and let silence fill the space between herself and the suspect as she focused on the action on her screen.

The elongated form of City Hall filled the screen, the camera's gaze centered on the steps that led up to five identical sets of double doors. Two men dressed entirely in black entered the field of vision from the side and Gemma easily identified Logan from his height. Both men had their helmets and safety glasses on, wore their rifles strapped to their backs and handguns in holsters on their right hips, and made a point of keeping their empty hands clearly in sight. They walked toward City Hall, stopping just short of the steps rising to the semicircular walkway that fronted the building and held both an American flag and the tricolor New York City flag to frame the front steps. This kept the men approximately forty feet from the bottom of the staircase. They stood motionless, their eyes fixed on the doorways.

A long minute ticked by, followed by a second.

This is taking too long.

Gemma exchanged doubtful glances with her colleagues, and was just about to unmute her headset and ask the suspect if there was a delay, when the middle door at the top of the stairs opened. The cameraman had seen it as well and zoomed in on the figure stumbling through the gap.

Rob Greenfield staggered as he cleared the doorway, almost going down to his knees as he reeled. At the bottom of the short flight of steps, Cummings took a step forward, but Logan locked a hand on his arm to hold him back.

Respect the space and the rules. Good.

He looked quietly watchful, but Gemma recognized Logan's stance from months of training with him. He was coiled, ready to spring at the slightest provocation.

Greenfield stopped for a moment with one hand on one of the tall Ionic columns, his head hanging low. The camera zoomed in, magnifying the dark red matted in his hair and the crimson rivulets streaking down his cheek.

"Look at that injury." Gemma glanced up to see Taylor nodding at his phone. "He got hit *hard*. And see how he's moving?"

"He's really unsteady," Taylor said. "He's likely concussed."

"He's not going to make it down those stairs." Garcia's gaze stayed fixed on the screen. "He can't walk a straight line out the door, forget about down a dozen steps."

"We need to get those officers up to him," McFarland stated.

"I agree." Gemma unmuted her mic. "Patrick, we need to get the officers up the steps to Greenfield. He's not well enough to make it down on his own."

"No." The word was a quiet snarl. "They stay where they are."

"But all they'll do is—"

"No."

Gemma forced herself to stop talking. The man wasn't budging and all she would do was put the remaining hostages at risk.

The team held their collective breaths as Greenfield staggered toward the stairs. He took a shaky step down onto the first tread and wobbled. But then he gathered strength, forcing himself upright and taking a second, steadier step.

Hope filled Gemma. *Come on, Rob, one step at a time. You can do this.*

A third step, then a fourth.

But Greenfield's step landed badly, and his left knee collapsed under him. Then he pitched headfirst down the steps, bumping and rolling, his skull striking solid stone again and again.

As her gasp of shock slipped free, Gemma remembered she hadn't muted the line again. But that was the least of her worries because Logan was on the move. He'd seen the fall telegraphed ahead of time and was sprinting across the walkway before Greenfield had collapsed. But the distance was too great and he couldn't get to Greenfield until he had come to rest at the bottom of the stairs.

In her headset, Patrick was screaming at her to get the officer out of there. She didn't even have time to respond as Logan lifted Greenfield, bent to drape him over his shoulders in a fireman's carry, and then jogged off across the walkway and down the steps. Cummings fell into step with him and they disappeared from view in seconds.

Gemma realized she'd come to her feet at some point in the last minute, but now she sank back down into her chair, her attention returning to the harsh breathing coming through the line. She inhaled to steady herself before addressing an armed man she knew was infuriated. "Thank you, Patrick, for allowing Mr. Greenfield his freedom. Now we'll be able to get him the medical help he needs."

"I told you no officers near the steps." The words were sharp and short bitten.

"That was our plan, but as you witnessed yourself, Mr. Greenfield was in no shape to help himself." She turned to the two council members, who stared at her with wide eyes. "Now Ms.

Baker and Mr. Robinson would like to talk to you about your request."

She pointed at Majority Leader Baker and leaned back in her chair as the two council members discussed the legislative process and how to fast-track a bill.

One hostage out, eight more to go.

CHAPTER 11

*A*s a first foray into municipal politics, it hadn't gone badly. Still, Gemma couldn't help but feel this attempt wasn't enough, and couldn't solve the problem fast enough to suit a man who threatened a life to get his own way.

What are we missing?

Gemma watched the two council members leave the vault, hurrying toward the exit on their way to convene an emergency council session off-site of City Hall, an ESU officer in their wake to keep the negotiation team up to date as to their progress. "This isn't going to work. We're banking everything on a bunch of politicians agreeing to repeal a good and reasonable law protecting the rights of citizens." She sank down into her chair. "And we know we can't set a precedent like this, or people will know they can use violence to get what they want, so we're playing along to buy time. But it's not going to happen and this is going to blow up in our faces."

"But, in the meantime, we appear proactive," Taylor said. "And that's keeping the hostage taker in check."

"Maybe. I think finding out who the suspect is might help a lot." She turned to Garcia. "As I see it, we're in a holding pattern for now."

Her lieutenant nodded his agreement. "We need to let the council do its thing. And I think some downtime for the suspect would be good. The longer we can stretch him without food or water, the easier he'll be to deal with as he starts to feel the pinch of his captivity."

"I don't know." Gemma shrugged when Garcia pinned her with a critical look. "That works for most hostage takers, but this guy isn't most. He's going to be prepared for a long siege. A few hours won't make a difference. A few days might, but there's no way the brass is going to want this to go on that long. This is a high-profile media circus that's closed down some of our busiest streets on a weekday. The brass and the A-Team are going to be under immense pressure from a public currently going through commuter hell and who will be pushing for a quick resolution to open up Lower Manhattan."

McFarland came through the vault doorway. "I have a preliminary report on Rob Greenfield. He's over at New York-Presbyterian with a grade-three concussion and doctors are concerned about an intracranial hematoma. They're working on him now. But getting him out of there when we did probably saved his life."

"It made the mayor unhappy, but it was the correct call," Taylor said.

"He certainly wasn't happy," Gemma agreed. "He's only thinking of Willan, but, for now, Willan is safe. I do think he should be our next extraction though. The suspect seems focused on him and that puts him at greater risk than Clara Sutton in my mind. I think her injuries will wait a little while. The suspect doesn't need her to make a point. The question is—does he only need Willan to put pressure on Rowland, or is there some other motive? Maybe he's trying to pressure Willan specifically?"

"It's not clear yet," Garcia said. "But you're right, the suspect does seem fixated on Willan."

"I'm going to do some research. We have a little time right now while the only current forward movement in this incident is out of our control. I want to see if we can find out more about this man. It might be the key to cracking this open." She pulled one of the laptops closer.

"I can give you a hand with that," McFarland offered. "What do you have in mind?"

"I think he's a cop. Specifically, an NYPD cop, or he'd be in another city taking a different group of staffers hostage. We need to create a list of potential suspects that include anyone who's been vocal about the end of stop-and-frisk or anyone who has been involved in a serious incident after the practice was abolished where stop-and-frisk might have increased their safety margin." At Taylor's frown, she clarified. "I agree with ending the practice. It was a huge breach of personal privacy and was clearly driven by a racial bias. But even you have to admit there is the odd incident where it might have increased an officer's safety to search a suspect."

"While obliterating the civilian's personal rights," Taylor muttered.

"Yes. As I said, I think it's a bad practice and I'm glad it's gone," Gemma agreed. "The de-escalation training we've all had has gone further to keeping the peace than stop-and-frisk ever did." She swung back to face McFarland. "Do those search terms make sense?"

"Yes. I think we should limit the time frame on a first search. This isn't someone who had an incident five years ago, and has been simmering over it since then. A recent event triggered this."

"I agree. Let's start off keeping the search to the past year. We can expand from there if nothing pops."

Garcia stood. "While you two do that, I'm going to make contact with Sanders and the rest of the command team to find out the overall progress and soothe any nervous fears. I don't want anyone getting twitchy while we're waiting. If Patrick is happy to wait, we should be too. Taylor, I'd like you to confirm our connection with the officer they sent to the council meeting, so we can keep tabs on what's happening. Make sure he understands we're going to need regular updates so we can keep the hostage taker calm if it starts to take too long for him."

"Yes, sir." Taylor rose and left the vault.

For nearly a full thirty minutes, the only sound in the vault was the tapping of keys, the scratch of pen on paper, and the odd mumbled comment. When Taylor returned to the vault, he gave

McFarland a hand with his research. Garcia wandered in and out of the vault restlessly. Gemma understood his distraction—at this point in a hostage situation, a negotiator had to be patient and let the situation play out. Often, less was more and there was nothing to be gained in smothering a suspect with attention. In fact, there was a lot to lose.

She leaned back in her chair and looked at her notes. She had three potential leads, all of them plausible, though one was stronger than the others. It wouldn't take long to confirm the details of the one incident—

Kalani appeared in the doorway. "Lieutenant, you need to come out here and see this."

Garcia pushed back his chair and followed her out into the front room. Gemma had already turned back to her laptop when Garcia's vicious, guttural curse filtered back into the vault. She looked up sharply and exchanged glances with McFarland.

"Get out there." McFarland cranked a thumb in the direction of the vault doorway. "We'll monitor from here. Fill us in when you get back."

Gemma jumped to her feet and jogged out of the vault. And stopped almost immediately at the sight of a group of officers, including Kalani and Garcia, gathered around a laptop monitor. As she came closer, she caught a glimpse of the scene displayed.

Rowland stood at the top of a flight of steps, a gaggle of reporters and cameramen below him, cell phones and microphones all held up to catch his every word. Gemma instantly recognized the wide steps, the row of four-story-tall Corinthian columns, and the massive wrought iron lanterns as the Thurgood Marshall Courthouse, conveniently located just outside the evacuated area, but still close to City Hall, the site of the action.

"He's giving a press conference?" The appalled question slipped out from Gemma before she could stop it.

"Sure looks like it," Garcia growled. "Who put him up to it? We never recommended anything of the sort."

"He never asked us about it. But if we wanted him to do this, it would have been a very carefully controlled message."

On screen, Rowland was holding both hands out to quiet the group around him. "Thank you for joining me today. I know there has been a lot of concern over the situation at City Hall and I wanted to reassure the people of New York City that the men and women of the NYPD are working to quickly and peacefully resolve the situation.

"We currently have a hostage situation involving a number of City Hall staffers. Earlier this afternoon, a man entered my offices and took hostages. The NYPD, including the Emergency Services Unit and the Hostage Negotiation Team, are involved, and their hostage negotiators have made contact with the suspect. At this point, the suspect has made demands and we are working toward meeting those demands or at least finding a compromise situation. I have the utmost confidence in the NYPD to end a difficult situation peacefully and without loss of life. But until then, the existing street and mass transit closures must be maintained, and I am grateful to the citizens of New York City for understanding and upholding these security considerations." He looked out over the mass of people. "I have time to take a few questions now and I'll do my best to answer them. Please understand this is an ongoing situation so I will not be able to share some information, but we will update on the negotiations going forward as we can." There was an unintelligible burst of questions from the reporters and Rowland held his hands up for silence. "One at a time, please." He pointed at someone in the crowd. "Yes, Chris."

"Do we know how many hostages there are, sir?"

"Eight, currently. One has been released and has been taken to NewYork-Presbyterian in Lower Manhattan."

"Goddamn it," Garcia snapped. He jabbed a finger at one of the officers standing nearby. "Contact Fisher. Tell him Rowland just leaked Greenfield's location. Reporters will be on their way there now. We need to make sure he's cordoned off." He turned back to the screen. "He also just said he wanted us to resolve the situation peacefully and then contradicted himself by saying someone's been sent to the hospital." He went silent as Rowland started talking again.

"—not made any request for ransom money. In fact, we do not believe money is the incentive. His request lies in another arena entirely."

"One you can contribute to?"

"One I am helping to facilitate, yes." He picked another reporter out of the crowd.

"You've referred to a single male suspect," a woman asked. "Is he working alone, or is there anyone else?"

"At this time, we understand it to be an individual male."

He started to scan the crowd, but the woman spoke up again. "A follow-up question, if I may. You said there are eight hostages. Do you know exactly who those hostages are?"

"We do, but I'm sure you understand that's not information we can share at this time. I will leave that information to the discretion of the NYPD to release when they feel they can. Yes, you in the blue."

A man just visible at the edge of the screen put down his hand. "Has the NYPD stepped back and they're just letting the suspect get what he wants? This guy sounds like a terrorist. What happened to not negotiating with terrorists?"

Gemma locked gazes with Garcia and she saw the same foreboding that clenched her gut.

"Let me assure you, we know exactly what this man is and what his motives are. We're willing to make some moves toward compromise, but that certainly isn't the whole game."

"So you intend a show of strength."

"That would be my preference, yes. The NYPD has the option of going in to retrieve the hostages. And, frankly, it's the method I'd prefer. I want my people out now. I've been assured it can be done safely."

Garcia's muttered response was unintelligible, but Gemma knew he was furious at Rowland for conveying the exact opposite of their clearly stated position.

"So, why the hesitation?"

Rowland stiffened at the term "hesitation." As she watched the feed, Gemma's breath caught. *He'll perceive that as a slight. An implication of his own weakness as the leader of the city.*

"Because the Hostage Negotiation Team wants to try." There was a thread of acid curling through Rowland's voice now. "But if this takes too long, let me assure you, I'll take it to the commissioner if I have to, and stronger wills will prevail. But we'll get our people out, one way or another. We're in charge of this, not him, and will show him that through force if need be. Thank you for your attention. We'll be happy to update you as more information becomes available."

One of the cops in the HNT headquarters whistled up at Garcia, who looked like he wanted to say something, but then simply threw up his hands and walked back into the vault.

Gemma followed him to stand in the doorway, tracking him as he paced back and forth. From the table, McFarland and Taylor watched with matching worried expressions.

"What happened?" McFarland asked Gemma.

She waited until Garcia passed her to cross his path and sink down onto her chair. "Rowland took it upon himself to run a press conference. He probably wanted to make himself look like he's in charge."

"He's not," Garcia muttered, turning to retrace his steps.

"No, but he wants them to think that. So, after he contradicted himself about how it's going so far, he made a power play. Insisted that we were in charge of the situation, not the hostage taker, and that we'd do whatever it took to get the hostages out. That he'd go over our heads to end this, if needed."

"That sounds like Sanders talking," Taylor said.

"*Doesn't it?*" Garcia threw out both hands as he stopped pacing. "That has to be who's behind this. Sanders probably got to him and told him to send a message to the city. Remind the citizens who's in charge. And Rowland is such a bone-deep politician, he forgot he's holding Willan's life in his hands and went right into campaign mode, like he's already looking toward his next election and needs a decisive win."

"Also, send a message?" McFarland looked from Garcia to Gemma. "Have they forgotten the hostage taker has access to outside media feeds? That's going to send a message all right, but not to the right audience."

Gemma shrugged. "He shouldn't have forgotten, but Rowland's so desperate to get Willan out of there that he's missing a lot of the nuances of this situation. Whatever the reason, he just tried to come off as the man in charge, and it's going to blow up in our faces because our suspect wants to think *he's* in charge. We won't know what damage he's done until we make contact again."

Garcia dropped resignedly into his chair. "No time like the present. Let's find out if the mayor has just spoiled hours of work."

CHAPTER 12

*G*emma had a bad feeling from the moment they called in and the phone rang and rang. And then went to voice mail.

She glanced up at McFarland.

He shrugged, but the way his shoulders rode up close to his ears belied his tension. "Maybe he didn't see the press conference?"

"Not a chance," Garcia said. "He watched Greenfield's exit on someone's cell phone. Every local network and likely at least half of the national ones would have carried the press conference. CNN lives for this kind of breaking news." Jaw clenched, he shook his head. "He saw it."

Gemma pointed at the phone. "Dial it again. We—" She broke off as a ring was interrupted by the phone connecting. "Patrick?"

"I'm here."

The voice was calm and without the fury Gemma was afraid she'd hear. Still, it was a little too stilted and Gemma knew instinctively they'd lost this round. Time to meet it head-on. "Did you see the press conference?"

"I did. Is the mayor there?"

"No."

"I'd like to speak to him."

"I'd be happy to talk to you about the press conference."

"No. I have . . . questions. For the mayor directly. Call me back when you have him on the line." He hung up.

"I'll get Rowland." Garcia pushed back from the table and stood. "I'd like to have a word with him anyway, and it's better if I do that a little more privately than this." He stalked out of the room without another word.

Gemma pulled her headset down to hang around her neck. "He's not as angry as I anticipated."

"Which is nothing short of a miracle," Taylor said. He took a long swallow of what had to be ice-cold coffee by this point. "What on earth was the mayor thinking?"

"You mean what was Sanders thinking." Gemma tipped her coffee cup toward her, swirled the dregs in the bottom of the cup, noting how the cream separated out of the rest of the liquid, and pushed it away untasted. "When Rowland first came in here, he was all bluster and 'get my people out of there.' We managed to beat that down somewhat, so he could have a calm conversation with the man holding lives in his hands. Or, rather, holding Charles Willan's life in his hands, as it was pretty clear he was the only one who really mattered to him."

"Which is crap, because every hostage in there is a citizen of this city and that's all that should matter to the mayor." McFarland kicked back in his chair, but looked anything but relaxed. "Yet he's focused on Willan."

"He can't move past the fact they're friends. And that played right into Sanders's hands. Granted, I was worried Rowland's bravado might get all the hostages killed, but the suspect is calm." Gemma's eyes narrowed as she stared down at nothing. "Too calm for my liking, actually."

"If he's calm, we may be able to reason with him," McFarland said. "Strike a deal with him."

"For what? The only thing he's asked for, both the mayor and the media have made clear he can't have."

"His freedom then," McFarland suggested.

The laugh that escaped Gemma carried a harsh edge. "He's a cop. He knows there won't be any freedom if any of us catch him. And he knows we're not going to just let him walk out of there."

"But he's not aware we suspect he's a cop," Taylor said. "He thinks he holds the advantage. He . . ." His voice trailed off as voices abruptly rose in the outer room.

Gemma swiveled in her chair to find Rowland and Garcia striding toward the vault. The magnanimous politician of the press conference was gone; now Rowland looked like a thundercloud. Garcia appeared just as forbidding. Gemma realized why when she looked past the two men to see Sanders marching behind them.

With a warning sideways glance at Gemma, McFarland rose to his feet, Taylor following his lead.

Gemma stood as well. "Sir."

"Mayor Rowland is back to make contact with the suspect." Garcia's voice was nearly a growl. "He says he's willing to work with the suspect to free the hostages."

"That's always been my first preference. But there may come a time when—"

"Sir!" Garcia's open palm landed with a slap on the surface of the table, rattling equipment and sending pens rolling. "As I said, I agree with you that there has to be a final option, but it's not one we're looking at now. Right now, we need to focus on getting them out alive. If we go in with guns blazing"—his gaze cut to Sanders, standing in the doorway—"we *will* have casualties. And I don't mean the suspect. He won't talk to us, only to you, so I need you to work on hostage extraction with us. We don't know how much time we have with them."

Garcia and Rowland locked gazes for a long moment, but it was Rowland who finally looked away. "All right. For now."

"Thank you." Garcia stepped back and let Rowland pass him to take his chair once again. He turned back to Sanders. "We'll let you know if the call doesn't go as we planned and we need backup support."

"I'd rather listen in to see how it goes."

Gemma looked up from getting Rowland settled and reconnected, and for a moment, she thought Garcia was going to outright refuse.

"If you want to listen in, do it from out in the main room." He motioned to the woman standing behind Sanders and following the conversation. "Kalani can set you up. We need the mayor to be able to concentrate and not feel surrounded. I'm sure you understand." He turned his back on the A-Team officer as Kalani escorted Sanders out of sight.

Garcia took his chair again. "Are we ready?"

"Yes, sir." Gemma faced Rowland. "Are you ready, Mr. Mayor?"

"Yes."

"Let me start the conversation so he knows I'm on the line with you." She nodded at McFarland, who put the call through.

"Is he there?" the suspect asked instead of a greeting.

"Yes, he is. Mr. Mayor?"

"I'm here," said Rowland.

"I saw your press conference."

"As you can see, I'm in your corner, Patrick, and I'm here to—"

"*Really?*" The calm voice rose, the single word crescendoing in pitch and volume. "Is that really how you—"

The line went dead.

Gemma clapped both hands over her headphones, pressing them tighter against her ears, trying to catch any whisper of sound.

Nothing.

Her head jerked up to stare at McFarland, but she didn't even need to ask him. The shock on his face told her something was wrong.

Garcia was out of his chair. "What the hell are you playing at, McFarland? Get him back!"

McFarland was frantically jabbing buttons, shaking his head in disbelief. "I'm trying. There's no line. It's dead."

"What do you mean 'it's dead'?" Tossing down his equipment, Garcia circled the table. Leaning over, he tried the connection himself, disconnected, and tried again.

"Lieutenant!" Sergeant Kalani came into the vault with a cell phone in her hand, Sanders right behind her. "The technicians isolating the mayoral office phone line called in. Something went wrong and they cut it by accident. They're working on reconnecting the line, but say it's going to be about twenty minutes."

With a vicious curse, Garcia threw down the headset and strode to Kalani, who extended the phone to him.

"Who is this?" he snarled into the phone. "I don't care what happened, just fix it. I've got a pissed-off hostage taker with lives in his hands, and every minute that goes by with no communication could be another life lost. I lose anyone because of this, it's on your head. *Get it done! Now!*" He thrust the phone into Kalani's hands and raked his own through his hair.

"Sir?" Gemma raised her voice to cut through the raging scream that had to be ricocheting around Garcia's skull. "What do you want for the next steps?"

Taylor laid his own headset on the table by his notepad. "I'm not sure we can afford twenty minutes. Sir, why don't I find a bullhorn and go to the front foyer. I could get close to the office without entering, and we could communicate the old-fashioned way."

"Or as you said before, right under his window," McFarland suggested. "We could at least let him know we're having technical difficulties."

"That's a negative." Sanders pushed his way into the room, passing Kalani on her way out. He sidled in between the mayor and Gemma, and bent over the blueprints, studying the layout of the first floor. The first floor rose a half story above the ground, with multiple wide, paned, arching windows lining every side. "He may be inside and out of the line of sight, but if he's smart, he'll be monitoring news coverage on the hostages' phones. My men are on the lookout, but they're busy and are spending their time watching City Hall. We can't be sure a news crew hasn't snuck onto a roof somewhere to film this. If he sees anyone approaching through their feed, anyone he doesn't anticipate, he'll shoot first and ask questions later. It's bad enough hostages' lives are at risk, we're not risking NYPD officers. How long has it been?"

Gemma glanced at the clock. "I marked the time as soon as they gave us the repair duration. Two minutes."

"If this doesn't resolve soon, I'm going to recommend moving in." Before Garcia could disagree, Sanders tapped two fingers to his earpiece. "All teams, report in." He kept his laserlike gaze pinned on Garcia as voices must have been responding to his command. After a full minute, he said, "Stay sharp. We've lost communications temporarily. We may need to move in. Sanders out."

"Are they picking up on anything?" Gemma asked.

"No. Several of the guys have eyes through the windows and there's no sign of movement. My sound tech is using a parabolic mic, and says he doesn't hear any sound of gunfire. You might get lucky after all, Garcia."

"I won't be if they can't get the fucking phone line fixed. It's going to complicate matters if he thinks we're trying to pull a fast one. He was about to lose it in there."

Gemma glanced sideways at Rowland—who sat frozen in his chair—and shrugged. The mayor was going to find out their opinion sooner or later. "When he first picked up, he seemed calm. But it quickly struck me that he was too calm. He had everything tamped down and was just holding on. But the moment Mayor Rowland came on, he lost it."

"Or would have, if the line hadn't been cut. How much more time have we got?"

"If they're on time, we have another fourteen minutes."

It felt like the longest fourteen minutes ever for all of them.

Sanders checked in with his sound tech twice. Silence still reported.

Gemma reviewed her notes four times before flicking her pen away and sitting back in her chair.

McFarland checked the phone line approximately every sixty seconds.

Taylor steepled his hands in front of his face, tipping his mouth against them, and closed his eyes. Anyone unfamiliar with Taylor might have thought he had checked out, but Gemma knew he was reviewing every word of their communication over and over, looking for any clue that might give them a leg up.

Garcia simply paced.

"Wait. *Wait!*" McFarland slammed one fist on the table. "It's back."

Gemma grabbed her headset and slid it into place. She pointed at McFarland. "Dial." She turned to Rowland. "Stay quiet unless I tell you to talk. You're a trigger point for him now and we need to keep him calm."

The suspect picked up halfway through the first ring. "What the fuck are you playing at?"

Gemma winced at the rage in his voice. "I'm sorry, Patrick." She kept her voice serene. "We're not playing games with you. We're having technical difficulties on our end that resulted in us losing you for a few minutes. As I said, I'm sorry—"

"Save your 'sorry,'" he snapped. "Is the mayor there?"

"Yes."

"Put him on." There was no mistaking the venom in the man's tone.

Gemma pointed at Rowland; but for the first time, he was speechless and just simply stared up at her, the color draining from his face. Her own temper slipping slightly, she tapped the mayor's forearm sharply. She pointed at the phone and mouthed, "Talk."

"This . . . this is Kevin Rowland."

"Mayor Rowland."

Some of the acid had mellowed in the suspect's tone, but instead of giving Gemma any comfort, it made the hair on the back of her neck stand up in alarm. Her gaze flicked up to Garcia, but his narrowed eyes were locked on Rowland, his face set in stone.

"I saw your press conference," the man continued. "It sounds like you're not leaving me any choice. I know who's in charge."

Rowland's frame relaxed slightly at the words. "I'm sure you understand. We've been dealing fairly with you, but you have to deal fairly with us as well."

" 'Fairly'? Of course."

Gemma's reaction to the calm in the suspect's voice was the opposite of Rowland's, and she found herself growing more and more tense.

"Would you like to speak to your first deputy mayor? I know you want to assure his safety."

"Yes, thank you, I would."

There was a moment of silence and then Willan's voice came over the line. "Kevin, it's me." His words were slightly distant with the echo of being on speaker.

"Thank God. Charles, we're going to bargain for your release. I'm going to get you out of there."

But Gemma was focused on the voice of the man no longer speaking. On his tone. His steadiness. His words.

"I know who's in charge."

"I know who's in charge . . ."

He was.

Gemma surged to her feet, reaching out a hand to stop a man a full city block away, even as she heard the metallic *click* of the gun's safety once again through the phone line. "Patrick? Patrick! I need you to calm down. We can help you, but only if you leave the hostages unharmed. You're not looking at serious charges right now, but if you harm anyone, I can't help you and there'll be no looking back. Don't cross that line, Patrick."

"That line was crossed before I ever set foot in this building."

The suspect's voice held a resignation that turned Gemma's blood to ice. *It was already too late.*

"Mr. Mayor, this is what your games have brought."

Rowland lurched to stand, his fingers clawed over his earphones, his eyes wide and wild. "Charles! Don't hurt Charles!"

In the background, Charles Willan pleaded that he had a wife and children waiting for him at home.

She could picture Willan's face as seen in the papers from charity events and news conferences. A tall, blond, fit man, his bright smile radiating strength and confidence. Only now there'd be no smile. She could see him, on his knees, his hands raised in surrender, as he begged for his life.

Her mother, standing tall and proud as she faced the man in the black mask. From her place on the floor, Gemma could see the tremor in her fingers. The man screaming at her to sit down and to shut up. Her mother holding firm, talking quietly, trying to convince the man to let the hostages go, that it wasn't worth hurting anyone, and that they could just take the money. The gun swinging up to point directly between her eyes.

A single gunshot blocked out all other sound.

CHAPTER 13

"*Charles!*" Rowland's scream was full of agony as he stumbled backward, knocking over the chair behind him so it crashed to the floor. The cord for the headset snapped tight and then yanked from Rowland's head to clatter to the table.

"Patrick! Patrick, talk to me." Gemma leaned over the table, both hands braced on the edge. "Patrick?"

But the only sound that came across the line was a quiet *click*.

Gemma's head snapped up to McFarland, but he shook his head. The call had been terminated.

Gemma sank down in the chair, bracing her elbows on the table to drop her face into her upraised hands, trying to block out Rowland's wails of grief or the scuffle behind her as Garcia tried to calm him. Gradually the sound decreased and Gemma realized Rowland had been removed from the room. She looked up and met McFarland's gaze across the table.

"Garcia and Taylor dragged him out," he said in answer to her unspoken question. "Even without Willan dying, we can't use him anymore. He killed any chance of that as surely as he killed Willan with his little power play during the press conference."

Gemma sprang to her feet, just needing to move. "Goddamn Sanders. We can hang this clusterfuck on him and his need to show force."

McFarland threw himself back in his chair, looking utterly wrung out. "You know what tactical is like. Some officers value the negotiation process. Some still think strength is the best way to end a siege. Sanders is one of those."

"And now Willan has paid for it with his life." She met his gaze. "Unless . . . you don't think that was staged? That he pulled the trigger near the phone, but not into Willan's head?"

McFarland shook his head. "No. And neither do you."

"No. Willan's gone." She reached for a bottle of water on the table and downed a quarter of it in one long series of swallows. But it didn't wash the sour taste of failure from her mouth.

McFarland righted Rowland's toppled chair. "What's next?"

He knew exactly what came next and Gemma knew it was a gentle way to give her a push to take the next steps after a significant setback.

Because what came next was saving the lives of the remaining seven hostages. To do that, they had to find leverage with this suspect, which was nearly impossible when they didn't know who he was.

Or did they?

Sitting, Gemma pulled her notepad toward her and picked up her discarded pen. "Next is regrouping and figuring out a new angle to get the remaining hostages out of there. *Immediately.* This guy is now going to figure he has nothing to lose. He's killed his highest-profile hostage, the rest could just be collateral damage. But we've seen this before. Some of the suspect's rage is going to be spent now, and that gives us a time-out before he starts to ramp up again." She scanned the research notes she'd made. "It's critical now to know who we're dealing with. I have a couple of possibilities as to his identification, though one is stronger than the other." She looked up at McFarland. "How'd you do?"

"I have a couple too, but I'm not convinced they're strong enough."

"Working on anything is better than sitting here wallowing. Let's hear them."

McFarland pulled his laptop closer and brought up his notes. "I have three politicians who fit the bill, but we're really looking in the world of law enforcement, so let's backburner them for now. First off, there's the president of the PBA, Monty King. King has been a vocal proponent of stop-and-frisk right from the beginning. Says it keeps cops safe."

Gemma was familiar with King, who was president of the Police Benevolent Association, the NYPD's largest labor union, for nearly ten years. "This seems extreme for King."

"I told you I didn't think this was a strong enough possibility. Still, let's keep him in mind. Then there's Fred Klegmann."

"I'm not familiar with him."

"You wouldn't be, but you might be with his daughter, Melissa. Officer Melissa Klegmann was killed at a traffic stop when she pulled over a car with a broken taillight and was shot by the driver through the open window as she approached. The incident was captured on her dashcam, including the license plate of the car. They tracked down the driver. Turned out he had twelve ounces of heroin on him, which made him guilty of a Class A drug felony, with a minimum mandatory sentence of eight years' imprisonment."

"And he thought second-degree murder with a minimum fifteen-year sentence would be preferable?" Gemma scoffed.

"Apparently. Anyway, Fred Klegmann has crusaded since for anything to improve the safety of cops, and was a vocal supporter of stop-and-frisk."

"He seems more likely than the first one. Klegmann's not a cop, but might be familiar enough with the police because of his daughter's profession. Anything else?"

McFarland paused, contemplating his list. "Nothing else strong enough. We're going to be short of time here, so let's keep it as clean as possible. I'll hold on to them in case nothing else rings true. What about you?"

"I have three, but I think only one is a strong possibility."

"Let's narrow the list down then. Who are your less likelies?"

"The first one is Detective Cynthia Rogers, who was stabbed during a drug bust six months ago. She was critical following the attack, but managed to pull through. She's been back on the job for about four months now. But we're not looking for a woman, so unless one of her male coworkers or relatives wanted to go this far, I don't think we're looking at Detective Rogers. Then there is Julio Hernandez. Hernandez is a beat cop out of the Seventy-fifth. He witnessed an illegal firearms sale in a back alley in Brooklyn, went after both suspects, and got caught in a firefight during the apprehension. Got hit in the shoulder, but managed to take the shooter down. Was pretty vocal about it afterward."

"Sounds like what he needed was backup more than the ability to search the suspects," McFarland said. "It was a firearms exchange, and he knew there were weapons."

"That's what I was thinking, and why he's moved down my list. But then we have Connor Boyle. Connor was an officer with the Midtown South Precinct. He was killed four months ago responding to the report of a robbery. He stopped a suspect, but didn't have cause to search him. That suspect then gut shot him, point-blank, before making an escape. He was never apprehended. Officer Boyle died at the scene."

"Officer Boyle is not our hostage taker then," McFarland said. "But maybe a fellow officer?"

"You're half right. I think our suspect is his father, John Boyle. Captain John Boyle, out of the Forty-first Precinct. Or he was, until he retired five months ago."

"That one hits all the right notes." McFarland bent over his keyboard, clicked a few times, and then turned it around so Gemma could see. "Here's Captain Boyle."

The man staring statically back at them was wearing dress blues with his captain's bars on the collar of a crisp white shirt. Over his left breast pocket lay his shiny gold-and-blue enamel captain's shield under a stack of NYPD medals Gemma recognized as she scanned the photo—an American flag breast bar, the World Trade Center breast bar, the Exceptional Merit medal, and the Medal for Valor. The captain was posed in front of the standard American flag/NYC flag backdrop of all official NYPD officer photos. However, instead of the smile many officers wore, his expression was serious, like he carried the weight of the world on his broad shoulders. His eight-point uniform cap covered hair already gone gray, and his light gray eyes stared out from under heavy lids in a wide face.

"This guy was no lightweight. Those are some serious medals for significant acts of courage. Did he retire with full honors?"

"Let me check." McFarland spun the laptop back around to face him and ran a quick search query. "Yes. On time, as expected. Nothing notable there. Some local write-up about a solid career cop." He whistled. "Here's something useful. He's third-generation NYPD."

"Which made his son fourth generation. Any other Boyles on the force?"

"The PBA newsletter only mentions the single son. No other family."

"So his son's death cost him everything," Gemma hypothesized. "A son. The potential for grandchildren and a continuing family line to carry on the Boyle name. The common NYPD history and the pride of all those generations of cops dating back to . . . World War Two? All taken away by a single bullet from a gun his son didn't know about because he couldn't search for it. Also, note that Boyle is an Irish surname and he picked Patrick, a classic Irish name, a saint even, as his pseudonym. What do you want to bet there is or was a Patrick Boyle in his family tree?" She sat back in her chair, propping her elbows on the arm and weaving her fingers together. "I can't prove it, but this is the guy, I can feel it. And keeping that in mind, we never had a chance at this."

"What do you mean?" McFarland asked.

"Think back to what he said when I was trying to talk him out of killing Willan. 'That line was crossed before I ever set foot in this building.' He knew when he walked into City Hall that he intended to take a life in exchange for the life ripped out of his arms. The only thing I think went sideways was he always intended it to be Rowland, the man who championed repealing the policy that directly led to his son's death. Willan was always on board with it though, so when it was clear it wouldn't be Rowland, he was satisfied with Willan. We were never going to stop Willan's murder. Rowland's press conference didn't change the final result. Maybe it moved it up in the timeline, but Willan was lost the moment he was taken hostage. No matter what anyone said, there was never going to be any dealing with Boyle."

"Do you think that's why he wanted Rowland face-to-face? So he could kill Willan in front of him?"

"I'm not sure he wouldn't have taken them both out, given the chance. But I do think his angle on it changed as his original plan morphed. Losing his son had to just about kill Boyle. Right from the beginning, he said Willan was going to die and it was all Rowland's fault. He considers Rowland responsible for his son's death."

"He wanted Rowland to feel the same agony by killing a lifelong friend and colleague. Rowland is divorced with no children, so Willan would be the target with the most impact."

"Exactly. And when we wouldn't allow the face-to-face and he'd been pushed as far as he'd go, he did the next best thing. Killed Willan while Rowland was on the phone with him and could hear the terror of his last seconds when Willan knew he was going to die. And then the gunshot that ended it all." She sagged back in her chair. "Rowland will never forget those sounds for as long as he lives."

She knew that all too well.

"Mission accomplished then, as far as Boyle is concerned."

"Which brings me to my next thought." Gemma flipped back a page in her notepad, picked up a pen, and crossed out a single name. Then she studied the list:

Clara Sutton
Angelo Carboni
Janina Lee
Elizabeth Sharp
~~Charles Willan~~
Jamal Bowen
Andy McLaughlin
Carlos Rodriguez

She tapped her pen beside the list of names. "What if he's completed his end goal?"

"You mean 'a life for a life'?" McFarland looked thoughtful.

"And now that's done, he hasn't got anything left. He killed with deliberate planning and intent. That's murder one. We don't exercise the death penalty, but it still could be twenty-five to life in prison. Which would be a death sentence at his age. And, as you said, a cop in prison? The prison population will make his life a living hell or just might end it prematurely."

"He may not care if he makes it out alive today. He's done all he can to avenge his son's murder. This is where things get dangerous because if he really doesn't care what happens now, he may not care if the hostages live or die." Gemma set down her pen and looked up at McFarland "We need to get him back on the phone now. ESU has ears on him, and there haven't been reports of any additional gunfire, so, for now, the hostages are likely untouched. However, he may think his best chance to end this as quickly and painlessly as possible is suicide by cop. To do that, he'll want to become public enemy number one. And the best way to ensure *that* will be to kill everyone in the room."

CHAPTER 14

"*R*eady?" Garcia asked.

"Yes, sir." Gemma nodded at McFarland, who tapped in the phone number.

The phone rang again and again, and went to voice mail.

"Dial it again," she said.

Voice mail a second time.

"Is he ignoring the call, or is it chaos inside City Hall and he's occupied?" Taylor mused.

"Or is he so pissed he pulled the phone cord out of the wall and we're SOL on communications," McFarland countered.

"My money is on him playing it cool," said Garcia. "He's reestablishing that he's the one in control. Just in case killing Willan didn't get that point through."

"Oh, he's made his point abundantly clear." Gemma's voice was flat as she struggled to keep her temper under wraps. The senseless loss of life enraged her, but a loss of control now could lose them the entire game. She could afford to let her guard down with her colleagues, but today she didn't even want to crack that door open, for fear of what might come flooding out. This entire situation was digging up too much of a past she didn't want to dwell on.

Lives depended on her remaining calm. She'd made a connection with him; now it was time to leverage that connection against him.

The hostage taker finally picked up on the fourth round. "Now are you going to believe everything I say?"

"I never doubted your word." Gemma spoke carefully, feeling like every word carried the weight of a human life. "That's not the issue here."

"No, what's at issue here is that I want changes made. I've got another seven lives here that can walk the same path as Charles Willan. Is Rowland still there?"

"No. We sent him away. You don't need him anymore anyway. You've made your point."

"You think you know me so well. How do you know I don't want to kill every living soul in this room, including me?"

Gemma felt her patience slipping. She was so tired of his attitude and his disregard for the terrified lives he held in his grasp. She turned to Garcia, but she didn't even need to voice her question. He simply nodded his assent.

Time to set him off balance. Time to take the upper hand.

"I think you only wanted 'a life for a life.' Now that you've avenged Connor, how would he feel about you killing others in his name? People who are innocent of anything having to do with his death. People who are public servants . . . just like he was."

Gemma counted in her head as the seconds of silence ticked off. *One . . . two . . . three . . . fo—*

The laugh came first. It wasn't the reaction Gemma expected. She foresaw shock, surprise, or the disconcerted stumblings of confusion. But not humor.

"Well, a point to you," he said. "How'd you figure it out?"

"That you're John Boyle? I had you pinned as a cop back near the beginning of our conversation. Then it was just a matter of figuring out which cops had an ax to grind because of the lack of stop-and-frisk. You weren't the only possibility, but to me, you were the right possibility."

"Maybe Tony Capello is proud of his little girl after all."

"He sure is." A movement in the doorway caught her eye and she turned to face Sanders standing in the doorway. The look on his face told her they were out of time. "John . . . I can call you that?"

"You've earned it at this point."

"John, I don't think you want to hurt those other people. You've hurt Rowland, taken a loved one from him, like you feel he took from you. The other hostages don't deserve to die. You've made your point."

Sanders shifted his weight from foot to foot, and Gemma knew she needed to end her call with Boyle to discuss strategy—before Sanders blew right in front of the suspect. "John, can I have your word you won't harm any of the hostages for now? We've done what you asked, and city council is discussing your proposal. Let me see if they're making any progress."

This time, the laugh that came across the line wasn't full of amusement, but darkness. "Sure, Detective Capello. But don't keep me waiting long." He hung up.

As one, the Hostage Negotiation Team turned to Sanders, who looked ready to detonate. "What the fuck are you all playing at? I'm sending my men in now."

Gemma stepped forward as if to stop him. "No, wait!"

Garcia held up a hand, waving her back. "Hold up, Lieutenant. We need to make sure we have the hostages' best interests in mind."

"Their 'best interests'?" Sanders stepped up to Garcia, close enough to bump his chest with his bulky vest and equipment. "He just murdered the first deputy mayor in cold blood. Everyone is at risk in there. Our only choice is to go in there and get them all out."

But Garcia didn't budge an inch, just stood with his eyes locked unblinkingly on Sanders. "Unless you've got a clear kill shot through a window—and I bet you don't—you're going to storm into City Hall, and by the time you make it down the hallway, they'll all be dead. We know he's got at least one high-capacity weapon in there with him, and unless he's an idiot, and that's not even remotely how he comes off, it's extremely doubtful he's going to run out of ammo. And once he's killed them all, he'll probably take himself out as well. Or you will. On the bright side, you'll save taxpayers the cost of a trial and life imprisonment, but you'll have to make explanations to all the victims' families." He took a step toward Sanders. "What's your rush, Sanders? Do you have theater tickets and you don't want to miss your curtain?"

"He needs to be stopped." Sanders leaned in close, his voice dropping to a growl. "I've been here before. I know what happens when we wait too long. And you're going nowhere fast."

"Actually, we're making progress," Gemma said.

Sanders didn't move from his posturing stance with Garcia, but shot her a sideways look. "How is that? You just lost a hostage."

"We got Greenfield out. And now we know who we're dealing with. You may even have known him. Captain John Boyle out of the Forty-first." She had to hand it to Sanders—he had an excellent poker face. Except for the slight widening of his eyes, she would have thought the name meant absolutely nothing to him. But that slight tell gave him away. "You *do* know him."

"Know of him, especially because of his son. That's our guy?"

"That's our guy."

Sanders shook his head. "Doesn't matter. Can't matter. He killed Willan."

"It all matters, especially when we're trying to connect with him. He's a father in agony because his son, his whole life and part of his identity, was taken from him. It doesn't excuse what he's done, but put yourself in his shoes. You're a cop, someone who's used to being the champion, who's used to saving people. Now you're the victim. You have the skills and the weaponry to get a little of your own back and to find vengeance for your son. Would you do it?"

"Of course not."

Gemma shook her head in disappointment. "Too fast. If you were honest, you'd at least consider it. We're all human, so it would have to at least cross your mind. But I hope we wouldn't make the same choice as Boyle. We're supposed to uphold the law, not shoot it down in flames."

"He made his choice, now I'm making mine. I'm in charge of this operation. You had your chance to talk him down. Now it's time to force his hand." Sanders stepped back from Garcia and turned toward the open doorway.

"Wait! What if I can talk him out of there? Just him? What if I offer him a way out? Then we'd have a chance to take him down, out in the open, away from the hostages. Or even if I could just get him near a window. Give me a shot," Gemma bargained.

Sanders stared back at her, unblinkingly.

She was losing him. Time for one last-ditch attempt. It was in his power to take the operation to purely tactical methods, but she had to try one last time. "If I can't make it work, then he's yours." She raised both hands, palms out. "And we'll step back and won't get in your way."

Sanders turned to Garcia. "Is she running the show now, Garcia?"

If Sanders was trying to bring Garcia low by implying that a lesser officer—and a woman—was in charge, his failure was clear from Garcia's response. "She's the one who connected with him. I tried, but it never worked. She's got a better feel for him now." Garcia met Gemma's eyes. "I trust her implicitly. If she says she can do it, she can." He broke away to face Sanders again. "Let her try."

Sanders was silent for a moment as he looked from detective to lieutenant and back again. "Fine. This is your last kick at the can. I'm giving you thirty minutes. Do it now, or not at all." Without another word, he strode from the vault.

McFarland let out a low whistle. "Didn't think you were going to swing that one."

"Trust me, I didn't either." Gemma sat and slid on her headset. "Okay, let's get him back. Clock's ticking."

"One sec." He ripped the top sheet off his notepad and held it out to her. "While you were doing the two-step with Sanders, I put this together."

Gemma took the sheet, flipping it around and scanning his handwritten notes. A smile slowly curved her lips as she read. It was a full grin when she looked back up at him. "This is perfect." She flashed the list at Taylor and Garcia. "It's a list of details about Connor Boyle, which could come in very handy. Okay, let's talk to him." She read down the list again as the phone rang in her ear, but her head came up when Boyle's voice came over the line. "John, my apologies for the interruption, but I know you must be eager to hear about council's progress. They're still talking, I'm afraid, but they tell me they have all hands on deck and are discussing the issue in depth. But while they work, I have something I'd like you to consider. Something I asked to bring to the table."

"You?"

"Yes, me personally. John, I'm a cop, just like you. Yes, you're retired, but we don't stop being cops just because we're drawing a pension. It's in the blood. In the bone. It's who we are. It's who Connor was." She paused, giving her words space to increase the punch. "We're 'on the side of the angels.'" She held very still, not even daring to breathe, waiting to see if he would laugh at her echo of his words, or if it would strike home.

"He was." The words were so quiet as to almost be a whisper.

Gemma flicked her eyes up to Garcia, who simply gave her a single nod of approval.

Got him. Interesting, though, that he no longer includes himself. Because of Willan's death?

"Connor wouldn't want you to kill in his name," Gemma continued. "*Fidelis ad mortem.*'" It was a phrase every New York cop knew, the mission statement every recruit learned—"Faithful unto death."

"Connor was. And he would want you to be. You've made your point, John. Now it's time to let the others go. You've had your 'eye for an eye,' don't you think?"

She let the seconds of silence tick by, knowing an open-ended question, followed by the weight of silence, could sometimes push a suspect harder than insistent screaming. She waited, hoping her intrusion into his emotions would play into her hands.

But the silence drew out too long. *Come on, John. Work with me. You're going to get everyone killed.*

She was drawing breath to fill the void when he finally spoke.

"You know as well as I do that the moment I let the hostages go, I'm dead. Who've you got running the op? Cartwright?"

It didn't occur to her to lie. He knew too much. "Sanders."

Boyle's laugh was harsh. "I would have been better off with Cartwright. Sanders is a goddamn cowboy. He must already be pushing to storm the place."

"You let me worry about Sanders. He knows we're talking. But you're right, he won't wait forever. Let me help you."

"What have you got in mind?" His skepticism came across loud and clear.

"You send out all the hostages and then you come out. I give you my word that no one will hurt you."

Skepticism gave way to a rolling laugh for several seconds before it cut off abruptly. "No. You must think I'm insane."

"Not at all. I think you're a man who knows how this works."

"You got that right. And because I know how this works, I know very well that Sanders will have his best sharpshooters on the surrounding buildings and will give the order to take the kill shot the moment they've got it. So . . . no."

"I'm not interested in killing you, John. I'm HNT. Keeping everyone, and I mean *everyone,* alive is what I do."

"No, you want them to take me into custody. And we're back to 'you must think I'm insane.' You know what happens to a cop in prison. I won't last more than a few weeks before someone shanks me. So again . . . no."

Gemma glanced at the clock at the head of the table. She'd already used a third of her allotted time. It was time for the last-ditch offer. "What do you need then? Transportation with a guarantee of safe passage to it?"

"You're going to arrange that? You know getting out of Lower Manhattan by road won't work. You could make it look like a possibility from here, but three streets over, in every single direction, will be blocked. And then we're back to prison."

"What if I bring in a helicopter?"

"Bring it in where? There's not enough room to land in front of City Hall."

"No . . ." She drew the word out, wracking her brain for a feasible location.

Taylor sprang out of his chair, grabbed the aerial map of the

Civic Center, and pushed it toward Gemma. He drilled an index finger at the intersection of Broadway and Park Avenue. The orientation of Park Avenue coming in at an angle to Broadway produced a wider-than-usual open intersection with no wires overhead to foul helicopter rotors.

That would do nicely. Gemma nodded her thanks. "There's enough space at the intersection of Broadway and Park. The area around City Hall Park is cordoned off, so it will be wide open. I could arrange for a pilot to fly in. You'd just have to give us a little time to make the arrangements."

Boyle was quiet for a moment, then heaved out a breath. "I want to think about it."

"I can give you some time for that." Gemma checked the time again. "Take fifteen minutes. I can hold Sanders off that long. But you leave the hostages alone, John, or I can't help you anymore."

"You have my word on it."

"Good. I'll call you back in fifteen minutes." She nodded to McFarland and he ended the call. She sat back in her chair. "That's it, right there. He's either going to take the bait, or Sanders won't give us any more time."

"Sanders is never going to let him get as far as a helicopter," Garcia said. "He's going to want to take him in. If he can't manage that, he's going to want to take him down. But I can talk him into getting a helicopter on-site as bait."

"He will only agree if no other hostage is harmed." Taylor reached for the map, pulling it closer to him, studying the intersection he'd suggested. "This location is going to be a tight fit, but a good pilot could manage it. He can set a flight path over City Hall Park and then set down between the streetlights." He looked up at Gemma. "Will you call Sanders now?"

"No. He gave me thirty minutes. When I call Boyle back, that will be just about time. Then we'll figure out how to make it work. But if Boyle won't go for it, I don't want to waste already-strained resources on a needless operation." She rolled some of the stress-induced stiffness out of her shoulders and stood. "I need some air." She picked up her phone, marking the time again. "I'm going to take five. I'll be right back."

For the first time since the operation started, she left the vault, pushing through the crowd of officers in the open office space, making her way outside. She stepped out on the sidewalk lining Broadway, turning her face up into the warmth of the last of the late-afternoon sun. The change in light made her realize how much time had passed since she'd entered their incident headquarters. They'd been inside a closed vault with no windows for hours and she'd been so focused she hadn't noticed the passage of time.

She was struck once again at the ghostly unreality of the quiet of the empty streets. One of the things she loved about New York City was the constant hustle and bustle of city life. Pedestrians jostling for space on the overcrowded sidewalks, street vendors selling their wares in the summer heat, and cars jammed in bumper-to-bumper traffic. Bike messengers weaving through vehicles and around those on foot with an adept skill that kept them not only on their bikes, but successfully zipping along. The smells of the food cart on the corner mixing with exhaust and human perspiration. The roar of an impatient driver taking off as the light turned green, music rising and falling from passing cars, pedestrians bellowing at drivers skimming too close, and dogs barking from a fire escape far overhead. And now . . . nothing. Standing, staring into the empty green space of the park, she could hear birdsong and the trickle of water from the fountain.

It was disconcerting.

Taking a deep breath of air that smelled almost-sterile without the overriding smell of traffic, she took a few minutes to walk down Broadway to the Woolworth Building. Standing on the corner, she tipped her head back, following the long line of pale limestone and shining windows up sixty stories into the blue sky.

It was amazing to think that a single episode in her life brought her to this place, standing in eerie quiet in the middle of the most populated city in America, waiting to find out what she'd need to do to save the lives of seven innocent people who wanted nothing more than to return to their families and forget about the horror of this day.

Not that they ever would. No one knew that better than Gemma.

* * *

She'd been at NYU, halfway through her bachelor's degree in psychology, and had been coming home late from studying in the twenty-four-hour Bobst Library. She stood on the A line platform in the West 4th Street–Washington Square Station, having just missed a train as she arrived. It was nearly one thirty in the morning and the platform was deserted except for a young man with a purple NYU backpack all too similar to Gemma's own. At first, she didn't notice him, due to her irritation at having to wait a full twenty minutes for the next train when she was beyond exhausted and stressed about her upcoming exams. But his pacing at the far end of the platform finally caught her attention. He'd stepped to the edge of the platform and stared down at the tracks, then peered expectantly down the dark tunnel for an oncoming train, only to glance back at the tracks and retreat. All while muttering as if giving himself a pep talk.

It was when he completed the cycle a third time that the back of Gemma's neck started to prickle with alarm. It wasn't just being in a deserted subway station with someone who was potentially unstable—she was a New Yorker and was entirely used to the characters who often rode the subway. Furthermore, her father was a cop and she had four brothers who had taught her how to protect herself. There was something about the young man—the misery that radiated from him, edged with both fear and indecision—that made her realize something was terribly wrong. By the fourth time he did it, as she studied the way he looked down at the tracks, she was convinced he was considering stepping in front of the oncoming train.

Gemma did the only thing Tony Capello's daughter would even consider—she walked over and struck up a conversation, blatantly challenging what he was about to do. The young man, whose name was Doug, had been startled and embarrassed, and had nearly bolted—which she knew would be a disaster, as he might simply pick a different station for the same goal—but Gemma was able to use her own experience at NYU, highlighting her own struggles and stresses, to show him he wasn't alone. And while suicide might end his own pain, it would only be the beginning of his family's agony to go on without him.

When the train pulled into the station, they were seated, side by side, on one of the station benches that ran down the middle of the platform. They picked up their nearly identical backpacks and boarded the train together. And the next morning, she met Doug first thing and accompanied him to NYU's Counseling and Wellness Services, only leaving him there once he went into his first appointment.

That win had changed the course of her life. Law enforcement had always been her goal, but she learned that day that negotiating with a person in crisis could proactively change a life in ways most reactive cop work couldn't. The losses and failures would come later, as they did for every cop, but that day set her feet on the path toward a career in the HNT. She'd never looked back. Neither had Doug, who survived that year at NYU and all the years that followed. And while he now lived in California, he remained a close friend.

Gemma's phone alerted an incoming text, bringing her back to the here and now. With a sigh, she turned her attention to the difficulties at ground level, and sent a return text to McFarland that she was right outside and would be there in two minutes as she speed walked to their temporary headquarters. She was back inside the windowless vault with minutes to spare and regretted hurrying. A minute or two more outside would have served her better than sitting inside watching the seconds tick by.

She called promptly at the fifteen-minute mark. She sat stiffly in her chair, dreading his refusal of her offer and the carnage that might precipitate. He had to take it; sending in the A-Team and the ensuing bloodshed would be a stain City Hall would never be able to shake. She loved this city and the grandeur of City Hall, and didn't want this to be a permanent part of its record.

Boyle didn't even bother with a greeting as he picked up. "I've thought about your offer. I don't like it."

Stifling a groan of disappointment, Gemma hung her head. She'd failed.

"But I have a counteroffer," he continued.

Her head snapped up. "What's that?" She was careful to keep any hope or excitement out of her voice.

"You want the hostages released."

"We want them released, unharmed, yes."

"Fine, unharmed. I'll agree to that proposal, but only on one condition."

"What's that?"

"Not so fast."

He's taking his time with this. Enjoying being in charge, being the one to give the orders and seeing everyone, especially someone he'd see as a junior officer, jump to his command.

"I want to work with you, John, but I can only do that if you meet me halfway. What is your one condition?"

"This is my final offer, take it or leave it. I send out all the hostages, one at a time, but to do that, I need one thing delivered here first."

"What's that?"

"You."

CHAPTER 15

"*A*bsolutely not!"

Gemma rubbed fingertips over the headache pounding behind her temples. She'd already gone around with Garcia on this, and now she was butting heads with Sanders.

"It's the only way."

"It's not the only way." Sanders slapped a hand over the butt of his carbine. "We'll go in and get them out."

Gemma bunched her fists at her side to keep herself from shoving Sanders in frustration. "We've gone over this. You're going to get them all killed. He wants me in exchange for all of them. It only makes sense. 'The needs of the many outweigh the needs of the few. Or the one.'" Gemma felt like an idiot quoting Mr. Spock to Sanders, but she was pretty sure he'd never make the connection between that quote and a fictional character. Besides, it succinctly summed up exactly how she felt.

She knew what it was to feel like her life was entirely out of her control and that help, if it ever arrived, would surely not come in time.

Two men bursting through Dime Savings Bank's doors just as she and her mother were next in line for the teller. Herding the customers and the employees at gunpoint into the center of the bank, to sit on the cold marble floor under the rotunda, towered over by a forest of tall, decorative columns.

One man keeping them at gunpoint. The other forcing the bank man-

ager to empty the tills and then open the vault and the lockboxes inside to remove all the cash and valuables. At first, both intruders were calm, and the man with the gun who watched them was careful to keep the barrel pointed at the floor.

Until the police arrived.

Then the arguing started. And the screaming that made her wince and shiver and curl into a ball against her mother to hide her eyes. Then the threats against the hostages to use them as leverage. The man who seemed to be in charge firing into the ceiling. The women screaming and crying and one of the men begging.

Her mother's stoic face as she set her daughter aside and stood, stepping forward to talk in that calm, rational tone of voice she used when her father got riled up about something at work. The man screaming in her face to stop, to sit down, and to shut up. Her calm and measured response.

Until he'd made her stop. Permanently.

How long had she sat frozen beside her mother's motionless body clutching her limp hand in both her own? Half an hour? An hour? When her father had followed the first wave of officers inside, he'd had to peel her fingers away from her mother's cooling hand. Only then could he wrap her in his arms and carry her to safety. Leaving the shell of the woman he loved behind forever.

There was nothing he could do for his wife. As an officer, he knew he had to abandon her there, alone and quiet in the whirlwind of chaos around her, until her body was photographed and removed to the cold, sterile morgue. To be closed in darkness in a drawer, that special flame, that spark that was Maria Capello, extinguished forever.

As a child, Gemma hadn't understood much of what had happened that day. But later, as an adult and as an NYPD officer, she'd considered the scene differently. The two partners: one the aggressor, the driving force, willing to do violence to get what he wanted; the other, the submissive who was willing to do what was needed to win the approval of his partner, but who drew the line at actual violence. The bulletproof vests the men wore, a precaution taken because they expected the possibility of a firefight. The watch sewn onto the back of one of the two men's black gloves, so they could mark the time from the moment they entered the bank to the time they'd estimated—seven minutes—for a police response. But when a passing cruiser had noticed the situation and called in backup early, their plan had gone to hell. That's when the desperation had set in.

And that's when her mother had taken too much into her own hands.

Gemma would have to be blind not to see the similarities between then and now. Her mother had stood up to protect the hostages. For years, Gemma had tried to guess at her motivation, just as her father must have. Was she trying to be the voice of reason? Was she trying to distract them from her daughter? Was she overconfident in her abilities because she was a cop's wife and felt she had a view inside the world of law enforcement from his stories? Had she not ascribed enough value to her own worth? Had she not thought about the risk she was taking and what it would do to her family?

Gemma had gone around and around on it, trying to discern what her mother had been thinking. And in the end, she knew no more than when she'd started.

But today gave her extra insight. Her mother had put the lives of the hostages before her own. It had cost her everything. Had cost her family everything. Now it was Gemma's turn. She had to hope her training, intuition, and strength as a strategist would help her survive. Because a second loss would damage her family in ways she couldn't bear to contemplate.

"Maybe we should get the chief down here," Sanders snapped.

"Chief Phillips?" Gemma knew this was an important operation, and Phillips had to be remotely monitoring it, but the police department would be better served by its chief handling the media end of this circus. And the mayor.

"No, I think this situation calls for the Chief of Special Operations. This does fall under his purview, after all. Should I call for Chief Capello?"

Anger rose up in Gemma to burn blisteringly hot. "You wouldn't dare."

"Why not? It's his department."

"Sanders is a goddamn cowboy." Boyle's words rang in Gemma's head. Out of the corner of her eye, she noted McFarland and Taylor were now also on their feet and she held out a hand, palm out, to tell them to stand down. "You know why," she bit out.

"Don't be an asshole, Sanders." Garcia grabbed Sanders's arm, twisting him around to partially face him. "You know he lost his wife to a situation not so different from this one. Don't leverage that pain to make sure you get your own way."

"Thank you," Gemma said quietly.

Garcia whirled back to her. "I'm still not letting you go in there."

"In where?"

As one, the officers turned to face the open doorway of the vault. A man stood there, dressed in a navy suit that screamed "public servant." In a fog of temper, Gemma had trouble placing him immediately, but Garcia was already moving forward, his hand extended. "Public Advocate Blackwell. This is unexpected."

"Mayor Rowland asked me to come down to assist with the incident. He is . . ." He paused, glancing over his shoulder through the vault doorway. "Indisposed."

Puzzle pieces clicked into place in Gemma's head. Rowland was so devastated by Willan's death that he'd taken himself out of the picture, sending instead the man who was next in line to succeed him. Willan may have been his closest confidant and right-hand man as his first deputy mayor, but it was the elected public advocate who was the first in line of succession if the mayor became incapacitated. Blackwell's statement was understated, but everyone in the room understood—for the time being, he was in charge of the city.

"Where aren't you sending her?" Blackwell asked.

Sizing up the situation quickly, Gemma saw a potential ally. She pasted on a smile and took a step toward Blackwell, holding out her hand. "Detective Gemma Capello, sir." They shook. "The suspect holding the hostages, John Boyle, has made a request to end the standoff. He is willing to send out the remaining seven hostages in exchange for . . . me."

Blackwell looked from Gemma to Sanders to Garcia. "And you won't send her in?"

"Sir, I'm sorry, but this is a police matter, not a political one," Garcia stated.

"That may be, but you understand the mayor and I have a vested interest in this situation. We've already lost First Deputy Mayor Willan. We can't afford to lose other staffers who were simply in the wrong place at the wrong time when this man . . ." He turned back to Gemma, a question in his eyes.

"John Boyle, sir."

"When John Boyle took the hostages captive. If this all goes to hell, it's going to be a media nightmare for the police department and the city. We need to do everything in our power to resolve this immediately. If this is the way to save all those people, and Detective Capello is willing to make the exchange, I don't understand what the issue is."

"Because the most important rule of hostage negotiation is to *not be* in the same room as the hostage taker." Garcia's voice was sharp, like he was struggling to keep his temper tamped down in the face of someone who could pressure them to overrule their decision. "We do all our communications by phone if possible. The only hostage negotiators who have ever died on the job have done so by trying to deal with a suspect face-to-face. Every. Single. One. I'm not sending my negotiator in with a suspect who just shot the first deputy mayor in the head."

Blackwell winced at the brutality of both tone and image, but didn't back down. "Don't you anticipate that's how he'll deal with all the hostages if Detective Capello doesn't go in?"

"The plan is to not give him the chance," Sanders interjected. "I have sharpshooters on roofs surrounding the building and a team ready to go in. We'll get the hostages out and neutralize Boyle."

"In time to keep everyone safe?" Blackwell turned back to Gemma. "What's the plan if you go in?"

"Once I'm in, he said he'll send out the remaining hostages, one at a time. We told him we'd bring in a chopper and land it at Broadway and Park."

A mixture of confusion and disbelief clouded Blackwell's face. "Your plan is to let him . . . escape?"

"No, sir. The helicopter is essentially a decoy to get him out of the building. Once he's out, the A-Team will surround him and take him into custody."

"I'm not hearing a downside to this plan so far." Blackwell pinned Garcia with a flat stare. "Your problem is that you just don't want her in the building with him."

"My *problem* is that there are no guarantees. I could send in one of my best negotiators, one I handpicked to be on this team, and he could kill her as she walks through the door and then kill all the hostages and himself."

"He's not going to do that," Gemma countered.

"And why is that?"

"It's about what we've set up for him. He's not going to suggest that the best way for him to get away is to saunter two full city blocks to the chopper on his own. He's going to have me with him." She swung to face Sanders. "I'll be his cover because he knows you won't give the order to kill the suspect when he's using another cop as cover. Especially when that cop is the daughter of the Chief of Special Operations."

Blackwell's eyebrows arched at that detail. "You told him this?"

"No, he recognized my last name. It's one of the ways I figured out he's a cop."

Blackwell drew back sharply. "The guy's a cop?"

"Yes."

"Why the hell is he doing this? What happened to 'serve and protect'?"

"His son was also a cop. He was killed on the job and he's lashing out." When Blackwell started to protest, she held up a hand to forestall him. "I'm not justifying what he's done, I'm just explaining so you understand this isn't a random event. I think now that he's claimed his 'life for a life,' all he wants to do is get the hell out of Dodge. I don't think he's interested in killing the hostages." She trained her stare on Sanders. "Unless we give him cause to, by going in there with guns blazing." She swung back to Blackwell. "I don't think he'll harm me either, though I admit that's just a gut feeling. It's one of the reasons I think I should be going in there."

"When is he expecting you to contact him again?"

"Anytime."

"How long will it take to bring in the chopper you mentioned? You are planning on doing that, right?"

"We'd need to make it look like we expect him to get on board and fly away, so all the pieces have to be in place," said Sanders. "He's close enough that he'll be waiting to hear it land."

Blackwell shot back his suit coat to reveal a jet-black wristwatch. "It's five-thirty. How long will it take to arrange?"

"About forty-five minutes to an hour to get someone in here and to get him safely landed in a tight spot."

Blackwell gave a curt nod. "Then get it arranged. What I'm hearing right now is that this is certainly not an operation without risk, but I don't hear any other better suggestions. And if you come up with an alternate idea in the meantime, let's discuss it." When Garcia and Sanders didn't move, his jaw tightened. "Or do you need me to call Doug to discuss it with him and to get the ball rolling?"

Gemma could see the casual way Blackwell dropped Chief Phillips's first name grated on both men, but they did an admirable job of covering it.

"No, sir. I'll start making arrangements." Sanders picked up his tactical helmet from the table and marched out of the room.

"I'll give you room to get ready," Blackwell said. "But I'll be back in about an hour so I can report on the operation to Mayor Rowland. He very much wants to see this man taken into custody."

"We'll do our best." Garcia gave Blackwell a curt nod as Blackwell left the vault. Garcia waited, watching the man exit the building.

Only then, did he turn back to his team with a vicious curse. "Okay, time to put our heads together. He may think he's running the show, but I'm not sold on this. We need to find another option or I'm calling off this entire operation."

CHAPTER 16

As a group, they came up with every idea they could think of, both the possible and the impossible. From using the helicopter to drop a couple of A-Team officers on the roof of City Hall before it moved on to land at Broadway and Park, to quietly picking the lock on the side door of the building out of sight of the prying eyes of any media cameras, to forcing a window in the east wing, to trying to gain entry through the sunken basement door.

But they kept circling around to the fact that Boyle was holed up in an interior room with a high-powered assault weapon, likely with his back to the wall and the open doorway across from him. Possibly using the hostages in front of him as human shields. He'd kill anyone unexpected who tried to get through that doorway.

It would be a suicide mission. Not to mention that if any of the hostages were caught in the middle, which was practically guaranteed, they'd be instantly slain as well.

The idea of having an A-Team officer circle the building to come up to one of the windows in the mayor's office to get a shot off down the hallway and into the conference room was similarly rejected. This was an ex-cop. He wouldn't be so careless as to expose his position to any exterior vulnerability and certainly would not take up a perch with direct line of sight to a window. Any similar attempt would simply end in at least one hostage being killed in retribution. If not all of them, in fact.

While they played for time, they communicated with Boyle as if the plan was green-lit and under way.

"I want to know what time you're coming in," Boyle demanded.

"You want me to think you're an unplanned infiltration and shoot you as you walk in the front door?"

Garcia's narrowed stare clearly communicated to Gemma that this was exactly why she was never going to set foot in the building.

"John, you know an operation this complicated may not go like clockwork, but we're doing our best to keep you updated on the details as we learn them. We expect the chopper to arrive at six forty-five. I'll enter City Hall at the same time."

"No. That's too late. Six-thirty."

"I don't know if we can make it happen that fast."

"You tell Garcia to find a way to make it happen that fast if you want these hostages to survive. I'll see you at six-thirty." He hung up.

"Jesus Christ." Garcia's fist came down on the desk, but from the look on his face, the aggressive action didn't release any of his tension. "You see why I don't want you in there?"

"We need to call him back and tell him we agree to six-thirty," Gemma said, keeping her tone level, knowing the situation had degraded to such an extent that she was now negotiating inside the vault, as well as over the phone line. "That will make him feel like he has some measure of control. Otherwise, at six thirty-one, he's going to start thinking about executing a hostage."

"Fine. Call him back. Tell him what he wants to hear. But we still need to find another way."

Gemma called Boyle and informed him they agreed to his request. In a show of good faith, when Gemma asked for another quick proof-of-life conversation with the hostages, he agreed without arguing. Not knowing how much Boyle had communicated to the hostages, Gemma quickly told each one that a deal had been struck, and they would be freed later that evening. The relief and joy coming over the line was gratifying. This was the point of the HNT: to bring hope from despair, to resurrect life from the ashes of death.

But that hope was entirely lacking inside the vault of the HNT headquarters as they came down to the final minutes before Boyle's deadline.

"I'm not saying it again," Garcia snapped.

"You told the public advocate we were a go." Gemma pushed back hard, feeling victory slipping through her fingers. "You're going to explain to him when he shows up in ten minutes that you pulled the operation at the last second with no other feasible way to replace it?"

"You're pulling the operation?"

Gemma, Garcia, McFarland, and Taylor looked up to find Sanders in the doorway. Logan stood behind him, his helmet and safety glasses already in place, ready to act immediately on Sanders's anticipated orders.

"Yes." Garcia straightened from the map of the area spread across the two tables. "I have word right from Chief Phillips that he doesn't like it. Yes, he'll only have one hostage instead of seven, but what's his next demand going to be? Now, instead of a bunch of unknowns, he's going to be making demands to the NYPD using the life of their officer as collateral. A life that the Chief of Special Operations, a gang squad lieutenant, a patrol sergeant, and an IAB goon will all be arguing to save at any cost."

Garcia's reference to Alex as a "goon" made her temper, already stretched thin, edge closer to snapping completely. She clamped her jaw shut and ground her teeth to keep herself from saying something she'd regret.

"What's Phillips's plan? To send in someone else?" Sanders asked.

"We discussed it, though he's not wild about that either. It still puts one of his officers at risk."

"I'll go," McFarland blurted. "We need to send in someone who's a trained professional and can deal with Boyle on the fly as the situation shifts. Realistically, it needs to be someone from this team. Someone who is not only a negotiator, but is familiar with the suspect. We know him now, have done the research to understand where he's coming from and a little of how he ticks."

Garcia discarded the idea with a flick of his hand. "No, we need you here to run the tech. We need to keep talking to him."

"Respectfully, sir," McFarland retorted, "that's bullshit, and you know it. Taylor could run comms, and so could Capello."

"If McFarland isn't appropriate," Taylor interjected, "I can do it. It can't be you, Lieutenant—you've already lost the connection with him. If you went in, instead of Capello, it could set him off." He glanced at the clock. "I need to go now though. We're cutting this close." He pushed back his chair from the table.

That was it for Gemma. They were talking around her as if she wasn't there. Her team was good, and the men in it didn't tend to treat her differently because she was a woman, but she suspected that played into part of their attitude now. She wouldn't allow them to discount her ability to handle the man inside City Hall. No one had a stronger relationship with him. More than that, her gender had absolutely nothing to do with her ability to do her job and do it well.

On top of it all, she was the only one in the room who truly knew the bone-melting terror of someone else holding your life in their hands, and knowing that life meant less than nothing to them. She was a fellow officer, and she was the daughter of a cop familiar to Boyle. She would play into that, making ending her life a more difficult choice for him. And in doing so, she might just save herself.

"Enough." She stood to tower over the men at the table. "It has to be me. I'm the only one he'll accept. You'll kill seven innocent people if you send anyone else in under a flag of truce. You'll kill them faster if you send anyone else in under a flag of war."

Garcia rose to his feet to face her. "And I'm issuing you a direct order. You will not go in there."

There it was, the challenge she knew could surface at any time. She really had no choice with what came next, not if she wanted to be able to live with herself afterward. She slid her hand down to the detective shield clipped to the waistband of her capris. She yanked it off and slapped it down on the table. Then she pulled her holstered Glock 19 from under her peasant blouse and laid it beside her shield.

Ignoring McFarland's indrawn surprised breath and Sanders's guttural curse, she met Garcia's shocked gaze. "Now I don't have to follow your orders." She looked down at her shield, pushing aside the arguments already screaming in her head about walking away from her life's work. "And now they don't have to argue for the life of a fellow officer. Tell them I went rogue. Take no responsibility for this."

"I could have you arrested for interfering with a police investigation, civilian," Garcia snapped.

Gemma couldn't help wincing at the moniker. Over twenty years working toward a goal, gone in a snap. "You could, but I know you're smarter than that and I know you value the lives of those civilians more than that. We're out of time and Boyle's out of patience. If I don't go in there, the hostages *are* going to die."

"So Tony Capello's daughter is going to play the hero?" Sander's tone carried the hint of a sneer.

"Only because Tony isn't here to do it himself," she retorted. "And if he was here, he'd be going in with me." She turned her back on Sanders to face the man who had been her commander up until minutes before. "I know you're torn. I know you're looking for a way for all of us to win, but there isn't one unless I walk in there because he won't accept anyone else. If it all goes to hell, blame me. Tell whatever story you need to make sure the team and the department come out of this clean. You know my family; they won't hold the department to blame. That's all on me."

She strode from the room, carefully meeting no one's eyes. As she cut through the outer office, she heard an explosion of sound come from within the vault, McFarland's voice loudest of all arguing, "You can't let her do this."

Too late. The damage is already done.

Don't think about it. Focus on the operation.

She pushed through the officers milling near the front windows—none of whom tried to stop her; for now, only the five men inside the vault knew what she'd done—and burst out through the front door, into the clear air of late summer, where she could breathe again. Dragging in a lungful of fresh air, she jogged across the street, as if expecting Garcia to grab her from behind to stop her. But when she mounted the curb on the far side and looked back, the door below the old Citibank sign remained closed.

She blew out a long breath and sent a silent word of thanks to McFarland and Taylor, who had no doubt kept Garcia too busy arguing to come after her. The only thing she was truly leaving behind was her shield; Boyle had already specified she come in unarmed. But the lack of her shield left her feeling naked and bereft. Her only goal from the time she was a child was to follow in her father's and then her brothers' footsteps to become an NYPD officer. Now she'd thrown it all away.

What have I done?

Deal with it later. You need to survive this first. Then you'll find a way to get it back.

She wouldn't allow herself to contemplate the possibility that wouldn't be possible.

She checked the time on the fitness band that doubled as her watch: 6:25 p.m. *Right on time.* Fixing her gaze on the building in the center of the park and taking a deep breath, she started toward City Hall. She entered the park past the deserted security gatehouse that guarded the small parking lot for City Hall staffers, still full of cars because of the rapid evacuation.

The regret she felt at giving up her shield faded slightly under the greater guilt over what she knew she was going to put her family through. After her mother died, her father had not spared himself a single detail of the last moments of Maria's life. Every conversation, every movement. With a strong personal connection to the case, Tony had not been allowed to interview the one surviving suspect, but that hadn't stopped him from questioning his daughter, gently, but in a way that drew all the details from the shattered ten-year-old. Then he'd read every report in the case file. He'd attended every day of court and had been there for the sentencing. Only after the man had been sentenced to twenty-five to life had he put the outward grief away and moved on to the greater responsibility of raising their children alone. But Gemma knew the grief had stayed with him for years, and still snuck up on him occasionally.

And now, because of this one decision, she would put him through it all over again. He'd relive every moment of that day twenty-five years before—like it was yesterday. And then on top of it, he'd go through the fresh hell of his daughter being a hostage again. She may be a cop now, but to her father, part of her would always be the terrified and traumatized ten-year-old he pulled out of the bank. The little girl who took a full twenty-four hours to talk after watching her mother's murder. The little girl whose whole center had been violently taken from her as she'd helplessly watched. The little girl who grew up and was now the same age as her mother had been that fateful day.

Then there were her brothers. They, too, had lived with the shock of losing their mother, though they'd been spared witnessing her death. They were the sons of a cop, and were well familiar with the violence that came with Tony's career, even though he'd done his best to shield them from it. They, too, would be affected by this, and she was grateful they would be there for her father, if anything went wrong.

The guilt weighed heavier as she thought about what she was doing to those she loved. She had no choice, but regretted they were collateral damage.

Despite the summer heat, she shivered slightly as she stepped into the shade of the large trees surrounding City Hall, and couldn't help the memories from flooding back.

The chill of cold marble under her legs. The sobs of a terrified woman and the ragged breathing of the men. The splatter of blood and—

"Capello!"

She turned at the sound of running feet to find Sean Logan sprinting across the street.

She drew herself up taller. "Back off, Logan. I have this under control."

He came to a standstill five feet away and pulled off his safety glasses so she could look directly into his blue eyes. "I'm not sure you do."

"This is how it has to be."

"Garcia's not wrong. The likelihood of this going south is pretty high."

"Am I just supposed to leave them in there to die? They've spent hours at the mercy of a madman with a gun, a man who is so focused on revenge that he doesn't care who gets in his way. He's killed already today. That's the biggest barrier in a hostage taker. Once that first kill is complete, the rest all come pretty easily."

He moved to put himself between her and City Hall. "So you get to be the sacrificial lamb? It's your life for all of theirs? Is this your way of atoning for the past? You were ten. What were you supposed to do?"

White-hot fury rose up in Gemma and it took all her control not to slap him across the face for . . . what? Speaking the truth? Climbing into her head? Putting voice to feelings she didn't dare touch?

The reason didn't matter. She had a job to do. She stepped past him.

He grabbed her arm, spinning her back. "Gem."

The last time he'd called her that, it had been on a whisper in the dark. "Don't call me that." She yanked her arm free. "We're done here." She stared pointedly at his carbine. "Unless you plan on shooting me, get out of my way."

"Goddamn it, wait a second. You're going in there with no communications, no vest, and no weapon. You'll be completely at his mercy."

"No gun, no wire, no phone. Those were his conditions. And the bulletproof vest would be useless when he's close enough to make a head shot. All it would do is hamper my own movements. But he can't take away my experience and my intuition. You say I'm walking in there with no weapons. I disagree. Think back."

She saw the memory in his eyes: The two of them grappling during a training exercise. His confidence that he'd be able to take her down simply because of his greater size. Her stubborn determination that her skills would give her the edge. The stunned look in his eyes when she pinned him to the mat.

It was a mistake he'd only made once.

He gave a sharp nod of acknowledgment. "Point taken. Even

considering that, you're still walking into a totally unpredictable situation. I don't know if you're the bravest person I know, or the most foolhardy."

She didn't even pretend to know how to take that. She just shook her head and turned away. "I have to go."

"Capello, just . . . be careful. Don't underestimate him. He's wily and I'm not sure he figures he has much to live for at this point. 'Head up and eyes open.'" He echoed the words of one of their instructors from years ago, a mantra he repeated to his cadets daily. Simple words that saved lives on a regular basis. Could save hers today.

Logan took a step back from her, gripping the butt of his carbine in one white-knuckled fist.

Not stopping her, but fighting the instinct to do so.

She nodded at him. Then she turned away, squared her shoulders, and strode toward City Hall, her gaze fixed on the front doors and whatever awaited her inside.

CHAPTER 17

She climbed the steps to City Hall with her hands in the air.

The ABC7 team was still set up in City Hall Park, and she knew if they hadn't still been broadcasting, they would have started again the moment she appeared. She was sure Boyle watched her approach, but she wasn't about to take the chance he might think she was approaching in any kind of aggressive manner. He could even have stationed one of the hostages to watch for her approach at the designated time, so she deemed caution to be in order.

She had already crossed the raised stone platform encircling the front steps, passing between the twin flagpoles. With her hands held up above her shoulders, she mounted the dozen limestone steps climbing up to the main entrance.

She kept her eyes fixed on the five sets of double doors that opened into the building. Even on her walk from the gatehouse to the front steps, she assumed she was being watched, and took care not to search the tops of the buildings around her for any sign of A-Team sharpshooters. She knew they were there. And she was willing to bet a year's salary that Boyle knew it too.

She lowered one hand to grasp the handle of the middle set of doors and pulled it open to step through into the cool dimness of the foyer. On her right stood a tall bronze statue of George Washington towering over her as he stood atop a marble pedestal. She gave herself a few seconds for her eyes to acclimate to the lower lighting, and then moved through a stone archway into the airy rotunda. A grand, floating staircase rose ahead of her to split into two, curving higher to meet again on the second floor. The domed, coffered rotunda soared far overhead, supported by a circle of classical columns and lit by a central skylight.

But Gemma only barely spared a glance for the classical architecture as she looked down the hallway to the left. Beyond paired wooden benches painted white to match the walls, a short fence of vertical black bars with a gate separated the foyer from the mayor's suite of offices. Behind the gate sat a sturdy security desk, now deserted.

Not that security had helped City Hall staffers today.

Boyle wasn't far away now.

"John? It's Gemma Capello. I'm coming in, just as I promised. I'm alone and unarmed."

She opened the gate and stepped into a hallway lined with massive gold-framed paintings of historic City Hall notables hanging over the wainscoting. The closed door directly in front of her carried a brass sign to announce the OFFICE OF THE MAYOR OF NEW YORK CITY. She tried the knob. Unlocked.

She cracked the door open a few inches and called out her greeting again, not being sure when he'd actually be able to hear her. She found herself in a well-furnished reception space with a classic wood desk for an administrative assistant. McFarland's research had borne fruit and they knew who the hostages were now, as well as their basic history, and how they fit into City Hall life. This room was Janina Lee's post, where she would greet the many high-status visitors who came to meet with the mayor. The woman Gemma had spoken to had been calm and collected each time, even if a thread of fear wove through her tone. Gemma had the impression she was a woman used to managing an overbooked schedule, as well as stressful situations, but still had the sense to know this one was entirely out of her control.

The reception room matched the rest of the building's Federal style from the wainscoting to the spare decorative touches to the comfortable wing chairs in the waiting area.

An open door to the left led to a large, sumptuous, unoccupied room that had to be the mayor's personal office. Lit well by tall, mullioned windows, even if framed by curtains, Boyle would have instantly recognized it would be a death trap under the eagle eye of a sniper.

Gemma turned to the doorway on her right and called out again, sure he'd be able to hear her at this point. "John? It's Gemma."

"I hear you. Keep coming. Down the hallway, turn right. First door on your right."

"Okay, I'm coming in. I'm unarmed and I'll keep my hands in view." She slowly walked down the hallway, quickly taking in the surroundings in case she was able to stage an escape.

All the rooms on the left side of the hallway had light spilling through their open doorways to signify bared windows. When the building was constructed in the early nineteenth century, commercial electric lighting was over seventy years away, so architectural designs were fashioned to allow as much natural light into the work space as possible. The few completely internal rooms would have been dark, dungeonlike spaces, lit only by candle or lamplight.

But now, this enclosed space was the only logical place for Boyle to be.

She turned the corner and found an open doorway to her right. It faced the corridor wall, ensuring no line of sight for an eager sniper. A single exit ensured no one could cause a distraction at one entrance to allow escape at another. She glanced back at the doorway into the reception room to find the EMERGENCY EXIT sign shining over the top lintel. Only one entrance also meant only one exit. The enemy could only sneak up on you from one direction, if they dared to try.

It made Gemma wonder how far in advance Boyle had planned this. Had he manufactured a visit to the mayor's office to get the lay of the land? Or had he been invited here as part of his law enforcement duties or as a reward for a job well done? He was a decorated officer, so it wasn't unlikely he had met the mayor here before. If that had happened, and if Rowland discovered he had played even the smallest part in the scheme, it would only add to his agony over the death of his friend.

She paused outside the open doorway. "John, can I come in?"

"Yes. But go slow."

She took one cautious step, then two, then three. And stopped in the doorway of the combination library-and-conference room.

The first thing that hit her was the smell, recognizable as freshly spilled blood. Overlaying that was the odor of waste products, released from a body as it dies.

She took in the scene in one quick, calculating scan. The room was approximately twelve feet squared. Unlike many of the outer rooms and hallways, which were painted an off-white shade, this room was all dark wood and rich red carpet. Overstuffed dark walnut bookshelves lined all three walls, with the somber tones of burgundy, navy, and brown leather spines. A high-gloss mahogany table on a bloodred area rug filled the middle of the space, surrounded by a dozen upholstered armchairs.

Those chairs were currently filled down the far side of the table with hostages, with two more squeezed into the end. They sat with their hands folded in front of them on the table, clearly in view. Boyle sat midway down the near side of the table in a chair pulled away and angled toward the door, a man casually at rest. That is, if you ignored the AR-15 he held trained on her, center mass.

The nightmare lay behind Boyle. She couldn't see all of him, but a man's crumpled form lay in the far corner. He wore a dark suit and she caught a glimpse of a bright blue tie layered over a white shirt now drenched with blood. She couldn't see his head and she wasn't sure if it had fallen from view behind the chair— or if enough of it was missing that there wasn't anything to see. What she did know was there was a spray of blood and gray matter over the books about four feet from the ground.

She was right. He'd been on his knees begging for his life when he'd been shot in the head. The thought brought her no pleasure.

"Gemma . . . I may call you Gemma?"

She met his gaze unblinkingly. "Of course."

"Then, Gemma, welcome to our little group. Now turn around, feet apart, and put your hands on the bookcase."

She did as directed, assuming the classic frisk position, staring straight ahead and not flinching as he approached and roughly patted her down with one hand. Occasionally, as he moved, the barrel of the AR-15 pressed against her back, and she prayed his finger wasn't anywhere near the trigger or she'd be finished in less than a heartbeat. Many men might have taken the opportunity to cop a feel, but Boyle completed the search with the impersonal precision of a man who'd done searches a thousand times before and saw her as a subject rather than a woman. Good, that removed a whole layer of threat.

"Well done, Gemma. This whole exercise would have ended right here if you'd lied to me about being unarmed." His voice moved away from her as he spoke. She heard the rustle of clothing and upholstery as he sat down. "You can turn around now." With the barrel of the semiautomatic rifle, he indicated the chair at the end of the table closest to her. "Please have a seat."

She took her time moving to the chair, pulling it out and sitting down, taking care to keep the chair on a slight angle, and not to pull it up to the table, to allow for a quick exit, if needed. As she did so, she cataloged John Boyle.

He'd aged since his official NYPD photo, and not gracefully. The pale face from the photo had taken on a paunchy heaviness and a slightly ruddy tone. Without the eight-point uniform cap, she could see his gray hair was thinning and he now carried weight that wouldn't have fit behind the smooth lines of his dress blues. It was clear his son's death had hit him hard physically, as well as emotionally. But his gray eyes, still so icy cold and flat, even if sunken, were sharp and calculating, and she suspected he was similarly sizing her up. He was dressed all in black, from his boots to his cargo pants to his T-shirt.

She cataloged the arsenal he carried as well, at least what she could see, and she assumed there was more she couldn't see as he sat in the armchair. He had a handgun at his right hip; Gemma was pretty sure it was a SIG Sauer P226, a standard-issue pistol in the department since the early- to mid-nineties.

As she had told Logan, all she had was her experience and her intuition. To say the deck was stacked against her was an understatement, but she in no way considered herself outgunned.

"I told you I would come unarmed and without a phone. When I said I wouldn't lie to you, I was serious. How can we deal with each other if you can't believe everything I say?"

"Because you're trained to tell me what I want to hear. That's who you are and what you do."

She forced herself to give a light laugh. "Have you met my father?"

"Sure."

"What do you think of him?"

"I don't know him well, but he's well respected and has a sterling reputation as a straight shooter."

"Then think of me like you'd think of him. He raised me. He taught me what it was to be a cop even before the academy. That's who you're dealing with."

Boyle nodded thoughtfully, as if accepting of her statement, even if his weapon didn't waver.

Gemma pointed at the AR-15. "We weren't sure what you were carrying. We got reports of a high-capacity weapon, but couldn't figure out how you got in past security with it. But, evidently, you did."

"That was the easy part. If you want to stroll past the officers manning the security booths and their scanners, you just need to look like you belong there and are carrying the weapons they expect. The protest was my way in."

On the floor, a specialized police equipment bag draped with a utility belt caught her attention. The crumpled black shirt on the chair next to Boyle was the final clue. Gemma remembered her father's comment about the sustainable-energy demonstration that was taking place at City Hall; suddenly she knew exactly how he'd entered the mayor's office. "Where did you get the police uniform?"

"Online. There are plenty of places that sell uniforms and

equipment. Even knockoff shoulder patches that look identical to the real thing. I haven't been retired so long that I've forgotten protocol. I blended right in. And there were so many patrol cops down here, they never noticed one extra."

"And you could stroll past security wearing your SIG and no one looked at you twice. But a patrol cop wouldn't be carrying an AR-15."

Boyle ran one hand down the body of the rifle, almost lovingly. "It's a beauty, isn't it? But I didn't have to carry it out in the open. It's a special model I bought at a gun show a few years back. The barrel comes off and slides into the stock and then the body folds where the stock attaches to the receiver. Folds into a package about a foot long."

"And that's why you had an equipment bag."

Boyle grinned. "I just nodded at the guy in the security booth as he waved me through. Then when I got inside City Hall, I told the security guard we had a medical emergency with one of the protesters on the front steps and we needed a defibrillator. He grabbed the one he had stashed in the security desk and ran out with it. He thought I was behind him."

"But you went into the mayor's offices and pulled the fire alarm. And the guard never made it back in because of all the people running out."

"Now you've got it."

"No, now it's time to discuss letting the hostages go, as we agreed. I'm here, so it's time for them to go." She motioned to the landline phone sitting in the middle of the table, surrounded by a number of cell phones, some streaming footage of the front of City Hall. "I have the number of the negotiation team. We can call them and start the ball rolling."

"So I can talk to Garcia?" His smile held absolutely no joy. "No."

"Then I can talk to him."

Boyle laughed like that was the funniest thing he'd heard in weeks. Then the rolling laughter shut off like a tap. The effect was frankly startling, even to someone used to dealing with all kinds of devious personalities.

"No." The calculating twist of his lips told her he didn't believe in her honesty, no matter what she'd promised him. "And risk that you and Garcia have set up code phrases to give him information that could lead to an incursion? You forget I was on the job for over twenty years. I know our protocols." His eyes narrowed. "I know what I'm up against."

Gemma sat back in her chair, resting her elbows on the arms and interweaving her fingers together over her abdomen, hoping it projected the attitude of someone entirely hands-off with the proceedings. "Which is why I'm being totally transparent. You call. If you get Garcia, ask for someone else. But it's time to hold up your end of the bargain."

He fixed her with a slitted stare. "You're pushy for someone with absolutely no power."

"I disagree. I have the power of our agreement, including all the arrangements I've made for you. Also, you're NYPD. I know us. You'll do what you said you will. It's one thing to give a line to a perp, it's another thing to do that to a brother- or sister-in-arms. You'll do as you promised. Then, once they're all gone, we'll get to the chopper. That's just you and me." She pointedly glanced at her watch. "But if we don't move soon, Sanders may unilaterally decide it's not going to happen and take matters into his own hands."

"With you in here too?"

"Trust me, Sanders would come in here with guns blazing, even if his mother sat at this table. He's on a mission." She stared pointedly at the phone. "I recommend starting the process of getting the hostages, and then us, out of here. I don't want to die because he has a twitchy trigger finger."

Boyle hit the SPEAKER button on the phone and looked at Gemma. She rattled off the number she'd memorized, the direct line to the HNT phone.

The phone rang once and then was picked up. "Hello?"

Gemma was relieved to hear Taylor's voice on the other end of the line. Garcia had wisely stepped back.

"She's here now."

"That's good, John, I'm glad to hear that."

As Taylor talked to Boyle, keeping his attention, Gemma stole a few precious seconds to study the hostages. The four men and three women looked like they'd gone through hell and back. Clara Sutton, easily identified by the bloody abrasion across her left cheek, was one of Rowland's interns. She sat in the middle of the table flanked by a pale woman in a stylish business suit, who wore her hair in a straight fall of black silk, and a black man in his fifties, with his hair close-cropped into a gradual fade. The woman on her left, whom Gemma pinpointed as Janina Lee, sat with her arm linked through Clara's before her hands were folded together. Clara sat close; she was almost slumped against Janina. The black man on her right was Jamal Bowen, Rowland's chief of staff. The last of Rowland's staff, Angelo Carboni, a senior adviser whose olive complexion and wiry salt-and-pepper hair reminded Gemma of her grandfather, sat on Bowen's other side. Andy McLaughlin, the sole Willan staffer, an intern, was almost at the far end of the table. He sat with his body turned toward the door, his frozen face angled toward her. *Doing everything he can* not *to look at what's left of his boss.* The last two hostages, Elizabeth Sharp and Carlos Rodriguez, both newly hired junior bullpen staffers, sat at the far end of the table, their chairs drawn as far away from the body as possible. Elizabeth looked like she'd been crying. Carlos, on the other hand, eyed Boyle like he was waiting for his attention to waver just slightly so he could jump the older man.

Gemma made a point of catching Carlos's eye and giving him a subtle head shake. She was just about to get the hostages released. The last thing they needed right now was a hothead blowing the whole plan to hell. His face tightened, but he gave her a brief nod and sat back in his chair.

She turned her attention back to Taylor, who was in the process of outlining the hostage release.

"—one at a time, every five minutes. That way, each will be well clear of the property before the next one comes out."

"No, that will take too long."

Taylor didn't even pause at the pushback. "Okay, then how about every three minutes. Does that work for you? We'll have officers at the southeast park exit to escort them out, but they won't come any closer. Once the last hostage is out, they'll fall back out of City Hall Park. Do you agree to those terms?"

"Yes."

"That's good. We'd like to start with Ms. Sutton. Can you send her out now? I'll stay on the phone with you for the entire process so you know exactly how we're doing."

"Let me help her." Gemma started to rise to her feet.

But Boyle stayed her with one hand. "No. No contact with the hostages. I don't want any chance you're feeding them information or a strategy of any kind."

Gemma lowered herself back into the chair. "I made you a promise. I'm not going to risk their lives by trying to put one over on you."

"Maybe not, but my suspicious nature's saved my life countless times out there." He pointed out the door toward the outer perimeter of the building. Toward the city. "I'm not giving it up now."

Gemma raised both hands in a gesture of surrender. "Fair enough. But I think someone will have to help her get on her feet and will have to give her some instructions. She doesn't look well."

Boyle stared at Clara, possibly really seeing her for the first time since he'd struck her, taking in her sheet-white face, bloody abrasion, and shuttered eyes. He pointed at Bowen. "You. Get her up and walk her to the conference room door. Then she's on her own."

Bowen nodded and stood. Curling one hand under her right arm, and the other around her waist, he half lifted her from the chair, Janina helping as much as she could from the other side. Clara swayed for a moment, then got her feet under her, smiling up at Bowen.

Bowen slowly walked them around the table, clearly repeating the instructions Taylor set out, asking her often if she understood. She said she did, but Gemma wasn't confident in her ability to manage on her own.

"You're sure we can't send her out with one of the other hostages?" Gemma pointed at the cell phones in the middle of the table. "You'll be able to see everything."

"No. That's not what I agreed to." He pointed the AR-15 at Bowen as they stopped near the doorway. "Let her go."

Bowen took an extra second or two to make sure Clara had her balance and then let go of her, keeping his hands in clear view as he stepped back.

The barrel of the rifle now turned to Clara. She flinched and stumbled away from him, reaching out one hand to catch herself on the wall and angling her face away, as if unable to face her coming death.

"Go."

Clara hesitated and then looked up slowly. When Boyle flicked the barrel of the rifle toward the door, she didn't need any more prompting. She stumbled out the door, heading toward the reception area, the foyer, and freedom.

"Time marked at six forty-five." With her eyes fixed on Boyle, Gemma listened to the woman clumsily making her way down the hallway; she was now second-guessing her previous estimation that Clara wasn't concussed. She was definitely going to require medical care. Fortunately, EMS would be waiting with the ESU at the park entrance. Clara just had to make it down the stairs in one piece. This time, Logan wasn't standing at the bottom of the steps waiting to catch her. She was on her own.

It took almost a full minute and a half, easily twice as long as needed, for her to appear through the front doors of City Hall on the streaming feeds. Gemma held her breath as Clara slowly walked to the top of the stairs. Each step was an excruciating exercise in care, but Clara made it down to the bottom without issue. When her head whipped sideways, Gemma knew the officers at the park entrance had called her name to show her where to go. The smile that lit her face was one of relief and joy, and she found the strength to half jog out of sight.

They'd done it. They'd successfully started to free the hostages. He wasn't going back on his word. Garcia would be utterly relieved, because she knew part of him still expected Boyle to renege on his part of the bargain. Now they just had to move the rest out.

One down. Six to go.

CHAPTER 18

*A*lex Capello pushed through the door of the command center for the Emergency Services Unit in 1 Police Plaza, NYPD headquarters only blocks from City Hall. The room was filled with officers in tactical gear awaiting instructions, a few patrol cops in their standard-issue blues, and a communication team monitoring all the ESU teams already deployed. The walls were covered with screens showing different angles of City Hall.

He spotted his father across the room, deep in conversation with Chief Phillips and his brother Joe. Alex wove through the crowd of officers and equipment, making his way toward the back of the room.

He felt the shift immediately as the officers around him drew back. In their sidelong glances. Heard it in the whisper of "Rat Squad."

He tamped down on his spike of temper. Now was not the time. He wasn't here as a member of the Internal Affairs Bureau. He was here as an NYPD officer. As a Capello. As family.

Joe spotted him making his way through the crowd, stepped forward, and sent a narrowed glare at a pair of officers standing nearby. "Stow it. For today, pretend he's not IAB. For today, he's one of us." One eyebrow cocked, he shook his head in disgust at Alex's Hawaiian shirt. "Even if he is wearing the ugliest shirt this side of the East River."

They stammered an apology and moved a few steps farther away.

Alex threw Joe a wan smile. "Thanks."

"You know IAB makes even straight cops squirm. The thought of losing their shields is unthinkable to them."

Alex bit off a comment—unless the cop was doing something dirty, IAB wasn't interested. They'd gone around on this before. Joe got it, but he was in the minority. Most cops thought IAB was out to find a scapegoat, and anyone handy would do. Nothing could be further from the truth.

"Which is more than I can say for some people," Joe said darkly.

"What does that mean?"

"You don't know?"

Alex tried counting to ten for patience, gave up at four. "No, I don't. Obviously. That's why I'm asking. What don't I know?"

"Maybe I should ask what you *do* know." Joe glanced at their father, still deep in conversation with Phillips, but purposefully keeping one eye on the nearest monitor. "Just to save time."

"I've been keeping tabs as I got in here. They're trying to keep all nonessential personnel out, to keep the chaos to a minimum."

"Not an easy thing on a day like today."

"No kidding. Since I wasn't called in, and I'm not an active criminal investigator, I had to do some fast talking."

"You could have called Dad. He'd have cleared a path for you."

They both turned to study Tony Capello. At sixty, he was three years away from mandatory retirement. Normally, he struck Alex as hale and hearty, a man who seemed too young to retire because he still had years to devote to his beloved city. Tonight, though, he looked worn and the smudges under his eyes were darker than usual.

"As Chief of Special Operations, his hands are full overseeing this entire op," Alex said. "I wasn't going to bother him. But once I heard the guy had asked for Gemma in exchange for the hostages, I was going to get in here, one way or another. I can't believe Garcia let her go in there. It is Garcia, right?"

"Yeah. And he didn't."

Alex cocked his head in question. "He didn't let her go in there?"

"No. He was against it."

Alex wanted to shove Joe in frustration. This was like pulling teeth. "He was overruled? By who?"

"In the end by her." Joe met his gaze and Alex saw temper sparking hot. "She gave him her shield."

"She what?"

"You heard me."

When Alex took a step toward their father, Joe grabbed his arm. "Wait a second. The shield thing isn't common knowledge. Garcia reported to Dad, but wants it kept on the down low for now."

"Garcia doesn't want to bring her up on insubordination charges if she stays in the department?"

"I'm not sure. Things are pretty chaotic over there. The guy gave them basically no choice—Gemma for all the hostages. They couldn't come up with another way to handle the situation, and Sanders was champing at the bit to storm in there and get the hostages out."

That was a name Alex knew well, and not necessarily for good reasons. "*Fanculo.* It had to be 'Shoot-'em-up Sanders.' "

"Which is why Gem probably felt she had to move so fast. And when Garcia changed his mind and suddenly wouldn't go for it, she handed Garcia her gun and shield and walked out the door. Garcia was sure the guy would keep all the hostages and Gemma, and just take them all out. You know what these situations can be like, once the first hostage has died."

"Died? Who?"

"First Deputy Mayor Charles Willan." Joe grabbed his forearm, hard, and squeezed, forestalling Alex's shocked exclamation. "I thought you said you were keeping tabs. That also is absolutely not public knowledge, but I know word of it is spreading like wildfire through the ranks."

Alex shook his brother off. "Does Rowland know?"

"Rowland was on the phone with Willan when the guy executed him."

Alex ran one hand through his dark hair, tousling the short curls further. "He's already killed one. Dad must be going crazy."

"He's trying not to show it, but he's terrified for her that she's in a hostage position again—with someone who's demonstrated his willingness to kill."

Memory dragged at Alex, pulling him back to that day twenty-five years before.

His mother had stopped by their elementary school as classes let out. She needed to run some errands and was going to take Gemma and Alex with her. Alex, nine, had begged and pleaded not to go. He could go home on his own. He was trustworthy enough to walk straight home and let himself in with the key she'd given him for his last birthday. The one he'd never used before.

Gemma had been happy to go with her mother for a girls' trip downtown, with the promise of a new hair scrunchie or tube of Lip Smackers as a reward for good behavior. His mother had reluctantly agreed—with a threat that if he didn't follow all the rules, he'd be thirty before she let him do it again.

He'd stood on the sidewalk, watching them walk away from him, his mother tall and stylish in a fashionable, swingy coat, holding Gemma's hand as she trotted alongside.

It was the last time he saw her alive.

It was one of the best days of his life. Freedom and responsibility. Feeling like a man and proud of his independence.

It was the worst day of his life. The gut-wrenching pain. The confusion. Feeling like a little boy, but this time, with no mama to reassure and soothe him.

After that, he and Gemma had walked home together, letting themselves into the silent house that never exactly felt like home anymore. The light had gone out of their lives, snuffed out by a man with a gun.

* * *

Here they were again. He couldn't even begin to imagine his father's agony. He'd never let it show—the cop was too ingrained in him for that—but deep down it had to be eating him alive.

Come hell or high water, they'd get her out of there. Or she'd get herself out. If there was one thing Alex had learned in the years following his mother's murder, it was that the lone remaining female in the family had the courage and smarts to run circles around the men. She wouldn't let them down—this time, most of all.

Alex glanced at one of the monitors and started when he caught movement at the front doors of City Hall. Then an older black man burst through the doors and jogged down the front steps before veering toward the southeast park exit. "That's one of the hostages. How many are out now?"

"That's number five of the seven live hostages in there. They're coming out every three minutes."

"So in six more minutes, Gem's going to be the only one in there."

Joe nodded.

"Then what?"

"The plan is to get him out into the open. They're bringing in a chopper and landing it at the intersection of Park and Broadway. But they don't intend for him to get that far. Once he's out in the open, they want to take him out."

"The A-Team guys aren't idiots. They have to know he'll be using Gem as a shield. They try to take him out, they risk taking her out too. Has anyone talked to Sanders?"

"Dad has."

The sound of a door opening had both men turning toward the entrance. A middle-aged woman, with her red hair pulled back in a bun and wearing the standard white shirt, black tie, blue jacket of the chiefs, entered the room.

"Deputy Chief Harrison's here," Joe said. "Phillips won't have to hang around anymore."

"You mean now that she's here?" Alex glanced from Harrison

to his father and then to Phillips. "They're pulling Dad off the operation because of the conflict of interest."

"It was fine until Gemma set foot in the building, but from that moment on, Phillips needed Harrison in here to make the calls. They won't be so cruel as to kick Dad out, but he won't be making the decisions. Harrison's sharp. She knows having Dad on hand can only increase their chance of pulling this off. You just can't replace that kind of experience. I wonder if she knew Boyle?"

"Boyle?"

"Sorry, still catching you up. Captain John Boyle, retired, out of the Forty-first. That's the hostage taker."

Alex stared at his brother as if he'd misheard him. "The hostage taker is a *cop*?"

"Yeah. Boyle lost his son four months ago while investigating a robbery. Connor Boyle apprehended a suspect, didn't have probable cause to search him for a weapon, then the guy pulled a gun and shot him. Connor died on scene. John Boyle thinks that ending stop-and-frisk caused his son's death, so he went after the man who championed getting rid of it."

"But anyone who lived in this city during the run-up to the election knows that was Rowland. How did he end up with Willan?"

"Bad timing. But once he had Willan, he made sure Rowland was there to know exactly what he'd done. Had him on the phone line with Willan when he executed him. Rowland is a mess right now, so the public advocate is standing in for him as needed."

"And he may be needed." Alex regarded his brother. "I assumed there was a gang connection. If the hostage taker is a retired cop, why are you here?"

"I was called in because there have been death threats made against Rowland from multiple gangs, so they were covering their bases while they didn't know who was involved. I was about to cut out, but then Gemma went in, and now I'm staying until this resolves."

Alex scanned the room again. "Where's Mark?"

"Down at the Fifth. Those boys are right in the thick of all this, and he wanted to be down at the precinct to help out his officers." He pointed at the monitor. "There goes number six."

A young man in casual clothes took the stairs leading to the front pathway at breakneck speed, then didn't even hesitate, just cut left and sprinted for the officers at the park entrance.

"So . . . just one more," Alex said.

"One more." The brothers locked eyes. "Then it's just Gemma and Boyle. That's when things are really going to come to a head."

CHAPTER 19

*G*emma watched Angelo Carboni—the senior adviser, who insisted on going last—take the outside steps so quickly he nearly stumbled, but then he caught himself on the second-to-last step, regaining his balance. With surer steps on level ground, Carboni loped down the path, disappearing from view.

Mission accomplished. All the hostages were out.

Now, on to the hard part.

In the background, Taylor was still talking to Boyle. "That's the last one. We're ready for you now, John. The helicopter is in place. You may have seen it on one of the live streams."

"I did," Boyle said, his eyes fixed on the phone as if he could see Taylor. "We're coming out now. Tell your men that if they try to be heroes and attempt to take me out, Detective Capello will die. She'll be at gunpoint the whole time, and the slightest stress will make me pull the trigger. Sure, I'd be dead, but so would Tony's little girl. Keep that in mind."

"Affirmative, John. We hear you."

"One other thing. I want everyone near City Hall moved back. There are officers at the park entrances to meet the hostages. There are probably snipers up the trees in the park close to City Hall. Get them all out. I don't want to see a single person when we come out of here. If I see one, I'll consider it a breach of our agreement and she dies. Move them now. We're coming out in three minutes."

Boyle reached over and cut the connection before Taylor could respond. Then he sat back in his chair to study her.

She was careful not to shift under his sharp gaze. "Thank you."

Boyle's brow furrowed. "For what?"

"For being a man of your word and for letting them go."

"Because I could have killed them all? You must think me a man with absolutely no code of honor."

She couldn't help her gaze sliding to the corner of the room where what was left of Charles Willan lay in a broken and bloody pile, just out of sight. Her gaze rose to meet his, but she let her silence speak volumes.

"Killing one man doesn't mean I don't have a code," he said. "I did that for my son. And for the other officers out there who are also in danger or dying because of Rowland's pet project."

"As you requested, the council is now looking at it."

He shook his head dolefully. "You really don't think I'm very smart, do you? Never forget I'm a cop. Yeah, I'm retired, but once a cop, always a cop. They may have been telling me what I wanted to hear, but they're not going to change it. And it was never anything they'd be able to change quickly enough to save the hostages. I knew you were playing for time."

Gemma sat back in her chair, crossing her arms over her chest. "And you played us right back."

He grinned. "Sure did."

"And now what?"

"Now we finish this."

"We're going out to the chopper?"

"Isn't that the whole plan? Going out?" He met her gaze, unblinkingly. "Getting me in range of the A-Team snipers?"

"No, the plan is getting you to the chopper. But you have to promise me one thing."

His eyes narrowed on her. "You're going to make stipulations now?"

"Only that you have to promise not to harm the pilot. He's just doing what he's ordered. You say you live by a code. Show me. Don't hurt the pilot."

"Oh, I promise not to hurt the pilot." He rose to his feet, keeping the barrel of the carbine fixed on her. "Get up."

Gemma rose slowly to her feet. There was something in his rapid agreement that set off alarm bells for her.

He was up to something.

Being honest with herself, she had to know he had some other plan. There was no way a man of his experience would put himself in this position without an escape plan. She didn't think his plan was to die here for his son, so he had to have an escape worked out in his original scenario. But she was pretty sure, whatever it was, he was abandoning it, or at least improvising and improving on it, because there was no way he'd have worked Tony Capello's daughter—and the safety she'd bring—into his schemes.

As she stood, she raised both hands into the air, where he could see them.

"Now turn around," he ordered.

She hesitated only for a moment, then turned, focusing on the fact that he would doom himself if he hurt her when his very survival depended on her being alive and able to escort him out of the building. She focused all her attention on every sound coming from behind her, trying to discern what he was doing. To her relief, every sound that followed was familiar to her. The *snick* and slide of the magazine released from the AR-15 and then the louder *crack* of the charging handle being pulled back to release the bullet from the chamber. The *ping* of the bullet ricocheting off the table to roll across the surface and fall almost silently to the carpet below. The *clunk* of the rifle being set down on the table.

Unloaded the AR-15 and put it down. He's abandoning it. Too big to take with him without also having to drag around a bag, but he doesn't want to leave it loaded so anyone else can use it as a weapon against him.

Next came the rustling of clothing, the sound of a snap popping, and then the *shush* of a pistol pulled from its holster. A second later, the cold metal of a gun barrel pressed against the very base of her skull forcing her head sideways into an awkward tilt.

She understood his placement of the handgun, and it shot a

bolt of pure fear into her gut. In this position, one shot and her brain stem would be obliterated. Lights out. Permanently. No chance of recovery.

His other hand came down over her left shoulder. "I highly recommend you don't try anything, Detective. I *will* pull the trigger. I've already killed in cold blood once today. What's one more?"

"Understood," she ground out, wincing at the pain radiating through her neck and skull. "You could pull back a bit. A fraction of an inch won't make any difference in a kill shot."

"Maybe not, but I'll start as I intend to go on, and I'll be exposed from our first steps out of this room." He gave her a rough jerk sideways, ignoring the catch in her breath at the pain as bone ground against metal. "Out we go."

Their progress was slow. He was pressed against her back, his fingers digging into her shoulder to keep her in the closest proximity to both himself and the gun he could manage. Being practically attached to him made for awkward walking, and the best Gemma could manage were slow, shuffling steps.

She took the opportunity to size up Boyle. A sideways glance was difficult and caused significant pain as the gun jabbed deeper, but she noted a khaki green cuff on the wrist of the hand clamped to her shoulder. He'd been wearing a plain black T-shirt before, but had taken the time to layer a long-sleeved shirt or jacket over it, surely for pockets or to cover the weapons he carried. And now she was this close to him, the press of his body against her back confirmed that the AR-15 was definitely gone. She couldn't feel the weapon or the strap and buckle of a cross-carry. So he was only carrying a smaller, concealed-carry type weapon, like the SIG. Or maybe he had more than one? All she could be assured of was the one pressed against her skull.

Had he left behind the greatest firepower because any shooting would be in close quarters or in only small crowds at best? Or so he could blend in with a crowd without attracting attention? The gun was compact, but was even that too much bulk to carry at this point? Her money was on the second possibility and confirmed her suspicions that he was proceeding with a plan, even if with some minor modifications. He intended to get back into the city's populace and get lost.

They moved through the hallway, back toward the reception area. They stopped in the doorway, and Boyle leaned hard against her, the barrel of the gun digging into her skull as he peered out over her shoulder and into the corridor leading to the foyer. But the emptiness and silence convinced him they were still alone, and he eased the pressure.

They cleared the foyer, skirting the sweeping double staircase on their way to the front door, and stopped just inside the doors opening out onto the outer steps.

He leaned in close to murmur into her ear. "Your friends better play by my rules, or this will be a very short trip for you."

A shiver ran down Gemma's spine, but she wasn't sure if it was in reaction to his undesired closeness or his words. "They will. They're not going to risk me just for you."

He chuckled. "Are you trying to hurt my feelings, or do you just have a high opinion of yourself?"

She gave as much of a shrug as she could with the weight of his hand riding heavily on her shoulder. "Just telling it like it is. They're not going to want to see me dead."

"I'm counting on that." Boyle tightened his grip on her shoulder, his fingers digging in brutally, as if he expected her to try to bolt as soon as they made it out of the building. "Here we go. Open the door and then go slowly."

She pushed the door open and they stepped out into the fading light of early evening, the sunlight still bright, even under the elongated portico. With her head awkwardly tilted, Gemma kept her eyes downcast so she could see the steps as they came closer and closer.

She stopped at the top. There was no railing, and the image of Rob Greenfield toppling down the steps came to mind.

Slowly and carefully. You trip and he'll think you're making a break for it and will pull the trigger. Then all ESU will be able to do is scrape your brains off the steps.

The thought of the ESU had her peering down the walkway toward the southeast park entrance. But where there had previously been a team of ESU officers, there were now just empty footpaths and roads with an open view toward the Brooklyn Bridge, the near granite tower with its Gothic arches just visible in the distance. A quick scan of the park and then above at the rooftops assured her everyone was at the very least out of sight. But like Boyle, she knew her every move was being monitored, both by the news media with zoom lenses and by the snipers with their rifle sights.

Do you see me, Dad? I'm okay. Stay strong.

Boyle gave her a nudge forward, bringing her gaze back to the task of getting down to ground level.

"You're going to have to back off a bit. You're going to decapitate me if you want my head to stay up here and the rest of me to go down a step."

"You're a lively one, aren't you?"

She couldn't see his face, but could practically visualize his half-smile from his tone of voice. That was good—the more he reluctantly liked her, the more hesitation he might have in killing her.

Because surviving the day was still completely up in the air.

"I'd say it's more practical than anything else," she replied. "We're both working toward the same goal, John. Getting away from here. Let's make it happen."

He didn't say anything, but the pressure of the gun barrel eased slightly.

"Okay, I'm taking the first step down. I'll go carefully, and if I angle slightly, you can step down with me."

Slowly, one step at a time, they progressed. As she stepped down, he stayed with her, remaining close so she still mostly covered him. She counted the steps as they went down. Her tenth step down put them onto the raised, semicircular walkway fronting City Hall. She could feel Boyle twisting slowly from one side to the other while keeping his head close to hers as he scanned for shooters.

"Head for the northwest exit. Stay as close to City Hall as you can." He accompanied his words with a push to her left shoulder to angle her toward the walkway running to her right, across the front of City Hall and out to Broadway.

She did as directed, staying in line with the bottom of the steps, but looked pointedly at the path across from them that led through the trees toward the intersection of Broadway and Park. "Wouldn't it be better to follow the footpath? We could take shelter in the trees."

"Aren't you supposed to be working with the A-Team, not against them? Don't they want me to stay out in the open?"

"I'm sure they do. But we're in this together now. I don't want to get shot. And from the distances they're working with, all it takes is one of us to shift a fraction of an inch and that's what'll happen. You know very well that your best way to survive this is for me to also survive."

Past the end of the steps, she stayed in the lee of City Hall as the northwest wing of the building rose in front of her. Then cutting left, she followed the line of the building to the corner. They edged around the corner cautiously, but, once again, there was no officer in sight.

"You're using the building to shield any shot that might come from behind. And me for any shot that might come from the front," she stated.

"That's the plan. I'm expendable. You . . . not so much. At least I'm counting on that. Chief Capello has already lost his wife to a hostage taker. He's not going to want to lose his daughter the same way."

"You're also counting on the fact that news crews are catching this live while we're out in the open, so my family is watching in real time. How did you know about my mother?"

"Anyone who knows Tony Capello knows how he lost his wife and nearly his daughter."

"It was a gift from the Almighty to you, then, when I ended up being the voice on the end of the line."

"It was something I could work with. The day hadn't been going quite the way I'd planned. Though, in the end, it still worked out okay." His tone took on a dark, cruel edge. "I intended for Rowland to die and was pissed when I realized he was out of the office unexpectedly. But now, he'll have to live with the pain of losing someone irreplaceable, just like I do."

Gemma stopped her shuffle and turned her head as far as the gun would allow to look back at Boyle. "I'm very sorry for the loss of your son," she said quietly.

His face contorted into a pinched mixture of pain and rage. "I don't need your pity."

"You're not getting it. But you and I both know the hazards of this job, and how life can change in an instant. I looked up Connor's record. He was a good cop, and, from what I could see, a kind man. He is not only a loss to you, but to all of us at the NYPD. We need officers like him."

The struggle to stay focused was clear on Boyle's face. *There it is, his Achilles' heel.* So she pushed a little bit more, intent on making a connection with him, willing to lay herself bare in the effort to save her own life. "I know what it's like to lose someone who's your whole world. It's been twenty-five years since my mother died. I don't think about her constantly like I used to, but still, at odd times, there's an unrelated trigger that brings her back to me. And it still hurts. It's too soon for you, I bet. For you, it always hurts." Not wanting to press further, Gemma turned away, giving him time to pull himself together.

They came to the edge of City Hall, carefully descended the three steps from the raised walkway down to street level, and shuffled from there into the shade of the trees lining the small, reserved parking lot. They moved in silence now, their motions more in unison. Gemma knew how far she could move ahead without having him try to snap her back, grinding the back of her skull against his pistol barrel. Boyle had learned to anticipate her moves, staying tightly against her, keeping her angled out toward the parking lot so he was less of a target. As macabre dances went, they were just about ready for *Dancing with the Stars.*

He caught her off guard when he stopped dead, grasping her shoulder while in midstep and slamming her back against him, snapping her head back against the gun.

She couldn't quite swallow the grunt of pain. "Change of plans?" she gasped. She tried to squirm forward just a fraction of an inch, so she wasn't in contact with his full body, but he held her fast.

He turned her so she fully faced the parking lot, an open space between two cars in front of them. "We're going to cut across here. We're going to do it quickly, because we're going to be exposed."

Meaning you're going to be exposed. I'll be in front; nothing will be in back.

"And we're going to stay close the whole time." He leaned forward, pressing his cheek against hers. "Really close."

Gemma fought back the urge to shudder at the forced intimacy. She understood what he was doing. As they were exposed down the pathway, any bullet going through his head from a perpendicular shot would also go through hers, likely staying the hand of any sniper.

"Move," he ordered.

She took small, quick steps, pushing between the parked cars and then out into the open space of the lot. This time, instead of leading, she was being pushed along by Boyle, fast enough that she nearly stumbled as they wound between two vehicles on the far side. She just managed to get both hands out against sun-warmed metal to stop her forward momentum.

"Keep going," Boyle growled.

Then they were back under the leafy canopy of the park. Boyle's body relaxed and he pulled back from her fractionally. She ignored the urge to wipe the back of her hand over her cheek to remove any damp traces of sweat. He might be trying to transmit confidence, but his body's reaction gave him away. Those thirty seconds had been terrifying for him.

Gemma looked past the PLEASE KEEP OFF GRASS sign to the grove of dogwood trees beyond. "Go through there, staying under the trees?"

"That's what they're meant to think. But no. This way." He turned her body to the left, pushing her forward.

At first, she was confused when she saw the structure before her: The three-sided permanent iron fencing was set up in an open rectangle. Another section of fence was removed, to lean against one of the other sides. The dual metal doors, easily each ten feet long and three feet wide, lay flush with the ground around it. There was an electrical panel attached to the iron fence, with twin metal loops that should have held a padlock. She couldn't see the sign affixed to the mobile section of fence now, but she knew exactly what it said—CITY HALL.

It was the emergency exit to the historic City Hall subway station, open at the turn of the twentieth century and closed now for more than seventy years.

Shock short-circuited her coordination, nearly making her stumble as his plan became clear. Why he'd taken hostages—he had her as protection now, but he'd planned on using one of the hostages right from the start. He knew all along he didn't have to get out of City Hall Park, even when she'd offered him a helicopter. He only needed to get clear of the building and about forty feet past it to be able to disappear into the bowels of the world below New York City. Because from there, he could get lost into the underground life teeming under the city streets and eventually escape nearly anywhere.

She'd been confident in her skills and intuition as a negotiator. She thought she'd succeeded in getting into his head and had figured him out. But the realization that he'd so handily one-upped her felt like he'd dumped a bucket of ice water over her head. Suddenly her control of the situation was slipping through her fingers.

Without a doubt, she was now completely on her own. She'd thought she might be able to depend on the ESU and the A-Team for backup support while they were in City Hall Park, but now they'd still be waiting for them to come through the treed section of the park.

By the time the A-Team realized they were missing and sent in officers on foot, they'd have vanished.

CHAPTER 20

Gemma had grown up hearing about the abandoned City Hall subway station and had seen pictures of its colorful vaulted and tiled ceilings, leaded glass, and brass chandeliers, but she'd never seen it for herself. She and Frankie had talked about going several times, but it was so popular, the handful of tours given annually by the New York Transit Museum sold out in minutes, and they'd never been lucky enough to score tickets.

"This is an emergency exit only," she said. "That control panel should be inaccessible. How could you know it would be unlocked?"

He scoffed. "I've been planning this for nearly four months. They run tours down there. They're running one tonight, in fact. A Transit Museum worker comes during the afternoon on tour day to make sure the site is safe—no flooding, no cracked or crumbling stairs, and to make sure the train platform and wooden bridge are in good shape. I got to the park ahead of time and waited for him to go in, expecting him around three o'clock. But he was early and he forced my hand."

"That's why you missed Rowland. He would have been back by three, but your timeline got moved up. You calculated the odds and decided to go for it. But you got Willan instead."

Boyle gave her a push forward toward the doors and she gritted her teeth and leaned back against him. She only hoped trying to slow him down to give the A-Team time to catch up wouldn't get her killed.

"Wait! How did you know the panel would still be unlocked?"

Boyle eased the pressure on her slightly. "Because the evacuation was called when I went in. The museum employee would have been forced to have a number six train stop for him because he couldn't come back up. The panel stayed unlocked because he couldn't come up to close the doors from outside. But since the park was deserted, the guy likely didn't worry about anyone getting into the site. And certainly didn't think the man causing all the chaos would view it as his escape route. The whole exercise nearly ran too long to make this work. Now we're going to go join a tour in progress."

When Gemma had accused Boyle of playing them for time, she hadn't realized his plan was this structured. But it was, and he had timed his exit precisely to line up with a prescheduled tour. The entire stop-and-frisk policy change requirement had all been part of an elaborate scheme to buy several hours and nothing more.

"You seriously think they'll be running a tour beneath City Hall when everything above it has been evacuated? Surely, it'll be canceled." Anger at being so convincingly fooled burned hot in her chest and played at the edges of her clipped words.

"I'm betting this is a situation where the left hand doesn't know what the right hand is doing. The NYPD probably doesn't know it's even scheduled, and the transit cops are busy dealing with pissed-off commuters whose evenings have been disrupted. I'm counting on it being a detail that's gotten away from them, if they knew about it in the first place. They'll still be letting the six train go through the loop, or they'll have to close down the entire line and several stations, as the cars won't have anywhere to turn around. I've seen how these tours are prepped. There have been two guys that come to check out the site beforehand. One guy is a stickler. He always locks the control panel before he goes in so no one can sneak in behind him. But that's extra work going in and coming out, locking and unlocking it again so he can close up in the end, and it takes him longer. The other guy never does that extra work. He goes in, leaves the panel open, checks out the station, comes out, closes the site, and then locks the panel. I didn't know today would even be possible until I saw who came to the station. Once I saw it was the careless employee, I knew I was good to go. Because once things started to get out of hand up here, he was never going to admit he'd made an error and left the station open to external access. He'd lose his job."

"He'll lose his job now," Gemma muttered.

"And because the transit museum is going to consider the site sealed with no access to the controls, thereby locking out the entire entrance, they're going to consider it safe to run the tour as planned, as it's completely separate from what's going on above." He leaned over and flipped the panel door open. "They're going to be wrong."

The open panel revealed a simple two-button switch labeled OPEN and CLOSED.

"You're betting an awful lot on the fact that someone will consider this area to be totally detached and inaccessible from City Hall. And if there is a tour going on down there, you think they're not going to hear the doors open?" Gemma asked.

"They're actually really quiet. It's an emergency exit, so they check it regularly to make sure it stays functional." When Gemma craned her neck to look back at him silently, he continued, "I told you—I've been planning this for a while. Now, enough. If you think I don't see you trying to buy time, you're sadly mistaken. I'm going to open the doors, then we'll tiptoe down those stairs— *silently*—and join the back of the tour. They won't even notice us. On the chance there is no tour, we're simply going to disappear into the subway system. It'll work for me either way."

He reached over and punched the OPEN button. Slowly, and with a surprisingly quiet *whir,* the doors lifted open, pushed by hydraulic hinges. With a last jab against the back of her neck, which had her stumbling off balance, he stepped back, taking the gun away.

Regaining her balance, she turned to face him. She'd been right about the jacket. He now wore a khaki military-style jacket with many pockets. He'd taken advantage of the seconds she'd taken to steady herself and turn around—he'd holstered his SIG

Sauer P226 and was now holding a compact Glock 42 he must have pulled from a jacket pocket. She rubbed the aching back of her neck. "That's why you kept shortening the timetable on us."

"Sure. I literally have a train to catch. We're just going to be a couple out for an evening tour. And because they've been on the tour, if the media is broadcasting our pictures, the tour participants won't have seen them." He raised the Glock so she couldn't fail to see it. "This is going to be on you. More than that, it's going to be on every person in that tour. Tell anyone what is going on, or make any move to escape, and you might survive, but they won't." He took a quick look at his watch. "It's seven-fifty. Time to move. The tour is almost over." He motioned with the Glock toward the stairs. "You go first. Be quiet and inconspicuous. If anyone figures out we've joined the tour partway, they die. You don't want that on you."

Gemma nodded and walked toward the open doorway. As they got closer, a flight of steps materialized from the darkness below, starting at street level and disappearing down into a dimly lit tunnel that curved to the left and out of sight. She paused for only a fraction of a second at the top, but it was apparently too long for Boyle, who nudged the small of her back. She threw him an irritated glance and took her first step into the tunnel. She went down a step at a time, Boyle staying only a tread or two behind her, taking care to keep her steps silent, grateful for the rubber-soled summer sneakers she wore to a family picnic. The flat-heeled boots she paired with the suits she wore for a regular shift—because you never knew when you might have to run after a perp—would never have been this quiet. Boyle ghosted along behind her on his rubber-soled military boots, reinforcing that this was part of his plan right from the start.

Gemma passed another control panel on her left, and seconds later heard the soft *whir* again as the doors closed with only a faint *thump*, leaving them in the cool dimness of the faint light coming from the tunnel ahead of them.

She followed the curve of the tunnel, taking care to check for anyone in sight ahead. But finding the tunnel empty, she followed it to the left and then down a new flight of steps. About halfway down the steps, Boyle's hand came down on her shoulder. She stopped midstep, reaching out with one hand to grasp the banister to make sure she didn't lose her balance.

They stayed frozen for a slow count of six, their ears straining for any sound. But the only voice they heard sounded far away and echoed distortedly. Gemma couldn't be sure how close the speaker actually was. All she knew was the speaker was male and was somewhere ahead and below them.

Boyle released her and she continued down the stairs until she stepped off the staircase into a wide, empty room with a high, cross-vaulted ceiling. The walls were covered with pale yellow enameled tiles, still surprisingly bright after more than a century. Above, the ceiling rose in a herringbone pattern of red tiles, tucked into the vault between ribs of the yellow and bright emerald. At the apex of the vaulted ceiling, a circular leaded glass window, inset with a floral pattern, filtered in diffuse light from above.

But the room was empty. Across from them, a doorway was boarded off, likely the second entrance into the station, which wasn't refurbished when the station opened for tours early in this century. Another flight of steps could be seen through a tiled archway, leading downward, most likely to the tracks themselves. This room must have been for purchasing tickets, long before the advent of tokens or turnstiles.

Gemma glanced back at Boyle, who gave her a head jerk in the direction of the stairs.

As she stepped into the archway and took her first step down, the voice became louder and more distinct. At the bottom of the steps, she could see the platform and just a sliver of rails, but no one was in sight. They crept quietly down the stairs. Gemma glanced overhead, knowing any sound they made would be amplified by both the arched shape of the passageway and the neat rows of shiny yellow tiles.

She hesitated on the last step, trying to peer around the corner. She was just able to see the back of someone in cutoff jean shorts and a rock band tour shirt with cities and dates listed in two columns down the back. Boyle pressed close behind her and she raised a single index finger. *Wait.*

The voice was speaking again. "If you look up at this leaded glass window, you can see that some of the segments still bear the tar left over from World War Two."

Gemma moved, slipping silently down onto the platform. About twenty people stood in a loose cluster, the rear of which was approximately five feet away. A man wearing a bright orange, high-visibility vest stood at the front of the group, his back to them with his head tipped up and one arm extended upward as he pointed at an arching leaded glass window overhead. The tour participants studied the glass overhead as he described its history. No one turned to look at her or in any way indicated they noticed movement.

"The windows were blacked out for safety." The tour guide indicated the line of brass chandeliers hanging suspended over the platform. "The design was intended to let natural light in from above to assist in illuminating the platform, but that same design became a concern when the risk of air raids arose because, at night, light from the platform could be seen out on the street through the glass blocks up above. The windows were covered with tar paint to quench the station and train lights."

Gemma slipped in behind the group, adopting a similar upturned pose. She fixed an expression of relaxed interest on her face, but that expression nearly slipped when Boyle came up beside her and casually slipped an arm around her waist and tipped his upturned face nearly to hers. Out of the corner of her eye, Gemma caught a woman nearby look straight at her, her forehead wrinkled in confusion. But then she shrugged and turned back to the historian leading the tour.

Thank God. You just saved your own life.

Gemma let herself relax fractionally. Had they pulled it off? But then she stiffened again as Boyle began to casually stroke his thumb up and down over her side. When she reflexively tried to pull away slightly, his fingers dug in, holding her close, and she was reminded that while he held on to her with his left arm, the index finger of his right hand was likely resting against the trigger guard of the Glock in his pocket pointed at any one of the people in front of them. She might survive a struggle with him, but some of these innocent people—rock band man or perhaps the older couple in matching "I ♥ NY" shirts to his right—might die. She forced herself to relax, to move fractionally toward Boyle. His grip on her lightened slightly, but not enough to doubt who was in control at that moment.

"If you've noted the artistry of the leaded glass, you'll see that it, like the rest of the station, is crafted in the Beaux Arts style, as were several other buildings in New York City at the turn of the prior century. Richard Morris Hunt's posthumous Metropolitan Museum of Art in 1902, or Charles Reed and Allen Stem's Grand Central Terminal in 1913, for example. If you consider the ceiling . . ."

He paused, turning in place, his hands raised toward the sequence of barrel vaults arching overhead across the tracks. The vaults were the same herringbone red tile as the ticket room, but every third vault was a bowed leaded glass window similar to the one over their heads. The center window stretched from the archway over the stairway where the words CITY HALL were spelled out in yellow and green tiles, all the way to a decorative brass plaque celebrating the launch of New York City's first rapid-transit railroad in 1904. Ornate brass candelabra hung from each tiled section of ceiling over the platform. Between the electric lights and the last of the daylight from above, the colored tiles on the arching ribs and slanted ceilings quietly glowed.

"If you consider the ceiling," he continued, "you'll see the Guastavino tile work continues in this area as well. It's beautiful and gives the station some of its Beaux Arts appeal, but, at its heart, it's a structural component of the station. It's a form of thin-tile compression vaulting that not only supports the ceiling, but beautifies the space. When George Lewis Heins and Christopher Grant LaFarge designed the station, they intended it to be the crown jewel of a system encompassing nine miles and twenty-eight stations." He paused and grinned as laughter rose from the crowd. "Nine miles and twenty-eight stations, doesn't that seem quaint? And tiny. The original line ran from right here at City Hall Station up to One Hundred Forty-fifth Street. Now we have four hundred twenty-seven stations, covering two hundred thirty-six miles of subway routes."

He stopped for a moment, his head cocked slightly as the faint sound of an approaching train reached their ears. "And speaking of subway routes, here's our train coming to pick us up. And that is the end of the tour. If anyone has any questions, I'd be happy to answer them now, on the ride back, or once we're at the Canal Street Station. And a reminder, because of the closure of the Brooklyn Bridge Station, we'll be disembarking at Canal Street."

Gemma looked sharply at Boyle, who continued to gaze placidly at the tour guide as if he didn't have a care in the world. Of course, this would also be part of his plan. With a hostage situation at City Hall, the Brooklyn Bridge subway station would be bypassed and they'd get off at the next station to the north.

He was rolling the dice and whether he came up sixes or snake eyes depended on pure luck. How fast would the ESU figure out they'd disappeared? How long before they discovered the unsecured emergency exit down into the subway system? And then, would they assume they were on foot winding through tunnels only used by the homeless or thrill seekers, or would they bet on them somehow being on a train?

If Gemma was in charge, she'd take both possibilities into account. And she knew her father would as well. But Tony Capello would be off this case by now and all he'd be able to do was wait for news.

And hope that the next time he saw his daughter, it wouldn't be at the morgue.

CHAPTER 21

*A*s the out-of-service 6 train came into view, Gemma hoped her face didn't reflect the relief that nearly buckled her knees. Or, if it did and anyone caught her expression, they would think she was simply bored by the tour and eager for it to end. Not that she was praying the train's arrival might avert a bloodbath.

The train came around the tight curve in the track and slowed to a halt, brakes screeching in protest. Two MTA employees hopped out at the far doors of the first car, where it was closest to the platform. Together, they picked up a short wooden bridge from a corner of the platform and carried it over to the middle door. They set it down, closing the gap between the door and the platform, making Gemma realize why the station had been shuttered—modern cars were built longer with additional doorways, making the curved station stop dangerously impractical.

While the car was prepared and the tour group milled restlessly on the platform, Gemma noticed Boyle's gaze shooting up the stairs to the empty ticket room several times.

He's waiting for the A-Team to storm down the stairs.

They'd figure out their escape route sooner or later, but first someone would have to notice the unlocked control panel on the old station entrance. Gemma fervently wished they'd take their time to avoid the tiny platform and its occupants becoming the scene of a tactical nightmare. She'd rather deal with Boyle on her own later when she could pick the time and place. One much more isolated than the crowded subway platform.

The tour guide and the MTA workers finally escorted everyone on board the train, the bridge's high-railing sides providing safe passage from the twentieth century to the twenty-first. Once in the car, everyone settled into seats, and conversation rose to fill the car with a happy buzz punctuated by punches of laughter.

A young man, seated directly across from them with his girlfriend, flashed her a saucy grin and leaned down to whisper something in his girl's ear that made her flush and give him a playful shove before settling back into the lee of his arm.

With an initial jerk, which had the occupants of the car swaying in unison, the train pulled out of the station, rounding the corner, and starting to pick up speed. Gemma finally let herself relax back against the seat.

They had pulled off his escape and bought a little more time. Now her next goal was to get Boyle out of this crowd of people.

To the outside world, she imagined, they looked like a winter-spring romantic couple, seated on the subway car, side by side, swaying together as the car banked around the tight loop or rolled over switches. Boyle sat with his arm companionably stretched out over the top of the seat behind Gemma's shoulders, his head bent close to hers as he kept his voice low, a look of doting amusement on his face.

But the pleasant expression didn't fool Gemma for one second. She knew the right hand tucked into his pocket kept the Glock steadily fixed on the young couple that only had eyes for each other. His silent threat was implicit: Behave, or the ramifications were entirely her fault.

Boyle leaned in closer, drawing her attention. From the set of his jaw and his shoulders, she could see he, too, had relaxed slightly, now that the immediate risk of discovery by the A-Team was over.

"Smile," he murmured, following his own direction. "We wouldn't want anyone to think you're not here willingly."

"I *am* here willingly. It was my choice, remember?" She smiled, but knew it didn't meet her eyes. Still, it was enough for them to blend in.

She stiffened, looking past him as the tour guide wandered in their direction, stopping and chatting with this person, then that one.

Keep moving. Don't stop here.

As if he'd heard her thought, and decided to ignore it, the man headed directly to them, a wide grin on his face. "Hi, folks. Did you enjoy the tour?"

"We did," said Boyle. "Thank you so much. It's clear you love what you do."

Gemma struggled to keep the surprise off her face as the two men made small talk, but then realized Boyle had determined there was no point in laying low and not attracting attention. By now, the A-Team had to be swarming the park looking for them, and could already be cautiously entering the tunnel. Of course, they'd be taking it slowly, as they'd expect bullets around every corner, expanding the lead on their escape as the train carried them away, far underground.

"I really do," said the tour guide. He turned to Gemma. "Did you have any questions?"

"I did actually." She treated him to a bright smile while her mind worked a mile a minute to come up with a question he wouldn't have covered during the majority of the tour they'd missed, calling out their absence, or at least inattention. "The station is wonderful, but I actually had a question a little broader than just that one location. It's more about the subway system back then. Even if it was tiny." She paused to give a light laugh, and he joined her. "How did they build the actual tunnels? I mean, today they use those giant boring machines you see on the six o'clock news. But those didn't exist back then."

"You mean the 'cut and cover' technique?" Boyle asked.

The tour guide's eyes lit up as if he'd discovered a kindred spirit. "That's exactly how they did it. Are you familiar with subway construction?"

"A little bit. My son is a history buff."

Gemma noted that Boyle described his son in the present tense, likely to avoid painful questions.

"He loves to tour the city's historical landmarks and I often go with him," Boyle continued. "I've picked up quite a lot of information about the city in the eighteenth and nineteenth centuries. But please explain the concept to us; you most certainly know more about it than me."

"You're correct that there weren't any powered boring machines back then. The New York subway system was dug by hand by approximately seven thousand seven hundred Manhattan immigrants. It was dangerous work, and safety regulations aren't what they are now. It's estimated at least sixty men died constructing those tunnels. They closed the street where they wanted the line to run, dug the trench by hand for the tunnel, then built a series of trusses and beams and rebuilt the road on top while they completed the work underground." The tour guide went on for several more minutes about the minutiae of tunnel engineering, but then moved on to an older man waving for his attention farther down the train.

As soon as the guide's back was turned, Gemma shifted away from Boyle, pulling out from under the hand he cupped around her shoulder.

"Uh-uh," Boyle scolded. "We need to make sure everyone thinks we're together and have been with them since the start of the tour. Do *not* attract attention."

Gemma dropped her gaze so he wouldn't see the temper and calculation snapping in her eyes. Yes, being in physical contact with him was unsettling, but she needed to play along. "What's your plan from here?"

"You don't actually think I'm going to tell you that, do you?"

"I think you need to give some serious thought to trusting me. We're in this together now."

"Hardly." The smile he gave her had a ferocious edge. "You're just itching to slap cuffs on me."

Over his shoulder, and out the opposite window, the glossy white tile walls of a subway station whipped past. The white-on-green BROOKLYN BRIDGE and CITY HALL signs, with their terra-cotta trim, went by in a blur so fast, Gemma wouldn't have been able to read the words if she wasn't already familiar with the station. She only had seconds to be struck by the empty platforms and deserted escalators before they shot back into the dark of the tunnel.

In the city that never sleeps, when subways ran 24-7/365, this kind of abandonment was eerie and always meant something terrible had happened. For the people who had tried to navigate their ravaged city following the 9/11 terror attacks, this kind of evacuation instinctively brought a gut punch of adrenaline-laced reactive fear.

She wondered if Boyle felt it too.

Speaking of Boyle, maybe it was time for her to take a different tack with him, to convince him.

She gave a skeptical snort. " 'Slap cuffs' on you? Only if I wanted to make a citizen's arrest."

He squinted at her. "Because you wouldn't arrest me as a detective?" He kept his voice a murmur she nearly couldn't hear.

"That would get me in trouble for impersonating an officer." She lifted the edge of her peasant blouse so he could see her unadorned waistband. "No shield."

"From your outfit, I can see you were off duty when they called you in. Unless things have changed drastically from when I retired, no detective would arrive for shift looking like that."

"You're right on that account. But I had my shield with me and my gun in the lockbox in my car." She looked up and met his gaze so he could have no doubt of her sincerity. "Garcia didn't want me to go into City Hall. After all the arrangements, he was going to scrub the exchange. So I took matters into my own hands."

He drew back slightly. "You handed in your gun and shield?"

"Yes."

"*Why?*" The single word carried the confusion of someone dedicated to a profession that chose him as much as he chose it. Someone who couldn't understand how anyone could possibly give it up voluntarily. Someone who came from a long line of NYPD officers and had brought up his own son to join him on the force.

"Because if you'd killed them because I considered the job

more important than seven human lives, I wouldn't be much of a person. I certainly couldn't be a Capello. Wouldn't be Maria Capello's daughter." She turned her face away to stare out the darkened window at the concrete wall flying by. "So I quit and walked out."

"Clearly, Garcia didn't stop you. Why?"

"McFarland and Taylor got in his way. Kept him occupied while I slipped out. *Bastardo.*" The last word was a whispered epithet.

When the silence weighed heavily between them in the middle of the babble of happy conversation, she finally looked back at him. He was studying her face, measuring every nuanced expression.

"You really did it," he stated.

She nodded. "I'm not sure my father will ever forgive me." She shrugged, letting a tiny fraction of the devastation that played around the edges of her control flicker over her face.

He sat back in his seat, staring at her in thoughtful contemplation, so caught off guard the hand in his pocket relaxed, the hidden gun falling to rest against his thigh.

Keep him distracted. "I read up on Connor. He was a fine man, and a good cop, but do you know the note in his record that impressed me the most?"

Indecision flickered over Boyle's face, the pull of being able to talk about his boy warring with the need to remain coldly in control. Love for his son finally won out. "What?"

"It wasn't his arrest record, although that was solid. It was what he did for a young struggling family. I'm sure you know the story. The one where he found that young boy walking the streets at night alone, on his way to a grocery store to buy food for his little brother because he was hungry."

"He took the boy home." There was a roughness in Boyle's voice that hinted at strong emotion.

"And when he dropped the child off, and found the family in difficult financial straits, he went out and bought groceries for them with his own money. So that those kids, that mother, wouldn't go hungry on his watch. That's a special kind of man." She paused, letting her words sink in. "Be proud of the man you raised."

"Always." It was nearly a whisper.

Gemma glanced at the time and knew they had to be close to arrival at the station. *Time to get back to the situation at hand.* "So, what's your plan? You had this escape in mind all along, so you must have a plan. We're in this together now, so I'd like to know it."

But he stayed silent, giving an infinitesimal shake of his head.

Something to keep working on then.

They broke from the darkness of the subway tunnel into the brilliance of the white-tiled Canal Street Station.

"Okay, folks, this is the end of the tour," said the tour guide as he held on to one of the vertical poles by the middle door. "Thank you again for your flexibility in the last-minute switch to this station. And thank you for your support of the New York Transit Museum. Please watch our website and our newsletters for more information on upcoming tour opportunities."

The train slowed to a stop and all three sets of doors slid open. Most people headed for the middle door, where the tour guide stood by the exit, personally thanking all the tour participants. Boyle cupped his left hand under Gemma's elbow and steered her toward the door at their end of the car.

They stepped out of the car into a station that was also one of the original twenty-eight, but now Gemma couldn't help but see the differences between the Canal Street and City Hall Stations. This station had the same type of rectangular tiles lining the walls and square pillars along the edge of the platform, but everything was in straight, boxy lines, and there were no graceful vaulted ceilings. Whereas the City Hall Station had been frozen in time in 1945, the Canal Street Station showed the wear of an additional three-quarters of a century of use. The decorative terra-cotta trim and plaques near the top of the walls along the platform were now faded and smudged with an oily black residue from decades of powder-fine metallic dust and grime blown into the air by speeding subway trains. Above the trim, parts of the black plaster wall had collapsed, revealing the concrete foundation beneath.

Gemma couldn't count the number of times she'd passed through this station before, but now she was seeing it in comparison to a historic crown jewel and couldn't help but find it sadly shabby.

Behind them, the familiar two-tone chime sounded and a recorded voice announced the closing of the doors. Seconds later, the out-of-service train pulled out of the platform. The tour participants, moving in pairs or loose groups, remained on the platform waiting for the next 6 train, headed for the turnstiles, or veered off toward the passageway that would take them to connecting subway lines.

Gemma glanced at the sign hanging overhead in the corridor stretching away to the right, guiding the way to connections to the J, Z, N, Q, R, and W lines. If Boyle was looking to disappear into the city, this would be the fastest way to get out of Lower Manhattan. Any of those trains would take them east into Brooklyn. Or if they waited, an in-service 6 train would take them north into the Bronx.

The more lost they got, they more jeopardy she would be in. And the less chance she'd have of help being nearby, with most of the city's law enforcement concentrating in Lower Manhattan.

"This way." Boyle's fingers dug into her elbow as he propelled her across the platform, following the crowd to the connecting lines.

"Wait." Gemma pulled back against him. "Are you insane?"

His eyes narrowed to slits. "Some might think so after today."

"They'll think it more if you get on another subway train."

He arched an eyebrow at the suggestion. "Trying to convince me to stay near your cop friends?"

"I'm not an idiot. Getting you out of the most heavily populated area would be the safest for me and everyone around us. If things go south and a firefight starts, I want less people as collateral damage, not more. But when they figure out you've gotten away by subway and you're down here in the system, they're going to position cops at every subway exit in the city and on every platform, and you're going to be a sitting duck on any line. Your only hope of escape, and my only hope of keeping anyone else from dying today, including myself, is for you to get out onto the streets, where you can get lost in the crowd."

His crumpled brow and squinted eyes told her she was getting her point through. He'd been thinking speed, but she was swaying him toward caution. He just needed a little more of a push.

"They're not going to expect you to be on foot. And then you're not forced into any particular route. You can pick your own and make changes as needed. What's your plan? To head for commercial rail and make your way out of the city on Metro-North?"

"Like I'd share that with you." He pivoted and yanked her along with him.

Gemma kept her face composed, but a bolt of triumph shot through her as he steered her toward the floor-to-ceiling, full-height rotating turnstiles that led to the outer stairs.

A burst of laughter had her looking up and through the vertical steel bars of the fence that separated the fare-paid area from the unpaid. Her steps faltered when she spotted the NYPD blue uniform. From the growled curse in her ear, she knew the moment Boyle spotted the transit police officer.

The man stood against the wall about ten feet from the turnstile, his thumbs hooked into his utility belt, his posture at ease as he laughed with two civilians. Gemma didn't recognize any of them, but with a force the size of the NYPD, it was impossible to know all her brothers and sisters in blue. Whether the other two were also officers, either off-duty or undercover transit officers, she couldn't say. But that single officer could pose a huge threat to herself and everyone around her if he was aware the most wanted man in New York City was only fifteen feet away. A quick glance at Boyle confirmed he knew it too.

Gemma paused as several people in front of her jockeyed for position at the turnstile and then nearly stumbled as she stepped forward, only to be tugged back by Boyle. He met her eyes, glanced toward the officer, over the crowd around them, and then back at her. His message was clear: There was no way for him to physically hold her and they would be forced to separate and move through the turnstile one at a time, only feet away from a fellow officer. If she tried anything—calling for help, alerting the officer that Boyle had a gun, sprinting away, or trying to trap him on the platform side of the turnstile—he would have no choice but to use lethal force to get away.

He'd already killed once today. She had no doubt he'd do whatever he needed to do to be free.

She gave him a curt nod. *Message received.*

Soon she was at the turnstile. Boyle released her, but she could tell from the way his fingers lingered and slowly pulled away, he didn't trust this wasn't all about to go to hell. Gemma braced her hands on one of the horizontal bars and pushed the turnstile, the section bars closing in behind her. Then she stepped through to the far side, stepping forward and then stopping, so Boyle actually collided with her as he came through behind her. She looked over her shoulder to make eye contact, her gaze steady, silently pledging she wasn't planning any tricks. With an armed officer only feet away, she felt the risk of a firefight was simply too high.

She started forward, already peering over the heads of the people in front of her, up the stairs to where softer evening light was brightening the far wall.

When the cry came from in front of her, she jerked her gaze back down to this level, just in time to slam to a halt before plowing into the man in front of her. The cop was already moving toward them, his thumbs pulling free of his utility belt, one hand reaching out and the other dropping toward his firearm.

Out of the corner of her eye, Gemma caught the change in Boyle's expression as it morphed from surprise to purpose, and she didn't even think. Even as he drew back his right arm to pull the gun from his pocket, she grabbed his wrist as tightly as she could. It was awkward, as Boyle still stood behind her, but she managed to forestall his backward motion and drew him toward her until the barrel of the gun, still in his pocket, jammed against her side. She froze, waiting for the shot.

It never came.

With a smile, a woman straightened and accepted the bag she'd fumbled from the transit officer. She was laughing as she apologized for her clumsiness, patted him on the arm, and thanked him for his help. With a nod and a smile, the officer stepped back again, his hands at his side, his posture one of attention, but not alarm.

Gemma forced her fingers to let go of Boyle's wrist and the pressure of the gun barrel fell away. She shakily released the breath she'd been holding and cast a sideways look at Boyle, only to find him staring at her, his brows drawn together in question. She turned away from him, leaving him to draw his own conclusions, and started to move once the group shuffled forward again. She passed the officer without looking at him, keeping her eyes fixed on the summer sunlight ahead.

Out to the street, to light and freedom. They mounted the steps, taking the first flight, then over the landing and up to the last flight.

They were halfway up when the buzz of static came over the transit officer's radio. "All Precinct Five and transit officers, be on the lookout for two individuals, expected to have traveled to the Canal Street subway station on an uptown six. The male individual is . . ."

Then they were out on Canal Street and Gemma didn't even look to Boyle for guidance, she just headed east, striding down the sidewalk as fast as she could. In the distance, she heard sirens, growing louder as they headed in this direction.

They were out and alone, where they could get lost in the crowded city.

She'd saved the hostages. She'd saved the life of every person on that tour.

Now it was just him and her, one-on-one.

CHAPTER 22

*B*oyle grabbed Gemma's hand, gripping it as they arrowed through pedestrian traffic down Canal Street. Her hand lay lax in his grip, and while she would have preferred he didn't touch her, she didn't try to pull away. He may have been sure she would cut and run and considered her his ticket to safety as an important and handy hostage, but nothing was further from the truth. As she'd told him, she had to look out for the safety of all the citizens around her, just going about their daily lives, leaving a late work-day or enjoying an evening out in the city. She had no doubt he would use whatever force was necessary to keep his freedom. And if he thought he was going down, she was sure he'd have no compunction in taking her with him.

Only blocks away, a new siren joined the street noise.

Boyle craned his head over his shoulder, searching for any sign of law enforcement. Jerking her along with him, they jogged across Centre Street, just catching the end of the light. They stepped up onto the curb, and cars immediately filled the gap behind them, streaming north and south, cutting off access from the subway station.

Only a handful of blocks south, the David N. Dinkins Municipal Building rose to fill the skyline, a stark reminder of how little distance they'd put between them and City Hall. From the tightening of his grip and his increased stride, Gemma knew she wasn't the only one noting it.

Gemma half jogged to keep up with him. She gave her hand a hard yank. It didn't pull free, but it was enough to catch Boyle's attention. "Slow down." She suited actions to words by dropping into a walk, dragging him with her. "Unless you want to look like you're running for a bus from here to . . . wherever you have in mind, we're going to attract attention more by looking panicked and running, rather than if we walked through the crowds. Now, where are you trying to go?"

"Off this damn island. That's all I'm telling you."

Off the island. Out of Manhattan. Probably over state lines. From Manhattan, it wasn't hard to do. It all depended on which bridge or tunnel you chose; New Jersey was right next door, and Connecticut was only forty-five minutes away. Was he planning on mass transit to take him out of Manhattan? Or did he have a car waiting for him somewhere, maybe with stolen plates so he couldn't be easily identified?

He sent her a slitted glare. "Don't try to convince me we're a team. You're figuring out how to take me down."

Time to set aside the more conversational negotiator tone and convince him she was more partner than adversary. It might be the only way to bring down his guard for the half second she'd need to gain the advantage. "Don't tell me what I'm thinking," she said. "I've put my life in your hands in an attempt to save others. That's my only goal. Remember? No longer law enforcement. I don't have a horse in this race."

"Bullshit. Your family is the 'horse in this race.' *Your blood* is the 'horse in this race.' "

The rage lighting his eyes came from a bone-deep understanding of that blood. Of continuing a family legacy, of the pride of your child following in your footsteps as you followed in your father's. She couldn't imagine the agony of losing that child, but she could understand that his rage was seeded in that tragedy.

She looked ahead, down Canal Street. They were well into Chinatown here, and the stores flanking both sides of the street displayed signage in both English and Chinese characters. But on the far side of Chinatown, the entrance to the Manhattan Bridge was just a few blocks ahead, curving toward the south. If he was going to stay on foot, that would be his fastest way off the island. Then he could get lost in Brooklyn.

If only she had a way to contact the NYPD, he could be trapped on the bridge. But even then, civilians could become involved and more hostages taken. No, she needed to keep it to just her. Then she could use skills she'd honed for years. The ones he wouldn't anticipate, which would put him at a significant disadvantage.

She'd studied Brazilian jiu-jitsu since before attending the academy. It wasn't a requirement, but the NYPD liked its officers to have martial arts training on the side. It not only taught them self-defense, but also calm, patience, and control. These were all vital characteristics in any police action, but especially useful in hostage negotiations. Brazilian jiu-jitsu had been Gemma's choice. It was known for teaching sensible ways to avoid a fight in the first place, but also for techniques that made it easier for smaller, weaker fighters to win in combat when that fight was unavoidable. While Gemma didn't consider herself weaker in any way, sheer practicality meant that with her five-foot-seven-inch stature and slim build, she had a greater challenge against larger, more muscular men. But her training taught her she didn't need to be bigger and stronger than her combatant overall, just stronger than his weakest point.

As Logan had learned the hard way. He'd upped his game with her after that.

To use those skills, she needed to get Boyle alone, where she could concentrate on only him. But where in a city of nearly 9 million people could she find that kind of private moment?

If she wanted to leave the NYPD out of it for now, they'd have to avoid the CCTV cameras. From her days working patrol, Gemma knew the city had thousands of closed-circuit TV cameras spread out over the five boroughs. With the two of them loose in the city, the NYPD would be scanning those feeds, trying to find their location and then track them. It would be impossible to avoid the cameras altogether, but she needed to keep her eyes open for them and then keep their faces off the feeds.

Boyle, however, wasn't thinking about eyes in the sky. His eyes were fixed on the distance, down toward the Bowery, where the triumphal arch and colonnade at the entrance to the bridge remained just out of sight. Gemma could read the intent in his preoccupied gaze.

Foot traffic was predictably heavy for a pleasant summer evening, with a mix of business types and family groups. The sidewalk was crowded, but Boyle had no intention of moving with the flow of traffic. They speed walked past open fruit stalls, odorous fish markets, kitschy souvenir stores with knickknacks and T-shirts emblazoned with New York City slogans, and window after window of sparkling designer knockoff watches and jewelry.

With a growl, Boyle pushed past a young couple strolling hand in hand down the middle of the sidewalk, ignoring the man's exclamation as Boyle's elbow knocked him off balance. Gemma kept her head down, not wanting to start something with a temperamental finance bro wanting to make points with his girl for bravery. All the while, her eyes never stopped moving as she searched for any means of assistance or anyone who could pose a threat. But the crowd around them remained anonymous.

As they approached the intersection at Elizabeth Street, the outer columns of the colonnade came into view. Boyle's pace picked up even more and Gemma had to do a half trot every few paces to keep up with him.

Across Bowery, in the direction of the colonnade, a flash of sunlight off a reflective surface caught Gemma's eye as they approached the intersection. It took her a moment to identify the source, but when she did, warning bells went off in her head. The lowering angle of the sun bounced its rays off the lens of the shoulder-mounted video camera of a news team. And not any news team, but ABC7's hotshot investigative team with the infamous Greg Coulter. Even from this distance, she could identify his station polo shirt in ABC blue, his pearly-white teeth, and perfectly coiffed hair. Because God forbid Coulter wasn't constantly ready for his close-up. The man beside him, with unkempt hair, a scruffy beard, a white T-shirt, and beige cargo shorts, balancing the chunky camera on his shoulder, was clearly the technical half of the team.

She'd seen Garcia bump up against Coulter in the past when the field reporter kept trying to insert himself into a standoff at a chic and popular restaurant. Coulter was a local hotshot, someone who believed reporters lived their best lives out in the field, and would follow a story aggressively to break it. That day, he'd been corralled to the sidelines, but Gemma had never been able to watch his reporting since then without remembering his aggressive and self-aggrandizing attitude. And his simmering fury at being kept from what he saw as his rightful prize.

If he'd been watching his own station's feed during the crisis, then he'd seen her walk both into and out of City Hall.

Between threat and assistance, this was definitely a threat.

She slowed, not wanting to stop and attract attention, and hauled on Boyle's hand. "Wait."

He ignored her, continuing his forward motion, half dragging her along.

"Stop! There's a reporter in front of us. If he spots us, we're in trouble." She stumbled as he pulled her off balance, nearly falling forward. When she looked up, and through the crowds, it was to find Greg Coulter pinning them with a laserlike stare. *"Cazzo!"*

With a shout to his partner, Coulter sprinted toward them. The cameraman swung the camera off his shoulder, seated it in one beefy hand by the handle, and bolted after Coulter.

Boyle took the two men in with a single glance and growled a curse to match hers. Without even looking, he pivoted left and stepped off the curb directly into traffic.

The car headed for him just barely stopped in time with an ear-splitting shriek of brakes and tires on asphalt, but Boyle didn't even hesitate; he simply ran across the street, dragging Gemma with him.

"Keep up!" he barked at her. "Or I'm going to shoot him, and I don't care who gets in my way."

"Tell me what you're doing ahead of time and I'll keep up," she snarled back, getting her feet under her.

Horns blared as they sprinted through traffic. One car came around the corner so fast, Gemma thrust out a hand to stop it—a reflexive motion that would have had no impact whatsoever on its forward motion—and her palm met the engine-warmed hood as it screeched to a halt. She had a flash of startled eyes through the windshield and then they were on the far curb and sprinting up Bowery. Boyle's legs were longer than hers, but she was a cop in peak physical shape, and she kept up with him easily, stretching her stride to match her pace to his.

A chorus of horns sounded and Gemma spared a glance behind—Coulter and his guy were about fifty feet back, winding through the stopped cars on Canal Street, heading straight for them.

Out of the frying pan and into the fire. Coulter was like a dog with a bone, and he would never let them go easily. In fact, he'd see this as his biggest opportunity of the year for a hot story. If he somehow knew Willan was dead, he'd be even more dogged. And if that camera was Internet-ready, and she'd be willing to bet her life savings it was, any footage they shot would be uploaded in real time and every cop in the city would know exactly where they were. They'd be surrounded in no time, and then how many would die? Including, possibly, herself.

No matter what she did, her goal of getting Boyle alone and taking him down with the least chance of civilian injury or loss of life seemed continually out of reach.

Unless they shook Coulter, the chances of this all going to hell had just gone up exponentially.

CHAPTER 23

A break in the traffic gave them the chance to cross the street in the middle of the block and round the corner to tear down Hester Street. They eschewed the crowded, slow-moving sidewalks and gained precious seconds running down the narrow separation between the two lanes of cars heading west.

Luck was with them as they hit the pedestrian crossing at Chrystie Street with the light, and they sprinted past mothers pushing strollers and elderly couples tottering across the street.

Ahead lay Sara Delano Roosevelt Park, the narrow strip of community green space that ran in a seven-block line from Canal Street up to East Houston Street in connected sections of playgrounds, basketball courts, and gardens. A cold shiver skittered down Gemma's spine at the thought of the families out for a breath of cooler evening air after a hot August day. Babies, toddlers, school-aged kids, out with their moms, or dads, or both.

"No." She tried to turn down Chrystie, to keep a buffer between this man and the people of New York City, but Boyle wasn't having any of it. He had greater bulk and inertia on his side, and where she would have dragged him toward the sidewalk, separated from the park by a wrought iron fence, he simply ran into her intended track. She had no choice but to allow herself to be driven onto the footpath that led directly into the playground or else she'd have gone down face-first into the interlocking bricks.

She was breathing hard and her mouth was bone-dry, but she

still managed a plea. "Don't . . . hurt them. Families . . . children." When he tossed her a look she read as belittling, still angry
she hadn't been able to sway him from this path, she went for the
kill shot. "You lost yours. . . . Don't make them . . . lose theirs."

Boyle stumbled and she knew she'd hit home. All she could
hope was it was enough. Her life in jeopardy was one thing. The
children who were just starting theirs was another. She knew and
accepted her risk; they were prepared for nothing more than innocent fun.

If he tried to take a child or family hostage, or pulled his weapon, she would have no choice but to stand between them. Literally.

So be it.

He dragged her into a playground full of shrieking and laughing children. Over the textured rubber surface that gave under
their pounding feet. Past the bright-roofed platforms, sank into
beds of sand and linked by short suspension bridges. Behind the
swing set, ducking around parents pushing their children into
flight, and ignoring the shouts to slow down. Then they were
through the open gate on the far side and racing through the
first of two basketball courts. There were pickup games on both
of them.

Boyle didn't hesitate, but cut directly through the middle of
the court, leading with one shoulder, plowing anyone out of the
way. A tall African-American teen was just pivoting to catch a pass
when Boyle shoulder-checked him, sending him sprawling with a
string of invectives. But Boyle didn't stop, heading for the far corner of the second court, to circle the adjacent handball courts.

Gemma didn't look back, but guessed from the cries and
shouts coming from behind her that Coulter was keeping up with
them and wreaking a similar path of chaos.

They caught another break with light traffic on Grand Street,
allowing them to cross against the light, heading around the
green-grassed soccer pitches of Lion's Gate Field on the Forsyth
Street side.

Gemma did a quick calculation from the city map in her head

built on years of living in Manhattan. Their best chance of escape at this point would be to try to lose Coulter at the Delancey Street–Essex Street subway station only a few blocks away, a nexus where four lines converged over two platforms and three sets of tracks going in six eventual directions. It also happened to be at the foot of the Williamsburg Bridge, so they could escape on foot into Brooklyn.

But what she wanted to do was counter to what everyone would expect. She wanted to take Boyle back into the city, not out of it. Everyone would be watching the subway lines, and the driving or walking routes *out*. Fewer would be looking *in*.

Which meant they needed to be last seen in that vicinity, but they would have to lose Coulter so he could report it, but not be able to trace them. Then they would go to ground. She needed to figure out where, but first they had to lose their tail.

She lost a precious second turning to look back, only to find Coulter and his cameraman still behind them. Their lead had widened to about eighty feet, but Coulter was definitely still in the running. And the cameraman had the camera back on his shoulder, one arm wrapped around it. The only reason for that was to film Coulter in action.

Pompous figlio di puttana. *If he spent less time in front of the mirror and more at the gym, he'd be able to keep up.*

They rounded the corner onto Broome Street and Gemma considered the narrow blocks. Another block and a half to the Allen Malls. Then two more should put them at Ludlow Street. If they could gain enough on Ludlow, when they turned east onto Delancey Street, it would only be a block to the subway steps. Then, depending on timing, they could get around the corner, or go down one set of steps into the subway and back out the other, confusing Coulter. It would have to be a snap decision at the time.

"Ihaveanidea." Her statement came out as a single multisyllabic word between harsh breaths. "We need to . . . lose him. Without him knowing . . . where we went."

"Yeah?" Boyle sounded like he was having difficulty drawing breath. Almost half a year off the force and four months in mourning. He was about to be their biggest liability.

"Delancey Street Station." She slowed slightly, allowing her to drag in a ragged breath. "Multiple subway lines . . . Williamsburg Bridge entrance. Lose them . . . they won't . . . know where we went. Gotta stay . . . in front of . . . them. Then we have . . . options."

Boyle didn't say anything, but he didn't dismiss the idea. Granted, he was probably trying to save his breath.

She'd take it.

They shot through the treed boulevard splitting the center of Allen Malls and continued down Broome. Some of the small shops here had closed for the night—a hardware shop with its blinds drawn, a fish shop that passed in a blur of empty cold cases, and a dry cleaner, with a rainbow of clothes in the window—and the streets were a little quieter.

At the bodega on the corner, they headed north up Ludlow, against the one-way flow of traffic.

"Here . . . We need to lose them . . . here."

Ludlow was deserted. Towering at least twelve stories above the narrow, two-lane street on their right was the side of one of the new luxury housing towers gentrifying the Lower East Side. Across the street ran a line of closed or abandoned shops, their dented metal roll-down shields spray painted in various colors with initials and graphics. Best of all, there was no traffic and no one in their way to slow them down. They needed to pour on the speed, to clear the corner ahead of Coulter so he wouldn't be able to track where they'd gone as he rounded the corner to Delancey himself and was confronted with too many escape routes.

They were about twenty feet from the end of the street when Boyle slowed, starting to drop back. Gemma gripped his hand, pulling him with her. But he shook her off, actually letting go of her for the first time.

As he stopped completely and turned in place, it hit Gemma full force that she'd made a terrible assumption. He hadn't objected to her brief plan and she'd taken that silence as agreement. But if she could see he was flagging, he had to know it himself, and that desperation clearly drove him to choose a different method to lose their tail.

Off to the side and several feet in front, she knew instinctively she was too far away from him, but she made the attempt anyway. Spinning and leaping forward, she aimed her shoulder at his, calculating that where she couldn't block, she could divert. With their differences in weight, brute force was her only option. But he'd already pulled the SIG from its holster and was braced to take the shot as Coulter arced around the corner, his cameraman only feet behind him.

"No!"

The shot exploded in her unprotected ears just before she hit him, hard, driving him off balance.

Too late.

Gemma nearly went all the way down, catching herself on one hand on the road as Boyle sidestepped wildly, trying to catch his balance. For a moment, she was disoriented as the world spun, her ears ringing with the explosive gunshot, and the familiar, acrid smell of metallic sulfur clouding the air. She pushed herself upright, finding her center and catching her balance, to see Boyle doing the same. Jerking her head to look down the street, she was horrified to see Coulter slumped against a grimy brick wall, his right hand pressed over his left shoulder. A dark bloom of blood spread out from under his palm. His cameraman had abandoned the chase and was bellowing for help.

Boyle grabbed her hand again, catching it in a cruel grip as he reholstered his weapon, jerked her around, and dragged her toward Delancey Street.

"You wanted . . . to stay in front of him. You got your . . . wish. And unless you want to get caught . . . as an accessory . . . to assault with a deadly . . . I suggest you keep up."

Gemma tossed one last glance over her shoulder at Coulter, who'd slid down the wall to crumple on the sidewalk, and the cameraman hunched over him. He would be able to get Coulter help. She had to put Coulter out of her mind.

Boyle obviously hadn't planned on ratcheting up his body count or he'd have taken Coulter out before now, as well as the cameraman. But he'd clearly been forced to change his plans on the fly, ensuring his safety when his own physical stamina—or lack thereof—became an issue. What she *wasn't* sure of was, had he missed a kill shot, or had he meant to simply disable Coulter? Either way, she needed to focus on getting Boyle off the streets and subdued. He had two weapons, and she had none. She could attempt to disarm him, but that had to happen where no one else could get hurt. Or killed.

She hoped Coulter didn't fall into that second category.

She hoped the same for herself.

CHAPTER 24

*T*hey had gotten away, but only barely.

The cameraman must have called 911 as they'd rounded the corner, because in less than thirty seconds distant sirens could be heard from north of Delancey.

Gemma let fury carry her, pushing her forward and driving Boyle along with her. When sirens approached from the north, she went south on Norfolk Street, crossing Grand and over to Essex, then followed it back to Canal Street. Once they again joined the evening pedestrians on Canal, they slowed to a walk to catch their breaths, looking like any other couple out for an evening stroll, albeit a brisk one.

Gemma was faced again with the task of getting him somewhere private, which was going to be difficult in the middle of Lower Manhattan surrounded by cars, taxis, and civilians on foot. She scanned the area around them, getting her bearings. They were just on the northern edge of Chinatown, with the majority of the Asian markets and restaurants behind them. But with growing hope, she realized that in her rush to get away from arriving first responders, she had them on the edge of Little Italy.

Little Italy. Where the Capellos had settled in 1885, when her great-great-great-grandparents had come to America as a young married couple. The tenement they'd lived in no longer existed, but her grandparents' apartment on Elizabeth Street still stood. Though now, instead of being over an Italian deli, an organic butcher shop occupied the ground-floor space, its windows full of signs about grass-fed beef and free-range chicken. She had fond memories of spending weekends with her siblings at her grandparents'. Of sitting out on their fifth-floor fire escape on hot summer evenings, reveling in the cool breeze wafting over her skin while she watched life teeming below. Of the wonderful smells coming out of the kitchen. Of working with her grandmother in that kitchen, side by side, often with Frankie joining in, learning the family recipes she still made today.

When her mother died, her grandmother had stepped in to carry the weight of motherhood, as much as she could—on weekends, her grandmother allowed her father time to recharge, and her presence added feminine touches and guidance for the lone daughter. God, she missed her grandmother, now six years gone.

But one of the things she'd learned from her grandparents was all the secret nooks and crannies and treasures of Little Italy. Sure, it had been twenty-five years, and nothing stood still in New York City, but in many historical neighborhoods, residents were loath to make sweeping changes.

That could play to her advantage. Step one, then, would be to get him into Little Italy proper.

In fact, she knew the first place she'd be able to find assistance— La Cassatella. Frankie's father's Sicilian bakery stayed open late in the summer months, serving iced coffee and pastries on their charming, seasonal sidewalk patio, its bright red chairs and overflowing planters of flowers a cheerful pop of color in the middle of city life. If she could somehow get Boyle over a couple of blocks from Lafayette and up Mulberry Street, perhaps she could find a way to get a message to Frankie. During the summertime, Frankie's father, Luca, came in early to start the day's baking and to open the bakery. Frankie joined him later in the day and would take over, staying until the bakery closed at 9 p.m. She glanced surreptitiously at her watch—8:20 p.m.—so not only would the bakery be open, it would be doing brisk *Ferragosto* business. The Capellos would not be the only Sicilians celebrating the Feast of the Assumption on such a lovely summer evening.

Okay, that was step one in the plan. Get Boyle over to La Cassatella. Keep him away from Frankie, because over Gemma's dead body would she risk her best friend's life to this man with blood on his hands, hell-bent on vengeance. And then get a message to Frankie. But what message and how?

"You need to get off the street until things calm down. Especially now."

"You're going to help me find a place to lie low?" The sneer in his voice accompanied the slight curl in his lip.

"Look, at this point, my goal is for you to let me go. My safety and that of the people around me are all I care about. Once you're gone, you're not my responsibility anymore. Then it's up to the NYPD, the state police, or the FBI if you cross state lines. Do we have a deal? I'll help you lie low until you can get away, and you'll let me go at that point and won't hurt anyone else?"

He took a moment to consider her, glanced over her shoulder toward the growing wail of sirens, and then back at her. "If you do anything to screw me over, all bets are off. You, and anyone else in my vicinity, will die."

Gemma gave a careless shrug she hoped didn't convey any of her actual misgivings about pulling this off. "Then we're fine, because I have no intention of dying today. Come on, this way."

She realized that while she'd been thinking, she'd overshot her goal by a block, so she steered him up Baxter. Up ahead, a tall, copper-domed building commanded the end of the street, another classic structure of similar architecture to City Hall. This was the old NYPD headquarters, the building that had served the force in the years following Teddy Roosevelt's years as commissioner. Now it was a condominium building, filled with luxury apartments, but it gave Gemma a boost to see it in the distance. A small link back to the life to which she fully intended to return. That she fully intended to live right now.

One block over on Hester and the next cross street was Mulberry, the heart of Little Italy. Her goal.

"Let's go up here," she said, pointing down Mulberry where it ran between an Italian café on one corner and a five-star restaurant specializing in seafood on the other. Just crossing the road brought scents wafting out into the street and Gemma's heart rate settled with the comforting familiarity.

Coming to Little Italy was a good idea—she knew the area and the people and felt more in control. But the negative side of it was the popularity of the area. It was feast night, and many Italians were out celebrating after the evening's *Ferragosto* Mass, and many more had come to join them from outside the neighborhood. Foot traffic picked up sharply and it slowed their pace. However, on the bright side, they were now lost in another crowd of people.

Gemma crossed the street, darting between two parked cars with Boyle to hit the sidewalk on the east side, in front of a clam house. Farther up the street, she could just make out the sign for La Cassatella, and the splash of red from the patio sprawling over the wide sidewalk.

She needed a plan, needed to find a place he'd see as a way to lie low, and she'd see as an isolated location, where she would try to apprehend him. She ran through area locations that had been as familiar as home to Gemma and her brother Alex as children when they had the run of the neighborhood. The cigar shop, with its interesting smells, and old Mr. Romano, who slipped them Pastiglie Leone confections that melted on their tongues. The century-old ravioli shop that specialized in every shape of hand-made pasta imaginable. St. Patrick's Old Cathedral, where their mother used to take them on holy days of obligation. The dairy on the corner that sold every kind of cheese imaginable, including their own fresh mozzarella daily. The . . .

Gemma turned her body's knee-jerk reaction to freeze in place into a convincing stumble and a glare back at the sidewalk that didn't have a single crack in it to trip over. *St. Pat's.* She remembered the layout in detail, as if it had only been weeks since she'd last been there instead of twenty-five years. She needed a space to get him alone and no place was better suited. Sure, it had a large, soaring sanctuary, with seating for easily 250, but it also had a walled cemetery and catacombs, with a series of crypts below. It was built in 1815, if she remembered correctly, and had been designated a New York City landmark before she was even born. There was no chance they'd made any significant changes on such a historic building, so her mental map would still be accurate.

Normally the church would be closed and locked by this time of night. But on *Ferragosto*, a special evening Mass was celebrated. As a result, the church would be open for another half hour. The biggest risk would be visitors or congregants lingering after Mass. Getting Boyle off the streets was paramount, but she needed to ensure she wasn't simply handing him new potential hostages to escalate the situation. But at this time of night, there would be few others present, and they likely would be heading home soon after.

It was a chance she had to take.

Now she had a destination. Next she needed to communicate it to someone else. And there was only one person she could bring into this situation. Only one person with the skills and family background who wasn't already involved in what was likely now a citywide manhunt. Because no one called Internal Affairs when the city was in crisis.

Alex was exactly who she needed.

Dusk was falling and shop and streetlights were beginning to wink on as they passed a florist shop and a designer Italian leather-goods shop. La Cassatella was next on the right, its small fenced patio spilling onto the sidewalk. It was crowded as always, but a wide path to the front door of the bakery was unobstructed.

Gemma gauged the distance to the patio. *Three . . . two . . . one . . .*

Just as they were about to pass the center walkway through the patio, Gemma stiffened, pulling back on Boyle's hand. "Don't turn around," she hissed. "There's a beat cop across the street."

Ignoring her advice, Boyle started to turn, but Gemma yanked on his arm. "Don't! You'll attract attention." She looked around frantically.

"Go in there." Boyle let go of her hand, but crowded her into the bakery's patio. Without another look at the phantom officer,

Gemma turned and made her way to the bakery door, and then inside.

Familiar sights and smells hit her simultaneously. The waft of freshly baked bread and cookies. The sweet aroma of sugar-dusted cannoli and tiramisu. The crisp nuttiness of biscotti and ladyfingers. And over it all, the rich tang of espresso scented the air. The bakery was done in tones of dark wood and Venetian plaster, with rich leather bench seating and recessed arches hung with oil paintings of the Italian countryside. The main counter ran down the left side of the café, with booths and tables running along the right side and into the back.

Frankie, wearing a red apron to match the patio chairs out front, and with her hair piled into a careless knot on top of her head, stood behind the long glass case stuffed to overflowing with sweets, manning the espresso machine as she chatted with a customer. Behind her, stacks of wide stoneware cups for cappuccinos and *Americanos,* tall glass mugs for lattes, and tiny espresso cups lined the back wall next to a row of tall coffee syrup bottles. As Frankie turned, she caught Gemma's eye and her face broke into a smile.

Knowing Boyle was behind her, but likely taking in every detail, Gemma let all the fear she felt for her friend's safety wash over her face and gave an almost-imperceptible shake of her head.

Confused, Frankie's smile dissolved.

Gemma turned back to Boyle, who was staring out the wide, front picture window. "Can you see him? Is he still there?" She pushed up on tiptoe, peering out over his shoulder. "He was over there, by the cigar shop. The word must be out now that you got away, or Coulter may have told them you were last seen in the area. They must be plastering your face on every screen and have a BOLO out for you, so everyone will be watching. Is he there?"

As Boyle continued his visual search, Gemma turned back to Frankie, who stood transfixed, a heavy coffee cup drooping in her hand, her fancy drink forgotten. Gemma met her eyes, mouthed the word "Alex" and made the sign of the cross. Then she turned away. That was all she could do. She wouldn't risk Frankie in any way by attempting more communication than that.

"I don't see him," she said.

"I don't either."

"I have an idea. St. Patrick's Old Cathedral is just uptown by about a block or two. What better place for literal sanctuary than a church? *Ferragosto* Mass always starts at seven so it will be over by now, but the church will still be open for a little longer. It's only a few minutes' walk. We have to get out of this crowd before someone recognizes you."

"Connor told me about that place. It's the one with the crypts in the basement, where they do tours." He gave her a yank, pulling her toward the door. "Let's go."

Gemma knew Frankie would have seen both the stranger and the rough handling. She'd watch them leave and note their direction. She also knew the Capellos weren't religious, so there would be no reason Gemma would make the sign of the cross. As long as she understood that single-word message, she'd be on the phone to Alex as soon as they were out the door. Then it was up to her brother to figure out where they might be going.

Gemma left the bakery without daring to look back.

CHAPTER 25

*T*he command center at 1 Police Plaza was buzzing with frenetic activity. Following the chase, information came in at breakneck pace from multiple sources that had teams of officers on the street and mobilized the A-Team to new locations. It was so noisy, Alex almost didn't hear his phone ring.

He stepped back from where he stood with Joe and his father, moving to an infinitesimally quieter corner. He pulled his cell phone out of the pocket of his cargo shorts. The name **Francesca Russo** was splashed across the display with a picture of the smiling blonde. *Must be calling for an update.*

He hit the TALK button. "Hi, Frankie. I don't have any updates on Gemma, if that's what you're looking for."

"I don't need an update." Frankie spoke very quickly, with an edge of breathlessness. "She just left the bakery."

"What?" It was so loud in the command center, he must not have heard her correctly. He made a beeline to the door and waited to speak until he was in the quieter corridor. "Did you say she was just at La Cassatella?"

"Yes. Alex, she was acting really strange. She looked . . . scared. Gemma never looks scared."

"Was she alone?"

"No. She was with an older man. I've never seen him before. In his fifties, maybe? He treated her roughly, and dragged her out of the bakery before I could talk to her."

"*Merda*. She didn't say anything to you?"

There was a pause before Frankie spoke. "Not directly. But I think she mouthed your name to me. That's why I'm calling."

She's reaching out, looking for help. "That's great, Frankie. That's exactly right. Do you know what's going on at City Hall?"

"Customers have been talking about it. A gunman took hostages in the mayor's office."

"Yeah. What's not common knowledge is that Gemma traded herself for the release of the hostages." He kept talking over Frankie's gasp. "And then he escaped with her into the subway system. They got off at Canal Street and were chased through the Bowery, but then managed to get away and disappear. Until now. You've given us a chance to get her back. Did she mouth anything else? Or just my name."

"No, nothing else. She didn't have more than a second because she was trying not to attract the guy's attention."

"She didn't want to put you at risk. Somehow she got him in there, and then could only take seconds to find an ally, when she's otherwise out there on her own."

"Maybe. She didn't say anything else, but she did do one other weird thing."

Energy shot through Alex's spine, jerking him upright. "What?"

"She crossed herself. Which makes no sense. Minus being invited to weddings and baptisms you guys haven't voluntarily set foot in a church in more than two decades."

Which is exactly why it means something. She's not preparing to meet her Maker; she's sending me a message. "Frankie, I have to go. You're amazing. Thank you."

"Alex, please let me know when you know something. Anything at all. I'm so scared for her. Gem is the bravest woman I know. If she thinks she's in trouble, it's bad."

"It's bad," Alex agreed. "I'll call you as soon as I know anything, I promise." He hung up and stood motionless for a moment, staring down at his phone.

Gemma was in Little Italy after a mad dash through the Bowery. After getting that far away, they'd looped back to an area no one would anticipate because it was so deep downtown and they'd just gotten out of there. *No better place to hide than in plain sight because everyone was looking for them somewhere else.*

His head snapped up. *Hide in plain sight.* That was it. The heat was on and every on-duty cop in the NYPD was out looking for them. At some point, Gemma should have been able to get away from Boyle, but hadn't. Alex knew his sister, knew how her mind worked. Without a doubt, she was sticking to him now because if Boyle was on his own, he'd be a huge risk to the citizens of New York City. While she was with him, she could at least exercise a modicum of control over his actions. And while the rest of the NYPD might not know his location, she was keeping tabs on him, and, in doing so, was able to communicate that location.

If she hadn't apprehended him by now, there was a reason. Alex was willing to bet a year's salary it was because Boyle was armed and she wasn't, so she was waiting for the opportunity to get the upper hand without getting herself or someone else killed. As long as he remained a threat to the people of the city, she'd be playing along with him and trying to keep him from doing any more violence. And biding her time to bring him down.

But she'd put out a call for help—to him. Because he was the only Capello not officially on duty who was still an NYPD officer. Because they'd always been close, but their mother's death had strengthened that bond and kept them linked through thick and thin. Because they shared a history.

He closed his eyes, thinking hard. She'd crossed herself. What was she trying to say?

Because they shared a history.

His eyes flew open. She was going to St. Patrick's Old Cathedral. The church his mother used to take them to on holy days of obligation. A sanctuary. And one that would be open for *Ferragosto.*

Unless he was wrong. Most Precious Blood Church was closer. Or the Chapel of San Lorenzo Ruiz. Or Holy Trinity Ukrainian . . .

Stop second-guessing. You're wasting time. You know how she thinks.

He pushed back into the conference center. He'd report what he knew—Gemma was in Little Italy, she'd had Frankie call him, and she'd crossed herself. In case he was wrong and risked wasting resources boxing in an empty church, he'd leave the NYPD brass to reach their own conclusions for now. If he was right, and he found her at St. Pat's, he'd call in backup immediately. He'd know one way or the other inside of fifteen minutes.

It was time to slip out.

But not before signing out a weapon. And two throat mics so communication between them and the op commander was possible. He'd grab a ride from the first officer in a vehicle he could see. He'd get down to St. Patrick's Old Cathedral and he'd find Gemma.

And they'd end this.

CHAPTER 26

*G*emma sighed with relief as they stepped through the heavy oak doors, out of the hot August twilight, into the cool, quiet of St. Patrick's Old Cathedral. Just inside the door stood a tall stone font with several inches of holy water. Out of a long-ago habit, she dipped the fingertips of her right hand into the font and crossed herself, the water cool against her overheated skin. Then she led Boyle across the narrow narthex and through the heavy, red swath of velvet drapes, pulled back to allow entrance into the sanctuary beyond.

As the Gothic Revival sanctuary opened up in front of them, its vaulted ceiling rising to soar stories overhead, Gemma was pulled back into a cascade of childhood memories: Sitting through Mass with her family, washed with the soft glow of the chandeliers that hung overhead, suspended between the massive columns marching down the nave. The fading rays of the sun filtering in colored ribbons through the stained glass to fall over wooden pews rubbed satiny smooth under her fingertips from centuries of use. The scent of Easter lilies wafting from the huge spray atop the altar, now draped with a snow-white cloth, the color of Resurrection, after weeks of Lenten purple. Waiting at the back of the sanctuary after her mother had slipped into one of the twin confessionals, straining to hear the soft murmur of her voice as she confessed her sins.

Gemma hadn't set foot inside this church since her mother

died. But even with all those years in between, she realized coming into this place made her feel closer to her mother than she'd experienced in a very long time. To her, the sanctuary emoted a feeling of security, and of being loved, because that had been her association all those years ago. Back when she'd come to Mass in her Sunday best, in a frilly dress paired with short socks and stiff, uncomfortable shoes, with her hair neatly brushed and pinned back.

And here she was, dressed in denim capris and sneakers, hot, sweaty, and desperate. Bringing an armed, violent man inside a house of peace.

Forgive me, Father, for I have sinned . . .

Her attention was drawn by the stillness and silence of the scattering of people seated in and around the pews, broken only by the odd murmur and the soft tread of shoes on the stone floor. She scanned the few congregants who remained after Mass, or who had wandered in to take advantage of the evening hours. An older woman lighting a candle by St. Francis to her left, and five more people sitting in pews, one couple and three singles. The organ in the balcony over their heads was quiet and there was no sign of anyone in the confessional. The church would be closing in about fifteen minutes, so people were on their way home.

This would be how she would get him alone. And she knew just where to do it.

Down below, in the catacombs, where the only occupants had already shuffled off this mortal coil. They would not be able to help her, but they also couldn't get hurt.

She eyed the inset, double wooden doors first at the top of one aisle, then the other. She remembered from a series of articles on the church's renovations a few years earlier that they'd closed the old, external staircase down to the catacombs and built a new internal staircase for all-weather congregant and tour use. But which set of doors would take them down? They'd simply have to pick one and hope for the best, slipping through the doors when no one was watching. But for now, they needed to wait out the parishioners.

Gemma glanced over at Boyle, whose gaze was passing over the congregants. "Come on," she whispered. "Let's sit down. We need to look like we belong here, and we need to wait until most, if not all, of them leave. Then we can decide what to do." She grabbed his arm, tugging him down the main aisle.

She slid into one of the back pews on the left-hand side, in a spot where she could watch the whole church. Clasping her hands in her lap, she let a wave of exhaustion wash over her. The exertions of the day were catching up with her—the stress of the negotiation, losing Willan, putting herself up in exchange for the hostages, the pressure to blend seamlessly into the subway station tour, and then the wild flight through the Lower East Side. The emotional weight of her most painful memories.

She let herself give in to the fatigue for a moment.

Just one moment to regain the strength she would need to stop Boyle, once and for all.

CHAPTER 27

Alex sprinted down Mott Street, his eyes fixed on the bulk of St. Patrick's Old Cathedral, just up the block.

He'd had the uniform drop him two blocks away in case Gemma and Boyle were somehow still out on the streets. If she was working to confine them in a closed building for a takedown, he didn't want to cause Boyle to flee at the sight of an NYPD cruiser. This way, he could blend in, mostly—since he was running full tilt, even if he was in street clothes—and not set off any alarm bells. He might have a firearm under his gaudy Hawaiian shirt, and his shield and throat mic and earpiece for Gemma in his cargo shorts, but he was grateful his picnic garb marked him as a harmless tourist. The last thing they needed right now was someone in uniform.

He dropped to a walk as he neared St. Patrick's. He strode up the sidewalk to the tall wrought iron fence about thirty feet in front of the main doors to the church.

Alex paused for a moment on the sidewalk, gazing through the gap of the open gate to the heavy church doors thrown open and the dim narthex beyond, remembering the many times he'd been here so long ago. Sitting with his mother on a hard pew so tall he could swing his legs, and her gentle hand on his knee to stay the motion. Music bursting from the organ pipes. The smell of incense and the smoke wafting from the swinging thurible. Finally being old enough to attend Midnight Mass at Christmas.

This was a place of safety, for both himself and Gemma, and he could see why she'd come here. To draw strength from the familiar, as well as to strategically draw the upper hand. And in adding him to the mix, an even stronger hand.

He crossed the wide stone walkway that stretched across the front of the church, flanked on both sides by shorter wrought iron fencing enclosing the church's burial grounds. He stepped cautiously into the narthex, but the narrow space was empty. He moved forward, staying in the shadows behind one of the red velvet curtains, and peeked into the sanctuary. He spotted his sister immediately, sitting at the back beside an older man, and felt some of the stress slide off his shoulders. She was still wearing the outfit she'd worn to the picnic and her hair was a little more disarrayed than usual. But from the small slice of her face that was visible, she looked calm and in control.

He had known she was uninjured fifteen minutes before, when Frankie had called. But in a situation like this, when circumstances could turn on a dime, fifteen minutes was an eternity where anything could happen. Seeing Gemma unharmed with his own eyes settled the jagged edges in his gut.

They would take Boyle down here. The challenge was going to be in not turning it into yet another hostage situation. He scanned the room, taking in the other occupants, intuiting his sister was biding her time, waiting for people to leave. Which would happen soon, but what if Boyle got restless before that? Alex could possibly help there.

Silently he pulled back from the doorway and left the sanctuary, knowing exactly what he needed to do. First off was to contact the command center—using Joe as a conduit in case anyone objected to an IAB rat calling the shots—and get the building surrounded. The fewer people inside the building, the better, to avoid the situation getting out of hand and Boyle becoming desperate. However, if Boyle got away from them, he wanted the A-Team on the surrounding rooftops to make the shot.

Next, he needed a priest.

Hopefully, not for Last Rites.

CHAPTER 28

*G*emma didn't hear the door open, but the flash of movement caught her eye. She glanced up, briefly registered a dark-haired man wearing a black cassock and cincture closing the doors on the left aisle, and went back to surreptitiously watching the occupants in the church with her head bowed.

It took her three whole seconds to connect what she'd seen with what she knew. As the identity of the priest crystallized, her breath caught. She covered the sound with a cough and forced herself to breathe normally. And when she was sure Boyle's attention was completely focused on the people around them, she glanced back up again, quickly finding the "priest" moving slowly through the sanctuary.

Alex.

Her message had gotten through. He'd understood and come. Now they were two against one, and for the first time since she'd walked into the subway station with Boyle, true hope for a successful conclusion rose. She waited patiently until he casually looked her way and made eye contact with her. He gave a tiny head bob, which looked more like penitence than an acknowledgment, and continued down the aisle.

She was unsure at first of his motive as he approached the first parishioner, had a quiet word with her, and then moved on to the couple across the aisle. The parishioner stood, gathered her things, and started down the aisle toward them.

He's clearing everyone out. He's making sure there isn't anyone for Boyle to take hostage. Or to get hurt.

"We need to move," Boyle growled under his breath, his eyes fixed on Alex. "Looks like they're getting ready to close down for the night, and I am not leaving this church."

"What's your plan?"

"Remember the crypts beneath this church?" His chuckle was dark. "What better place to hide until things cool off than with the dead? Stay into the night, leave before dawn. Disappear in the dark."

Perfect. But she couldn't look too willing. "There are other places we could go." Turning slightly, she cast her eyes up behind them to the balcony above them, where the massive gold pipes of the organ rose to the ceiling. "What about the organ loft?"

His sneer was derisive. "Afraid of ghosts?"

Gemma let herself recoil slightly, causing him to reach out to clamp an iron hand over her forearm.

"You are. You're going to have a very bad night then." With his other hand, he pulled back his jacket, showing the butt of his SIG for her eyes only. "I suggest you come with me now or there'll be trouble." He looked up and over the sanctuary. "Maybe we'll start with the holier-than-thou priest."

Ice-cold fear washed over Gemma. She'd drawn Alex into this because she needed help, and, together, the two of them could beat Boyle. But the thought that she might have brought her brother here to die wasn't something she'd anticipated and it nearly stopped her cold. She purposely bolstered her tone with a bravado she didn't feel. "No need for another notch in your belt. The catacombs it is."

Boyle looked over at the far side of the church. "Then lead the way. Go light one of those candles over there. That will put us close to that door on the far side from the priest. There are only two side doors out of here, so we've got a fifty-fifty chance. If this isn't the way down to the catacombs, then we'll double back to the other doors."

Gemma nodded and shot to her feet. She stepped past him

back into the main aisle and then circled behind the last pew on the far side. Passing the paired, ten-foot-tall ornate wooden confessionals, she walked up the side aisle to where the Virgin Mary stood surrounded by candles, some already lit by congregants, their flames dancing in small glass holders. She selected a long wooden stick, its end already charred, and held it in a flame until it, too, burned bright. She lit a new candle, then gave the stick a few quick flicks to make sure the flame was extinguished before slipping it, charred end down, in the glass holder as Boyle joined her.

She took a quick look over her shoulder, but Alex stood with his back to her, speaking to the last parishioner near the back of the church. Her gaze shifted quickly to Boyle as the blunt barrel of the gun in his pocket pressed against her side.

"Now," he said. "While no one's looking."

She stole noiselessly down the aisle and pushed one of the two doors open to slip through, Boyle right behind her. Holding the handle, she seated the door silently back into place.

They were in a small vestibule, a later addition to the original early-nineteenth-century construction, that ran along the side of the church, dropping into a set of stairs leading downward into darkness.

They'd found the way to the catacombs.

No longer needing to hide it, Boyle pulled his SIG Sauer from his holster, eschewing the more compact format of the Glock in his pocket for the power and damage potential of the 9mm. Boyle planted his free hand at the small of her back and gave her a push toward the stairs. She half trotted for a few steps and sent him a narrowed glare over her shoulder. "No need to get rough."

He raised his gun so she couldn't miss his intent. "This isn't a committee. Go. We need to be out of sight before anyone else comes down here."

Turning away from him, Gemma started down the steps. Newly built, the stair treads were quiet under her sneakers and in seconds she was at the bottom and passing through a doorway into the dim undercroft.

Gemma had only a few seconds to observe everything in front

of her, knowing this was going to be her chance to take him down with no civilians nearby. Even though Alex had his back to them as they left the sanctuary, she was confident he'd followed their movement. Which meant he'd be right behind them.

The narrow undercroft filled the basement from one side of the church to the other. A flagstone floor stretched from the foundation to the chiseled fieldstone wall that separated the small gathering space from the catacombs themselves, once the original outer wall. The massive double doors to the catacombs, held in place by long decorative strap hinges that stretched nearly edge to edge, were thrown open, the darkness of the catacombs stretching beyond.

Boyle followed behind her, pulling the door shut after him, quenching all the light from above. Now the only light came from the red EXIT sign hanging over the doorway, giving the room a creepy crimson glow. "There we go. Get used to the dark. If the place was empty, the lights would be off, so that's how we'll wait. I don't want any light showing under the door attracting that priest's attention and bringing him down here."

Gemma took in the gaping maw of the doors leading into the catacombs. There, in the more complete dark, she'd make her move.

Like Logan had, she was counting on Boyle to underestimate her, even if only for the first second or two of the fight. Of course, she wasn't dealing with a random street brawler while out on patrol; she was dealing with an NYPD cop. One who might have gone slightly to seed with his retirement and the loss of his son, but who would have defensive moves as an automatic reaction. And he was easily about sixty pounds heavier than she; she had her work cut out, she had no doubt. Not to mention the first thing she had to do was get the SIG out of his hand. Martial arts could only take her so far. The first thing to avoid was a bullet to the brain.

But before that, she needed to make it far enough into the catacombs that if Alex followed them, the light from the open door wouldn't be visible to announce his arrival.

She stepped toward the doorway into the catacombs and made a show of pausing halfway there.

Boyle's hand landed on her shoulder and clamped on with an iron grip. "Keep going."

"I will. It's just . . . you know . . . dead people."

"Dead people are the least of your concerns. Now move." He pushed her forward.

Gemma reached out a hand to the wall of the arched passage into the catacombs. Part of the original construction, the wall was easily three feet thick, built out of mortar and mismatched field-stones. She paused, taking the moment to reinforce Boyle's perception of her hesitancy, but also to review her memories of the catacombs' layout.

She'd been in them several times, but that was more than twenty-five years ago when the door in the front walkway off Mott Street had led to the centuries-old stone steps down to the cata-combs. Still, these were in a historical landmark building; there was no way the footprint of the catacombs had been changed. Her one brief glimpse told her they'd refreshed the surface of the walls and redone the floor, but she was betting those would be the only changes. Closing her eyes, she drew a floor map in her head: A rectangular layout echoing the nave of the church above. There was a long central corridor, with sealed family crypts for up to a dozen members about every ten feet. Side offshoots at each end led to long corridors that ran parallel to the central pathway, each with more crypts running along the inner walls. At the far end was the original staircase, which ran up to the street level, but was now closed and abandoned in lieu of a safer entrance. Several open vaults held stone sarcophagus-style tombs and could pro-vide niches in which to hide. The most renowned vault in the church, that of Thomas Eckert, the Civil War hero, was famously unsealed, but she was sure it would be locked and inaccessible.

Take one of the side aisles and head toward the back of the catacombs.

Keeping one hand on the wall, Gemma rounded the corner to the right, moving slowly forward in utter darkness, trusting her sense of touch more than anything else. The faint red glow from the bottom of the stairs quickly dissipated inside the catacombs; she might as well have had her eyes closed in the inky blackness. The wall here was polished and slick under her fingertips with periodic breaks, but was a flat surface, with no recesses, and stretched all the way along the corridor. When she judged they must have been almost to the far side, she put out her left hand in front of her, and a few more steps brought her palm against smooth plaster.

They'd reached the crypts.

Now she just needed to take them farther in. She purposely kept them against the right-hand wall, knowing he was holding on to her with his left hand, while his right hand held his gun. Their path kept his right hand close to the wall, something she planned to use to her advantage.

It was impossible to know how far into the catacombs she'd taken him, but Gemma waited until she estimated they were at least halfway along the corridor, if not more.

It was now or never. She had to trust that if she got into trouble, Alex would move in to help.

She let her footsteps drag slightly, and then pretended to stumble in the dark. The move propelled her forward, down, and out from under Boyle's grip, giving her enough room to pivot, weave her fingers together, and swing with all her might at where she calculated his right arm and hand would be.

CHAPTER 29

*H*er joined hands hit flesh, just before the jolt of slamming into the plaster wall ricocheted up her arms. Boyle's grunt of pained surprise was followed by the satisfying sound of metal striking the stone floor and skittering away.

He'd lost his hold on the gun, which was now somewhere on the floor in the dark.

Finally a fair fight. Now she just had to keep his hands busy enough he wouldn't have the luxury of time or the freedom of movement to go after the Glock buried deep in his jacket pocket.

She reached out for where she gauged his right elbow might be, touched the edge of his jacket, and recalculated, feeling a spurt of triumph when she found it on the second try. She hooked her hand behind his elbow, yanking him forward and toward her right side, tipping him off balance. Then she ducked under his arm and lunged forward, wrapping both arms around the backs of his thighs, halfway up from his bent knees, and lifted him. Already off step, Boyle completely lost his footing and toppled backward, going down hard on his back. Gemma just barely got her arms out from under him as he fell, but she let herself go down with him, and then was on him in an upper grappling mount.

She had no weapon or handcuffs, and she was easily only two-thirds his weight. While she had no idea how much training he had, it wasn't zero. But she was realistic. All she really needed to do was subdue him until Alex showed up. And if she couldn't do that, then she needed to trap him in the catacombs until backup arrived.

The basics of the art were so ingrained in her that instinct took over. Use leverage, timing, and energy efficiency to compensate for her smaller size. Immobilize, control, and exhaust him. Stay low in the mount, using her hips and legs to anchor herself to him. Minimize the distance between them to minimize any damage he could do.

If she was right on top of him, he wouldn't have room to pull back and undercut her, so she went low. She lay over him, using her hips to pin his down as she slipped her feet under his bent knees and hooked them around his shins. She planted both hands on the floor on either side of his head to brace herself. Boyle immediately tried to buck her off, but she stayed connected, so he grabbed her at the waist, his fingers digging deep with fury, and tried to lift her off. It would have worked as long as he was able to bench-press her full weight. But she slid her right arm under his head, jamming his skull against her shoulder, pushed off the floor with her left hand, and used her legs to lock them together, forcing him to bench-press their combined weight to move her. When that didn't work, he tried to roll her in the opposite direction. She simply switched his head to her opposite shoulder and changed hand positions, jamming them in place on the floor.

His guttural curse brought a feral smile to her lips. *Gotcha*, bastardo.

She knew he was simply going to regroup, so she went on the offensive. She quickly grabbed the collar of his jacket in a palm-up right-handed fist on her left side of his neck. Releasing his head, she threaded her left hand under her right forearm. He made a wild grab for it, gripping his thumb and several fingers around her wrist, but she moved her right knee forward to trap his arm against her ribs and wrenched her wrist free. She shot her hand under her right arm to grab the collar of his jacket, palm down, just to the right of his neck. She knew he foresaw the cross choke when he wrapped his right forearm over both of hers, trying to block her, but a single arm wasn't enough. Using the collar for leverage, she leaned forward, expanding her chest, and heard the change in his breathing as it became strangled with the force of her compression.

All she needed was about five or six seconds and it would be enough for him to lose consciousness; then she could get him completely subdued until Alex got here. But having his arm locked beneath her right knee meant she didn't have time to get her ankle hooked around his leg on that side, when, with a giant heave, he threw his weight to the left and she started to roll. She lurched onto her right knee while still keeping her viselike grip on his collar, blocking the roll as her body bridged over his.

It should have been a simple correction—maintain the hold on his collar, yank him to line up with her knee, roll back over him and complete the chokehold. But as she braced and tried to haul him up, he didn't move. As her own inertia instead carried her forward, she realized her mistake—in the dark, his head had jammed against the invisible crypt wall, trapping him in place while she threw her weight forward. She never would have tried the move, if she had been able to see her surroundings, but now it was too late—she was tumbling, and she couldn't maintain her hold on his collar as she rolled onto her back.

Then he was on her. His fist came out of the dark and pain sang through her nerve endings as he connected with her right cheekbone in a brutal cross jab, bouncing her head on the tile floor.

Before she learned jiu-jitsu, being on the bottom of a fight would have been a terrifying position. But she knew what to do in this situation, and being far enough away for him to whale on her with his fists wasn't it. She wrapped her legs around him, crossing her ankles behind his back, reared up to wrap her right arm behind his neck, pulled him in close enough to smell the stale waft of his breath, and rolled back to the floor, pulling him down on top of her. In too close quarters to hit her with any force, Boyle tried to wind his arm under hers. She quickly counteracted by weaving her arm under his, putting them back into the same position. But when her sweaty palm slipped on the back of his neck and he slid free and back, she reached a hand out, connecting with his chest and pushing him a few extra inches away, while she unlocked her ankles, giving her room to pull her knees up and ram them into his chest. She heard his grunt as she made contact, felt his fist skim her chin, and knew she'd escaped the force of what might have been a knockout punch.

Time to wrap this up before he managed to overpower her with the bulk and strength clearly on his side, or he decided he could subdue her for the precious four or five seconds it would take to reach for, orient, and find the trigger on the Glock.

Alex, where the hell are you?

He could only be minutes behind her, and he couldn't fail to find them as they fought in the dark. And, hopefully, he'd have the sense to bring a light source. Or backup. Or weapons.

Or all of the above.

She could try a triangle chokehold by trapping his head under her locked thighs, but that would be damned hard when she couldn't see her opponent. Still, it might be the best way to hold him.

His weight thrust forward against her, so she snapped her knees open and he fell against her at the sudden loss of support, and she struggled to wrap her legs around him again. But this time, he was ready and threw himself toward her right side, scrambling to land perpendicular to her body. She countered by digging the fingers of her right hand into the soft flesh of his elbow and slammed her left forearm against the base of his neck, the initial target she'd missed in the dark. She brought up her right knee to nail him in the hip. When he jumped away from it, she jammed her heels into the floor and rolled him, flipping his body up and over the forearm locked against the back of his neck. He somersaulted over her to go rolling away in the dark.

Her triumph in the moment was cut short by the sound of a gun scraping along the floor, dragged by his body. She rolled to her knees and lunged for it. But when one of Gemma's fingers closed over cold metal, the other closed over Boyle's overheated hand. Her sweat-slicked skin couldn't get a solid grip on the gun, but she wrapped her fingers around the barrel and levered sideways as hard as she could and the gun skittered away again.

She was just about to reach for it, but an elbow bludgeoned her from out of the darkness, connected with her nose, and snapped her head back. The force of the hit knocked her backward and the shock of pain loosened her grip enough that Boyle was able to roll away. Then there was the sound of scrabbling, followed by retreating steps toward the back of the church.

As she planted her hands to push herself to her feet, her index finger brushed metal. She thrust her hand forward to grasp the discarded gun, her fingers finding the top of the grip. She transferred it to her right hand, feeling the familiar shape and heft of the SIG Sauer, a gun she'd shot many times, as it was one of the department's designated choices for a service weapon, even if the Glock 19 was her preference.

He still had the Glock in his pocket. Now they were both armed, so at least the fight stayed balanced.

She needed to move. He might already be working his way up the center aisle to the stone doorway and escape.

Eschewing a two-handed pistol grip to keep one hand on the crypt wall to guide her way, she silently crept down the corridor, back the way she'd come, grateful once again for the soft-soled sneakers that allowed her to move silently. She had the advantage of knowing the layout of the site, and moved stealthily, pausing only briefly every four or five steps to listen for any sign of Boyle.

She rounded the corner to the smaller feeder corridor. Could she see minute traces of the red EXIT sign in the darkness just there? Was that the doorway?

The gun held steadily in front of her and her left hand running along the wall, she picked up her pace. It wasn't the crypts and the corpses that gave her the creeps down here. It was the madman she couldn't find in the dark.

Her fingers ran around a corner and she knew she'd hit the doorway. *Finally*. She followed the wall line and took the corner.

And ran full tilt into something hard enough to steal the breath from her lungs.

CHAPTER 30

*G*emma reared back, and was just bringing the SIG Sauer up, when a voice hissed her name in her ear and her body sagged in relief.

Alex had arrived. Finally.

His hand locked around her wrist and he pulled her back into the empty undercroft, pressing them both against the fieldstone wall so they couldn't be a target from inside the catacombs. Alex had lost the cassock and was once again in cargo shorts and his Hawaiian shirt, now sketched with sinister patterns in the diffuse red illumination.

He scanned her quickly from head to toe. "You okay?" He kept his voice low so the sound couldn't carry inside the crypt.

She nodded.

He squinted at her and lightly touched his fingers, just under her nose. They came away wet with blood.

Maybe not so okay, after all, after a few shots to the face. But she didn't have time to worry about it now. "I took a couple of hits, but it's nothing major. He's still there."

"Just him?"

"Yes." When his gaze darted down toward her gun, Gemma said, "I got this away from him. But he's still got a Glock 42, so consider him very dangerous."

"Understood." He slipped his Glock into the holster at his hip and dug into one of the pockets of his cargo shorts. He pulled out a U-shaped band connected to an earpiece and a battery pack/receiver. "Put this on."

Gemma recognized it immediately, realizing Alex wore an identical throat mic and likely had under the priest's cassock, but it had been hidden by the high collar. She handed him her gun and took the communication equipment. She quickly fit the transducers into place on either side of her windpipe, clipped the push-to-talk button to the collar of her blouse, and slipped the receiver into a back pocket of her capris. She slid her earpiece in and suddenly the operation around her went live as she heard A-Team members being assigned locations both at street level and rooftops around the church. Several names she knew flashed by, including Logan's, who was across Mulberry on top of a six-story apartment building, with a view of the north cemetery and all the rear exits.

Alex had set all this up. A single clue and he'd known where she was, what she needed, and had found a way to make it all happen. Take that, anyone who considered him nothing more than a rat from Internal Affairs. He was as good a cop as any of them.

She pressed her TALK button. "Gemma Capello, signing on," she said very quietly, her eyes on Alex.

He gave her a thumbs-up and handed her back the SIG. She was live and they were good to go. "He's still in there?"

"Yes. He got away from me in the dark. I don't know how much ammunition he has in the pockets of his jacket. He might be able to sustain a firefight. Biggest problem in there is the multiple corridors. He could slip by us. Maybe we should wait him out until more people arrive and then go in and get him."

"That would work fine if there was only one entrance, but what about the old street entrance off Mott?"

"That was closed off years ago."

"From outside access. But did they block it off from the inside, or is that old staircase still there at the end of the main corridor? If it is, people might not be able to get in, but he may still be able to get out."

Gemma's heart sank. She had been counting on the fact there was only one way into the catacombs, but Alex was absolutely right. If they just killed time sitting here waiting for him to come out, he could be away and out on the street in minutes. Yes, the A-Team was setting up, but what if he got by them? It was all happening too quickly. In ten more minutes, she'd say there was no problem, but right now was when they could lose him.

"We have to go in," she said. "We have to contain him. Even if it means just holding him until backup arrives."

His lips a tight line, Alex nodded.

"You remember the layout?" she asked.

"Yeah. Any light in there?"

"Not right now, but we'd be idiots to keep it dark. Let's light it up. Then we can see him and each other so we don't take each other out."

"Agreed." Alex glanced back toward the staircase, at the panel of switches there. "We'll hit the lights and go in. We'll be able to tell right off the bat if the main aisle is empty. You go left, I'll go right, and we'll meet at the back near the external stairs up to the street."

"And, hopefully, he won't have run up the main corridor and out. Any sound in there is going to echo, so go as quietly as possible and listen for him to make a move." Gemma activated her throat mic again. "Detectives Capello are entering the catacombs to contain the subject. We're going 10-7," she said, using the radio code for "out of service."

"10-4," came the response.

Sanders. Even with that short answer, she'd know his voice anywhere. Of course, he'd be here running the op.

"Ready?" Gemma whispered.

"Give me a few seconds to get to the other side of the doorway so we go in simultaneously. See you on the other side. Be safe."

"You too."

Gemma dialed down the volume on her earpiece so she'd be able to hear the slightest noise in the crypt as Alex crossed the open doorway in a crouched position, then straightened on the other side. When he was in place, Alex gave her a thumbs-up.

She went over to the light panel and held up three fingers.

Three . . . two . . . one.

She hit all the light switches simultaneously and the room was flooded with brilliant white light, painful in its intensity after the near-total darkness. Gemma had to blink against the brightness as she moved to stand on the far side of the doorway.

Alex nodded to her. *Ready.*

They moved together, guns extended, swinging around the corner and into the arched doorway.

Ahead of them stretched the main corridor, with its arched ceiling and recessed lighting, brightly illuminating each crypt and the spaces between. In the distance, an open doorway gaped, the first few steps of the original staircase visible before disappearing up into the gloom. The corridor itself was empty.

If Boyle hadn't found the staircase before, he would be able to see it now, but that couldn't be helped. If it was permanently sealed, it could be a way to trap him. If it was only locked against outside access, he could use it for escape, so they would have to try to keep him away from it. But she knew with three main corridors, two side corridors, numerous open vaults, and an unsealed family vault, there was still a chance he'd get past them. If so, she had to hope by then that the A-Team was ready with a shot to disable him.

She moved silently down through the arch and then paused at the corner, Alex across from her. Leaning as far over as she could, while still staying protected by the wall, she peered down the right hallway, checking the way for Alex. The Eckert crypt was at the left end of the hallway, a short series of steps leading down to the cast iron door, and she could now see the smooth wall she'd used as a guide was actually the front tiles of a columbarium. But the space was deserted, with no sign of Boyle, so she gave Alex a thumbs-up. He did the same for her and gave her the same signal. Simultaneously they cleared the corner in their own direction, separating to start their own searches.

The access hallway was only about twenty feet long and Gemma covered it quickly, hugging the fieldstone wall at the west end. She noted there was also no sound. Neither from Alex nor from Boyle.

The corridor wall cut in, where it turned to the east, and instead of a sharp corner, there was a long stone sarcophagus. Gun extended, Gemma crossed to that side of the corridor and eased around the top of the sarcophagus. A second sarcophagus was set perpendicular to the first, with an open area in the lee between them. At least over the top of the sarcophagus, the open space appeared empty. She would have to check from the other side of the sarcophagus, but first, she had to step into the long run on the north corridor.

This was where things got dangerous. If she was caught in a section of the corridor where there were only closed crypts, she'd be a sitting duck, with nowhere to take cover if bullets started flying. But the same could be said for Boyle. The only difference was her first choice would be to try to take him down, but not out, giving her the chance to take him into custody, whereas he'd be aiming for a kill shot right from the start. She had to make sure she wasn't on the receiving end of that shot. His skill with a gun was already an established fact, and after their fight, he'd be in a killing rage and would show her no mercy.

She leaned out again and got a quick lay of the land. Empty. Down the right-hand side of the deserted corridor, there was a run of sealed crypt doors and then a gap in the wall that would be one of the open vaults. He could be hiding in there. And if he wasn't, it would be a good place for her to take cover in case he popped up.

But first, make sure he wasn't right under her nose. Crouching down, she circled the sarcophagus and then eased around the far corner, to find the area clear. Moving into the space between the sarcophagi, she leaned cautiously around the second tomb. No Boyle.

Still crouched, she checked the long corridor again, then stealthily half ran down the corridor, stopping just before a pair of inset tombs in an open vault. A quick glance over the tops of the tombs showed an empty space. She then went low to check out the space between the tombs. Also empty.

She slipped inside. She could stand erect inside the open vault, with several feet of space between the two tombs, both topped by massive slabs of marble inscribed with names, birth dates, and death dates. Between them, at the far end of the vault, stood a life-size crucifix, its wooden cross bearing the crucified Christ, his head bowed and his body limp in death.

The catacombs were so quiet, Gemma could swear she was the only one there, but she knew better. In this life-or-death game of cat and mouse, the slightest move could spin the dial toward death.

Keep going.

She checked the long stretch of corridor toward the back, found it empty, and quickly covered the distance to the cross corridor at the end of the catacombs. She leaned ever so slightly around the corner, more and more of the perpendicular access pathway coming into view. Empty . . . empty . . . the gaping maw of the rear staircase. He could be up there.

Gripping her gun firmly in both hands, she took the corner to find a deserted passageway running all the way to the far side of the catacombs. She slunk over to the open doorway at the end of the main corridor. Inside, she could see the original entrance to the catacombs and the crumbling original staircase marching up into darkness. There were no electric lights inside the staircase, leaving it shadowed in gloom. The question was, what was inside that gloom?

Only one way to find out.

She took a step toward it.

The explosion of a gunshot boomed, reverberating through the empty space and echoing off every surface, so Gemma couldn't determine where it originated.

Before she could even shout her brother's name, he bellowed hers and then the sound of pounding feet filled the air. Back toward the entrance. She turned and sprinted for the archway, cranking up the volume on her earpiece as she ran, knowing Alex would be alerting both herself and the team. Was that just a flash of Alex at the far end as she rounded the corner?

"Suspect on the move!" His voice filled her ear.

Keep talking. Tell me where to find you. Tell me you're okay.

Adrenaline gave her feet wings and she tore down the cata-combs, out through the undercroft, and back up the steps.

Another gunshot, this time from the direction of the nave. A second answering shot.

He could have gone outside. He must know if another cop is here, he could be surrounded. Didn't head to Mulberry, tried to take cover in the church.

She paused as she got to the double doors, checked the church, and then swung into the nave.

A quick scan told her the sanctuary was empty.

"Outside now." Alex's words were cut by harsh breaths. "Asked the monsignor to lock the front gates. Can't get out. He's head-ing into the north cemetery."

She hit her TALK button as she sprinted through the nave to-ward the main doors at the back. "10-4. In pursuit. We can corner him there."

"I have men in position." Sanders's voice this time. "Who has eyes on the north cemetery?"

"Logan here. I do. West side, as far as the farthest stand of trees."

"Morgan here. I've got the east side."

"We have you covered," Sanders said.

Ahead of Gemma, one of the front doors stood open, the space beyond them now dark, as dusk had come and gone. She paused long enough to check for threats and to confirm the six-foot-tall front gate was closed and locked. It was, which only left the shorter, decorative wrought iron fences on either side separating the flanking cemeteries. She went through the outer door in time to see Alex in the dimness landing on the far side of the fence closing off the north cemetery.

Terrified bleating came from deeper into the cemetery, and Gemma caught the ghostly blur of three white sheep galloping into the rear, darkened corner of the cemetery. The farm animals gave her a jolt of surprise until she remembered the church's landscaping "crew," the permanent residents of the grounds dur-ing warmer months. Hopefully, they'd stay out of the way.

Transferring the gun to her right hand, she bolted for the fence, leaping onto the handicap ramp and pushing off with all her might, bracing her left hand on the top of the fence to help her clear the row of decorative metal spikes. She felt the brush of metal as she went over and then landed with a stumbling step, letting her inertia carry her toward one of the obelisks. She stopped, her back to the memorial, looking side to side, but not seeing her brother.

"Alex." She kept her voice low, knowing the transducer would pick up her words. "I'm in, and behind the obelisk near the fence. Where are you?"

"Farther in. Behind the tall headstone with the Celtic cross on top. He's crouched down behind the bigger tomb with the pitched roof."

Thankful for the modern security lights mounted high on the historical building that threw scattered light through the trees of the cemetery, Gemma leaned out and identified the landmark. "Got it. You go west. I'll stay on the east side."

"10-4."

"Who has him in sight?" Sanders again.

"He's blocked from my angle." Morgan's voice.

"I have him," Logan said. "He just dropped a magazine and is loading a fresh one. He's not going down easy."

"We've got this," Gemma said. "We have him contained. Do not jump the gun. We can bring him in."

"And risk two officers?" Sanders had clearly had enough.

"Give us a chance," Alex said.

There was a pause before Sanders replied, "Do it now, do it fast, and do it safely, or I'm giving the order. Logan, are you ready?"

"Yes, sir."

"You are a go. Neutralize the target the moment you feel one of our officers is in jeopardy."

"Yes, sir."

Goddamn it. Now we have to finish this in a rush because Sanders is twitchy? Can't he see his cowboy attitude is putting us in more danger if the end goal is everyone coming out alive?

The light in the cemetery was patchy, but she was sure every sniper on the A-Team had night vision. They'd have a crystal-clear view of the entire scene.

Fine. All cards on the table then. Be a negotiator.

She didn't hit the TALK button. If she was going to try to negotiate for this man's life, she was going to keep Sanders on the outside. "John? John, I know you can hear me. It's time to end this before you get yourself killed."

"So I can spend my life in jail? It's freedom or nothing, Capello."

"You're not going to get free. You know that. And you'd know I was lying if I tried to sell you a line. Honesty always, remember?"

"Yeah. I remember."

"Then let me tell you, you're surrounded. Sanders has men on the rooftops watching. Throw down your gun and come out. I promise, you'll be treated with the respect due to an officer. Once NYPD, always NYPD." Leaning out around the obelisk, she saw Alex on the move, taking advantage of her distracting Boyle, and getting closer.

"*You* might think that, but it doesn't mean everyone else will."

"We've all lost brothers-in-arms. We've all lost family. Give them a chance. You lost your son in a line-of-duty death. They won't forget that." Gemma moved, quickly running between markers, crouching down behind a weathered headstone, with a skull sprouting angel wings etched on the top.

"Maybe not, but the warden and guards and prisoners won't care."

She could see Alex now, pressed flat behind a tall, rectangular column on a wide base. Another fifteen feet and he'd have line of sight on Boyle. If Boyle wouldn't come quietly, he could be disabled with a carefully placed shot to his right shoulder, rather than killed outright. She knew Alex's skill with a weapon, and knew he could do it.

She needed to keep Boyle talking while Alex got into place.

"John, I understand your pain. You know as well as I do, they're going to arrest you, but there are mitigating circumstances, and you have a solid career and multiple commendations behind you. Let them, and let me, speak on your behalf."

"Why would you do that?"

Alex darted behind another headstone. Nearly there.

"Because you're one of us, and any one of us could be you."

"Not good enough."

Running out of time. Time to twist the knife. She thought back to the personal details McFarland had dug up. "After Connor was killed, you accepted the Medal of Honor posthumously on his behalf. That's the highest medal the NYPD can bestow and it says something about how special he was. Meet me halfway and finish this peacefully for Connor and for his memory. He wouldn't want you to do this for him."

"Maybe not, but what's the point without him?"

His toneless words, shaded with resignation and bone-deep sorrow, sent a surge of alarm through Gemma.

The grief in his eyes when he told her about Connor. His glowing pride in the man he'd raised.

Already too late.

Boyle burst from behind the tomb, leaping to stand on the stone lid, his gaze trained on Alex, who was already shifting his stance to take his shot.

Gemma lurched to her feet, sensing his intent. He wasn't going to hurt Alex. That wasn't his goal. But he was absolutely going to make it look like it to force Logan's hand. She hit the TALK button for a last-ditch, personal appeal. "Sean, don't do this. He's going for suicide by—"

Boyle launched himself off the top of the tomb, his gun coming around to train on Alex.

The shot rang out. Boyle jerked in midair, his trajectory changing from the force of the bullet, to crash to the ground closer to Gemma.

Gemma ran the rest of the way and crouched down to press two fingers to where the pulse in his neck should have been. A deeper shadow fell across her. She raised her head to find Alex standing over her. She shook her head.

He turned away with a vicious curse.

Gemma sank down into the grass beside Boyle. Blood drenched his shirt and jacket around the entry wound. Logan's aim had been true. A single shot, center mass, to neutralize the target. Boyle had been dead before his body hit the ground.

Gemma glared up at the rooftop of the building across the street. A dark silhouette stood tall at the edge of the roof, backlit by the glow of city lights, towering stories over her. She couldn't see his face, but she knew Logan was staring directly at her. At his handiwork.

The case was over. Boyle wouldn't hurt anyone ever again.

How could a win feel like such a devastating loss?

CHAPTER 31

Gemma opened the gate into her father's backyard and slipped through into the warm, quiet darkness of the August night.

"You're sure you don't want to go inside?" Alex asked from behind her.

"I will. Just . . . not yet." Gemma couldn't put into words the feeling manifested in the tightness of her shoulders, the knot in her stomach, and the sweat dampening the back of her neck. Not even for Alex, and no one could possibly understand more than he could.

She'd given the case her all, but still couldn't shake the bone-deep disquiet at its conclusion.

If you'd given it your all, would two men be dead and a third be fighting for his life?

She pushed the thought away. Second-guessing herself at this point would only lead to sleepless nights and a dragging weight she couldn't lift from her shoulders. She needed to find her balance; then she could reflect on the day's events with a clear head.

Alex nearly bumped into her when she stopped long enough to toe off her mesh sneakers. Letting her hot, tired feet sink into the soft grass, she couldn't help the sigh of relief that slipped past her lips.

She was home.

She hadn't lived in this house for years, but somehow her tiny Manhattan apartment had never given her the same emotional connection as this beloved family home. Tonight she desperately needed that connection.

She picked up her shoes and carried them over to the picnic tables, still arranged for their family meal. They'd been covered with food, plates, and glasses when they'd rushed out earlier in the afternoon, but Rachel and Alyssa had cleared the mess. Now the empty tables echoed her desolate mood and she wondered bleakly if the Sicilian Feast of the Assumption would be an annual reminder of her failure.

She fell into one of the chairs, listlessly tossing her sneakers into the grass below, and blew out a long, exhausted breath.

"You can't beat yourself up over this." Alex dropped into the chair opposite her. The moon overhead in the clear sky was nearly full and washed the backyard in a silvery glow, though Alex's face was unreadable in the dim light.

"You think so?"

"I know exactly how your mind works. You're taking responsibility for everything that went wrong tonight. How about taking responsibility for everything that went right? Like the seven hostages you saved."

"And the citizens of New York you kept safe while you were out on the streets with him."

Gemma whipped around at the sound of her father's voice.

Tony stood on the patio with her brother Joe. She'd been so stuck inside her own head she hadn't even heard them come out of the house.

Tony crossed the grass to lay his hands on Gemma's shoulders and bent to press a kiss to the top of her head. *"Mia passerotta,"* he whispered as his hands squeezed tight. Tight enough for her to feel his fear.

Guilt bloomed at the pain in his voice paired with the endearment. It had been years, probably more than a decade, since he'd called her his "little sparrow," as he'd done often during her childhood. If she'd only suspected she'd put her father through absolute hell today, this was confirmation. Laying a hand over his, she held on for a moment with her head bowed.

When she finally let go, he tipped her face up to his and took a moment to catalog her injuries. She'd cleaned off the blood, but her right cheek was swollen and mottled with dark bruising. She suspected she'd have a hell of a shiner by tomorrow morning, and might never hear the end of it from her brothers.

"Did EMS see to that?"

Gemma nodded. "Paramedics checked me out on-site. Gave me the all clear."

"Good." Tony circled the table to Alex, to claim the chair to his right. Gemma couldn't hear her father's low words to her brother, but from Alex's sheepish smile, she deduced praise for going after his sister and throwing himself into the fray.

Joe pulled out the chair beside Gemma and sat down, holding her gaze. Grimly he took in her battered face. "I hear Lieutenant Garcia didn't condone your operation."

Gemma glared at her brother through narrowed lids. Leave it to Joe, the most hard-nosed of the Capello brothers, to start right in on her, before even her father could take her to task. Though she suspected Joe's anger was less grounded in what she'd done than in how her actions had affected her family, her father most of all. According to Alex, Joe had been with their father for the entire op, and had not only experienced her defection and subsequent disappearance, but had watched his father suffer through it as well. Now he wanted his pound of flesh for what she'd done to all of them.

No point in beating around the bush: She'd known from the moment she laid down her shield, her family wouldn't agree with her decision. She met his glare head-on. "No, he didn't."

"You've been on the force for . . . fourteen years? But even though your lieutenant has more than twice your years in blue, and has earned medals for exemplary service, you still thought you knew better than him?"

That stiffened Gemma's spine. Seniority didn't necessarily mean insight into one particular man. And it certainly didn't replace human lives. "Yes. We'd exhausted all possible options. It all came down to me in exchange for seven lives. Me, an experienced negotiator and a fellow officer, someone who could work with the situation rather than be a victim to it, like the seven hostages were."

"And you don't think he was taking that into account when he made the call *not* to send in one of his team members?"

"You weren't even there. How do you—"

"Stand down, both of you." Tony leaned forward, first meeting the eyes of his oldest son and then his daughter. "We've all been there, out in the field, when you've only got seconds to make a decision that could go either way. We've made those decisions and we've had others disagree with them. The only way to truly understand that decision is to have been there at the time."

Joe shook his head in disbelief. "Why are you giving her a pass on this? I would have thought you'd be angriest of all at the break in command structure."

"Don't get me wrong, I'm not happy about some of Gemma's choices today. But I'm also the one with the most experience around this table. I know how complex these situations can be, and how they can take on a life of their own. You make your best decision at the time with the information you have, and with what your gut tells you is the right call." His gaze moved to Gemma. "Sometimes you pay for that decision afterward. And sometimes your family also pays." He met her eyes, held them, and she felt the suffocating weight of the torment he'd suffered that day. "You knew what your decision would do to us." His gaze shifted first to Joe, and then to Alex. "To all of us."

"Yes." The word was a ragged whisper as she looked around the table. She cleared her throat. "I didn't have any choice." She faced her father. "Moreover, you would have done the same thing. If it had been you instead of me in that situation, with a cop who has already crossed the line and a room full of innocent hostages in play, are you telling me you'd have let them die?"

Several seconds of silence passed as their gazes held. Then Tony frowned. "No."

His single-word answer took the air out of Gemma and she sank back into her chair. "Of course, you wouldn't. Because leaving the innocent to die, no matter what the circumstance, is not you, not if you have a chance of saving them and then yourself. It's not me." She met Joe's level gaze. "It's not any of us."

Some of the tension reluctantly eased from Joe's shoulders. "No, it's not."

"Garcia came to see me tonight," said Tony, drawing her attention. "After Logan took Boyle down."

Gemma winced at Logan's name, but did her best to cover it. "What did Garcia want?"

"To make sure you got this back." He pulled her shield out of his pocket and slid it across the table to her. "Your service weapon is inside, in the gun safe."

Gemma stared at her badge, dumbfounded, her jaw sagging in disbelief. "I resigned. I countermanded his direct order and walked away from the NYPD."

"He doesn't see it that way. Didn't you notice no one questioned you this evening, or took you into custody for being an accessory to a crime?"

Gemma blinked at him, realizing that in her focus in completing her task tonight, the fact she was no longer NYPD hadn't truly registered during the final operation. That persona was bone deep and had been her life for so long, she couldn't truly fathom not being a cop.

"Garcia didn't tell anyone," Tony continued. "Outside of your team and us, no one knows."

"Sanders knows. So does Sean Logan."

"If Logan is smart, he'll keep his mouth shut. The same goes for Sanders. By giving you back your shield, Garcia is accepting responsibility for the wrong call and wiping the slate clean. Consider yourself *extremely* lucky."

Gemma picked up her shield. The NYPD blue enamel was nearly black in the dimness, but the gold glinted in the scant moonlight. She closed her hand over it, feeling a missing piece of her most elemental self slide back into place at the familiar texture of ridges and letters under her fingertips. Relief and a sense of belonging. And such gratitude. Garcia and her father had given her life back to her.

She looked up to meet his eyes. "Thank you."

"You're welcome." He held her gaze. "Don't do it again. There won't be any second chances."

"Understood." She scanned the backyard. "Were you waiting for me?"

Tony nodded.

"How did you know we'd come here? We could have split up and gone home."

"A father knows. After today, after how today ended, you weren't going to go home to sit alone. You'd need family."

"*After how today ended . . .*" Anger swelled in her again. "Such a senseless waste of life."

"Willan?" Joe asked.

"That goes without saying. I'm actually referring to Boyle." She could hear fury leaching into her tone, but couldn't hold it back. "He didn't need to die. We had him cornered. I told Logan we had him. He didn't have to take the shot."

"He was ordered to take the shot, and he followed that order." Joe's voice was flat and pure no-nonsense cop. "Sanders was past taking any further chances. You'd bought his reluctant patience up to then, but he was done. Boyle had managed to get as far as the cemetery. If he got past you two and back out into the city, he might have slipped through. He'd already killed and shown no compunction at shooting civilians. He was a risk, so Sanders made the call he felt was necessary."

"Logan could have taken him down with an extremity shot. He didn't have to end him."

"Logan's beyond good, but even he would have trouble making an extremity shot at night on a target who is leaping through the air. In taking that shot, he saved Alex's life."

"*Cazzate,*" she spit back. "Look at Boyle's actions through the whole day. He killed with intention just once, and that was in retribution for his son's death. From that point on, the only other person he injured—not killed, but injured—was in self-defense. Boyle wasn't a spree killer. He was a cop lashing out in a targeted approach. He was never going to do anything to Alex, because Alex was NYPD and Boyle respected the force. But he needed it to look like he would make the shot so Logan would take him out, saving him the hell of incarceration. He put the end of his life in a sniper's hands, knowing it would be fast and as painless as possible. I knew that was his goal and tried to stop it."

Joe leaned forward, propping an elbow on the table, his brow furrowed. "What's going on here? Why are you so angry?"

"Because we'd already lost Willan and possibly Coulter. Why lose one more?"

"That's not it," Tony countered.

"That's part of it."

"But not all."

Exhausted, Gemma bowed her head to stare at her shield, still clutched in her right hand. "No, it's not." She looked up, her gaze shifting from Joe, to Alex, and finally to her father. "He was one of us. He gave his life to the job, and then he gave his child." She swallowed hard. "He could have been you."

Tony held very still. Too still. "Me."

"How would you react if one of us went down in the line of duty, in a death you felt could have been prevented? How would you react to the loss of a child?" She turned to Joe. "Or you, if Sam or Gabe were killed?" To Alex. "He was one of us." Her voice dropped. "And what did our understanding of his pain get him? A bullet." She faced her father. "I'm a hostage negotiator. We try to bring everyone out alive. It's what we do." A shiver ran down her spine as she realized she'd inadvertently echoed Boyle's own words. "Yes, he deserved a trial and jail time for what he did, but I was trying to bring him out alive."

"Logan was just doing his job," Alex said. "Don't be pissed at him."

Gemma shrugged dejectedly. "I guess I'm just looking for a target and he's handy."

Tony reached across the table and took her hand in his. "I was terrified for you today. But also proud that you'd so selflessly put yourself in harm's way to save those people. Because as terrifying as it was for me to relive the day your mother died, it had to be worse for you. I'd only ever seen it from the outside. You'd lived it. I suspect that was the real reason you had no choice."

She latched onto her father's hand as if it were a lifeline. "I didn't analyze it at the time, but you're probably right. In the end, I didn't really have time to think about myself. I spent the whole time watching out for everyone else."

"Speaking of watching out for everyone else," Alex interjected, "how are the hostages?"

"They were all checked out by paramedics. Two of them were taken to the hospital for additional tests or treatment. Clara Sutton, the hostage who was pistol-whipped, was treated and released. She'll be fine. Janina Lee, Rowland's admin assistant, is pregnant—" At Gemma's harsh, indrawn breath, he patted her hand. "She's fine and so is the baby. It was just a precaution."

"She never said anything," Gemma stated.

"She said she didn't want to do anything to draw attention to herself. And she's only a few months along, so she wasn't showing. But she told the paramedics right away and they decided to err on the side of caution, which everyone agreed was best. Everyone else is fine. Rob Greenfield has a grade-three concussion and they're going to monitor him overnight, but he'll go home tomorrow."

"What about Coulter?"

"Last I heard, he was in surgery, listed in serious, but not critical, condition. His cameraman got help to him fast, so that's in his favor. Rowland is devastated by Willan's death, but insisted on being the one to tell his wife and kids. There'll be a big public funeral for him, probably next week, with a departmental presence, so you'll hear more about it once arrangements are made. Now you need to shut it down for the night." Tony looked at Alex. "You too. You're both to report for a debriefing tomorrow at headquarters at oh nine hundred."

"Yes, sir."

"I know Alyssa is expecting Joe home later on, but will you two do an old man a favor tonight?"

Gemma exchanged glances with Alex. "Of course. What do you need?"

"Come inside, decompress, and then bunk down here in your

old rooms. I just . . . need that tonight. Need my kids under my roof."

Gemma climbed to her feet and circled the table to stand behind her father's chair. She bent to wrap her arms around his shoulders and pressed her cheek to his, his day's worth of stubble a gentle scratch against her skin. *"Sì, Papà."*

Tomorrow there would be situation reviews and debriefings. There would be lessons to stockpile for new cases, and strategic planning to improve the next outcome. But for tonight, she would put it all away.

Tonight would be for family. For her father, who raised her and gave her a life's work. For her brothers, her fellow first-responders-in-arms, who shared her passion. For the memory of her mother, who gave her life trying to protect others.

Arm in arm with her father, they went inside. As Gemma paused to close the door behind her, she looked one last time over the site of her family's celebration. A day that had started with such hope, but had morphed into a twisted shadow of the worst day of their lives.

We'll rebuild our tradition next year.

She closed the door, turning away from the memories of the day, and joined her family in celebrating the bonds that still held fast.

Acknowledgments

Exit Strategy is my first solo novel, but I was incredibly lucky to have many of my usual writing supporters with me on this journey. My sincere thanks to those who helped launch the NYPD Negotiators:

My husband, Rick, who not only brainstormed parts of the novel with me, but was my guinea pig/alpha reader while I was crafting the initial proposal, and my travel companion on a whirlwind trip through New York City to scout every scene in the book and to walk Gemma's exact path through the city.

Fellow Seymour Agency sibling and longtime writing buddy Marianne Harden, who gladly jumped in during the proposal planning to assist with presubmission editing and polishing.

Son-in-law to be, Shane Vandevalk, for sharing his considerable knowledge on all things firearms-related, including taking me to a range and putting a gun in my hand for the very first time.

Fellow Kensington Books author and New York City native Laurie Chandlar, who was invaluable in helping me plan our trip to New York City. She was then instrumental in boots-on-the-ground troubleshooting of an issue concerning New York City Hall as we stood on the front steps before enjoying a tour of the building. A history buff, Laurie also assisted in my research of the historic City Hall subway station in the New York Transit Museum archives.

Rebecca Haggerty, archivist at the New York Transit Museum, for allowing me to invade the archives to do research on the City Hall subway station, and for sharing its colorful history and wonderful architecture from the turn of the twentieth century to the present.

Assistance from facets within and around the NYPD to ensure this book was as factual as possible: the NYPD Office of the Deputy Commissioner, Public Information; Sam Katz from the Detectives' Endowment Association, Inc.; and particularly Lieutenant Jack Cambria, the former commander of the NYPD HNT (2001–

2015). After their invaluable assistance, any and all mistakes are mine alone.

My critique team, who barely had time to recover from the last novel when I was already placing Exit Strategy in their capable hands. To Lisa Giblin, Jenny Lindstrom, Jessica Newton, Rick Newton, and Sharon Taylor, thank you for always going above and beyond to give me that extra push (sometimes even a week or two after reading the manuscript as new ideas came to you) to make the book a richer experience to not only write, but read.

My agent, Nicole Resciniti, who was with me from this project's inception—from the first phone call discussing the possibilities of this series, to early edits where she helped strengthen the germinal first chapters, to making the final deals for the series. My thanks for all your hard work; I literally could not have pulled this off without you.

The entire Kensington team, including Norma Perez-Hernandez, Louis Malcangi and his talented art department, and the publicity team—Larissa Ackerman, Lauren Jernigan, and Crytstal McCoy— for unending support during the entire process.

My editor at Kensington, Esi Sogah, for having faith in this new series and enthusiastically sharing her knowledge of the city and its people. It's been a wonderful experience moving into this new world with you, and I'm looking forward to where we can take Gemma and her family in the future.

Please turn the page for
the latest K-9 mystery
from Sara Driscoll

NO MAN'S LAND
On sale now!

CHAPTER 1

Urbexing: Urban exploration, usually of abandoned or nearly in-accessible man-made structures.

Sunday, October 7, 10:47 AM
Massaponax Psychiatric Hospital
Fredericksburg, Virginia

"**I**s this how you usually get into these places?" Meg Jennings pushed through the ragged tear slicing diagonally across the lower half of the towering chain-link fence. She ducked low, to avoid the jagged edges that threatened to catch the long dark hair she'd tied into a ponytail and to tug at her backpack.

"This is easy, compared to some." District of Columbia Fire and Emergency Services firefighter Chuck Smaill grinned down at her. "It's a small price to pay to get a look at some truly creepy stuff."

"You're really selling it. And as a duly sworn member of the FBI, I won't even ask if we're trespassing. I think it's better if I'm left officially in the dark on that point." Meg straightened and turned to the man standing beside her. Several inches taller than her own nearly six feet, DCFEMS firefighter and paramedic Lieutenant Todd Webb had the build of a man used to physical work and the short-cut dark hair that spoke to how often he wore a firefighter's helmet. "Todd, give me a hand with the fence for Hawk?"

"Sure." Having preceded her through the gap, Webb grabbed

one edge of the chain link and curled it back as Meg mirrored his actions on the opposite side.

"That's good. Okay, Hawk, come!"

The black Labrador trotted through the gap, his tail waving jauntily. Without his standard uniform of the FBI's Human Scent Evidence Team's navy-and-yellow vest, he sported only a bright red collar and rubber-soled Velcro boots to protect his paws.

Once he was through, Meg let go and the chain-link fencing vibrated back into place with a discordant metallic twang.

Smaill held his arms wide. "Welcome to no man's land."

Meg eyed the property around them. "No man's land?"

"It's an urbex term."

"Urban exploration has its own terms?"

"It has a language all its own. If you got on any of the urbex forums, you wouldn't understand half of what they say because they all use the lingo. Like 'blagging,' 'lift surfacing,' and 'tankcatting.' In this case, no man's land is the dead space between an outer security fence and the actual site or building. So, welcome to no man's land."

Meg took in the prickly weeds and overgrown grass, their lush green fading with autumn's cooling days. "Um . . . thanks?" She tipped her hand over her eyes, squinting past the open space to the red brick structure rising into the cloudless sky. "That's really fantastic Gothic Revival architecture. Such a shame it's practically falling down in real time."

Smaill's eyebrows shot up to disappear behind the sun-streaked blond hair that fell boyishly over his forehead. "You recognize the architecture?"

Webb laughed and bumped his shoulder affectionately to Meg's. "Oh yeah, she loves old buildings. I can't count the number of times she's had me pull to the side of the road so she can admire some old Victorian manor out her window. The older the better."

"Hey, at least I don't make you jog with me at six in the morning like I do Brian. He tends to pick parks for jogging, but I love going through the oldest neighborhoods in DC. Those classic

houses have a special glow as the sun is just clearing the treetops."
Meg considered the red brick structure. "And it's not hard to nail
this one. See the decorative pointed brick crowns over the windows? The front-facing gables on the top floor in that steep roof?
The main central castle tower? Classic Gothic Revival. But this
building is more than its architecture. Do you know anything
about it?"

"I always find out about a site before I visit," Smaill said. "Makes
the hacking more interesting because you know what you're ex-
ploring. Also makes it safer because you get an idea of the setup
and might foresee some of the hazards. When this place first went
up in the decade following the Civil War, it was the Massaponax
Insane Asylum. See how it's built? As a big center structure with
the two wings on either side?"

"Yeah. The architect didn't quite get the symmetry down,
though."

"He wasn't trying to. The wing on the left, the big one, that was
the men's wing. The more modest wing was for the ladies."

"And here we are without McCord, the walking Civil War ency-
clopedia," Webb deadpanned. "Even without the numbers he
could spout off the top of his head, I'm betting the Battle of Fredericksburg and the rest of the Civil War left a large proportion of
the surviving male population with some nasty mental health is-
sues."

"Got it in one," said Smaill. "Back then, they didn't know what
was wrong with those men. PTSD wasn't defined until after the
Second World War. In the First World War, they recognized the
issue as 'shell shock,' but they still didn't know what to do about
it. Now imagine how unprepared they were to handle it in the
1860s and 1870s after Sherman's March to the Sea, the destruc-
tion of South Carolina, and the retaking of Fort Sumter that
ended the Civil War."

"So instead of dealing with it, they locked those men up here,"
Meg said. "Out of the public eye."

"Here and many other places. Hardly seems like the right way
to treat veterans who barely survived the effort to protect their

country. Granted, some days I'm not sure we do that much better now. Come on, let's get in there."

The group followed a scant path that cut across what was once a well-tended lawn, now given way to weeds and brambles dotted with fallen amber leaves.

When Smaill had invited Webb on one of his urbex outings, Webb had suggested that Meg and Hawk come as well. Having met Meg and Hawk six months before at the site of the National Mall bombing, and then being with her for several other cases, Webb knew urbex would be exactly the kind of search-and-rescue—or SAR—practice that kept Meg and Hawk at the top of their game. Meg agreed wholeheartedly. From then on, it was just a matter of matching schedules between a firefighter, a firefighter/ paramedic, and a SAR team. A common day off between the first responders finally meant they could make the trip together from DC to Virginia.

"What's that mean?" Webb pointed to a faded metal sign attached to the brick near the front door featuring a yellow circle overlaid by a triad of downward-facing rust-colored triangles. "It's almost like a radiation hazard warning, but not quite."

"I've run into that one before," said Smaill. "It's the civil defense symbol for a fallout shelter from the Cold War."

"Duck and cover," Meg murmured. She scanned the lower windows—some were cracked but mostly intact; others were boarded up. "Can we get in the front door?"

"Last time I was here, someone had forced the lock on it and it was standing open. Hopefully no one has secured it since then. I'm not sure who owns the property now. I know there were rumors someone was going to buy it, gut it, and reno it into swanky condos, but clearly that hasn't happened yet."

"It's a great property." Meg scanned the front of the building, each floor marked by a horizontal stripe of white stone transecting the brick, and windows topped by decorative arches of alternating white and black blocks. "The outside is really stylish."

"And the inside is really a mess," Smaill countered. "But if they took it back to the studs and built it out again, it could be spectacular." Bracing one hand on the wrought iron railing, he climbed the stairs to the front door, with Meg, Hawk, and Webb following.

The heavy wood door formed a Gothic arch with a pointed apex. It stood open, leaving a gap of several feet to the doorjamb that allowed daylight to stream inside.

"When we're inside, be constantly conscious of your surroundings. For instance, places where the floor has given way can be treacherous. And if some spots have collapsed already, there are likely others that could go with only minimal stress. Eyes and ears open at all times. If anything looks dicey, don't push it." Smaill looked down at Hawk. "He's ready to go in?"

"All he needs are his boots. We can't afford for anything to injure his feet and risk taking him out of future searches. But he's used to working rubble wearing them. I'm going to keep him on lead unless I'm concerned he's going to get caught on it. Then I'll let him loose."

"There might be a few places where he'll do better without it, but you know best. He'll come when you call him if he's off leash?"

"Just you wait," Webb said before Meg could answer. "That dog is so well trained, he can practically bring you breakfast in bed. Don't worry, he'll be great."

Smaill pushed the door open a few more inches and stepped into the gloom. "Then let's do it."

They moved from the brilliant technicolor of fall into what was originally monochrome hospital beige, now spoiled by dark splotches of rust and mildew and brilliant palettes of paint. It took a minute for their eyes to adjust to the lower light, but then details began to emerge.

The foyer ceiling was at least twelve feet high, but the white-washed patterned tin, originally lovely curling scrollwork, was torn apart with whole sections ripped clean away, and the remaining areas were invaded with creeping rust stains. Paint peeled in ribbons from the walls around slabs of plaster that had lost their battle with gravity and crumbled to the floor years ago. The floor, once a utilitarian linoleum, was now an uneven spongy layer that

tore in soft spots under their steel-toed hiking boots and was lit-
tered with papers and scraps of wood. The wall opposite the door
was covered in clashing colors of spray paint, with the most recent
artistic offering, **WRekeR**, in large red block letters with a white
border over older faded stylings.

Webb whistled. "You weren't kidding. It's a mess. It looked way
better from outside."

"This is nothing," said Smaill. "Wait until you see some of the
hospital wings. Come this way."

Turning to the right, they entered a cramped office with a rubble-
covered floor. Open cubbyholes of worn, faded wood lined the
walls above where desks once stood. Overhead, a gaping gash in
the ceiling revealed a glimpse of the floor above, and pipework
for the sprinkler system and wiring for the ceiling lights dangled,
free-floating, overhead. A single intact bulb hung from a rusty fix-
ture.

Meg and Hawk wandered over to where a pile of heavy, yel-
lowed papers was tossed carelessly in a corner. She squatted down
for a better look at reports edged with mildew. "When did this
place close?"

"Sometime in 2003."

"These are handwritten ward reports from the 1970s. I'd have
thought this stuff would have been destroyed because of privacy
regulations."

"Apparently not."

Meg turned to her dog, who was pulling slightly against the
leash, his head turned to peer down a long hallway stretching
into the men's wing. "Do you smell something, buddy?"

"Mildew, dead critters, and rotting wood." Smaill picked up a
curled black-and-white photo from inside one of the cubbies, holding it out by one corner for them to see. The picture showed a section of brain with a long, thin protrusion thrust deep inside. "For
sure he smells something. You say you've explored ruined buildings before?"

"Yes, but usually freshly ruined. Explosions, fires, natural disas-
ters. Nothing like this. It's something new, which is good for

him." She gave his leash a light tug as she got to her feet and Hawk came to stand beside her. She pointed up at the ceiling and the rooms visible overhead. "Are we going up there?"

"You bet. Down into the basement too. It's pretty creepy down there."

"Lead the way."

They made their way down a hallway where paint curled from the walls as if bubbles had formed and popped, revealing the scarred wall beneath. Overhead, a line of rusted fluorescent lights marched in a drunken line along the gloomy ceiling. Weak daylight tumbled over the floor through open doorways leading to exam rooms.

"Hawk, come." Meg paused in the doorway of an exam room, scanning the interior. Lines of rust ran down one wall in rivulets to disappear behind a steel gurney. An overturned wheelchair with only one rubber wheel remaining sat beneath a cracked window. Beside it, ragged holes in a tangled pile of moldering blankets indicated the resident rodent population. A rippling, faded poster listing the classification criteria of *DSM-IV* mental disorders was still tacked to one wall, and a vacant doll head lay on top of a narrow white-laminate medical cabinet, the gash of its mouth grinning into eternity.

"That's creepy as hell."

Meg glanced over her shoulder to find Webb close behind her. "The doll?"

"The doll head. What happened to the rest of it? I thought this place was for adults."

"There were women," Smaill replied. "So there may have been kids too." He paused, frowning at the doll. "That's a nasty thought."

"Sure is."

Farther down the hallway, their progress abruptly halted at the gaping hole that stretched the width of the hall and dropped all the way down into the depths of the basement. Long slats of wood subfloor drooped into the gap, hanging nearly to the floor below.

Meg stopped a few feet back and was surprised when Hawk didn't stay with her but instead leaned toward the hole. A gentle tug at the leash brought him to her side. "How do we get around that?"

Smaill pushed open a door to their right that was nearly invisible in the gloom. "Up this way. Get out your flashlights and watch your step. Things are going to get a *lot* less stable. I'd recommend taking Hawk off his leash now. He's going to need complete freedom to navigate."

Meg pulled a flashlight from her backpack and shone it past Smaill. Not only was the stairwell beyond the doorway dark due to the lack of windows, but most of the middle of the staircase had collapsed, leaving a curl of steps clinging to the outer wall as it rose up into the shadows. She stepped into the stairwell to peer at the pile of torn wooden steps, fractured railings, and crumbling plaster. "That's more like what I thought we'd be dealing with. You're sure it's safe?"

"The steps are built right into the wall. Use your light, watch your step, stick to the wall, and you'll be fine. Don't trust the railing on the wall to hold you if you slip, or you'll end up on the pile below." Smaill gestured at Hawk. "He'll be able to manage?"

"Better than us. He has four feet and a lower center of gravity." She unhooked Hawk's leash, coiled it, and stuffed it in an outside pocket of her backpack. "Todd, you go first, and I'll send Hawk up after you."

Webb pulled a compact flashlight out of one of the pockets of his cargo pants and turned it on. He started up the stairs, his long legs carrying him easily over the first step piled high with rubble. The step groaned under his weight, but held. Keeping his light trained on the step above, Webb moved slowly and carefully into the dark. He stopped partway to push enough debris off the step to make room for his boot, and it tumbled onto the wreckage below with a crash. Halfway up, he turned around. "It's more stable than it looks. Send Hawk up."

"Hawk." Meg waited until the dog's gaze swung up to hers. "Go to Todd."

Hawk neatly jumped over the first step and then continued toward Webb, who shone his flashlight down on each step to guide the dog's way.

"You're right," Smaill said. "He's more sure-footed than I am. You next, and I'll bring up the rear."

Climbing the stairs was a slow, precise process. Place a foot, test your weight on the step, then transfer that weight. No sudden moves; just gradual, steady progress. But within three minutes they were on the upper landing gazing down at the ruins below.

"Are we going to be getting down the same way?" Webb asked.

"No. The other flight of stairs in this section is at the end of the wing. It's cut off from the main entrance by that cave-in, but there are a couple of emergency exits with crash bars on the ground floor we can force open to get out. Come on, things get interesting up here."

Smaill led them through the upper areas of the wing. Each room was lined with windows, and the light streaming in chased away the gloom. But the remnants of life here only accentuated the creepiness hinted at below:

A multistall bathroom where the sinks had been ripped from the wall and thrown to the floor in front of stalls so rusted, it were as if they'd been sprayed with blood.

A wooden prosthetic leg lying alone in a corner of the corridor, its painted surface so old and worn that it looked like mummified skin.

A ward room with the twisted remains of a bedstead crumpled near a pockmarked radiator sagging away from the crumbling wall.

A skeletal stainless steel table in the middle of a surgical suite, standing beneath a darkened lamp.

But creepiest of all was the morgue they discovered in the basement after they had descended a much sturdier flight of stairs. The room retained most of its working components, so it felt as if the staff had just stepped out and would return momentarily. A compartment door stood open, the stainless steel slab with its integrated neck support pulled out, ready to accept the next corpse. Sturdy glass organ jars were clustered on a nearby countertop beside heavy rubber gloves, tossed over the edge as if just removed. An organ scale dangled beside a deep sink, its needle several degrees off plumb as if ghostly flesh lay within its bowl.

But throughout their exploration, Hawk seemed distracted, his attention always focused down the corridor or out the nearest door. Meg was constantly calling him to her side when he wanted to wander away from the group.

"What's up with Hawk?" Webb crouched down beside the autopsy table and gave Hawk's back a good rub. "I've never seen him this distracted. Do you think he's picked up on something?"

"As Chuck said, I think he's smelling a dead rodent somewhere." She held still for a moment, considering her dog. "But his head is definitely not in the game. So why don't we let him show us?"

Webb straightened. "Let him lead the way?"

"Sure, why not? We don't have a set search plan here. We haven't found whatever he smells yet, so he'll only lead us somewhere new."

"That works for me, as long as it's safe," Smaill said. "And you said he'll come if you call him if he gets into trouble."

"Definitely. We're in the basement, so there shouldn't be any gaping holes dropping a story or two. But he's a wizard with voice commands, and on top of that, we have his 'don't mess with me' name."

Smaill glanced at the dog and then back at Meg. "'Don't mess with me'?"

Webb laughed and clapped him on the shoulder. "Don't worry. This is your first foray into canine search-and-rescue. Spend time with Hawk and it'll become second nature."

"That's the name I use when Hawk has to follow my commands with zero hesitation, even if it looks like I'm throwing him straight into the path of danger," Meg said. "Like the time we were doing a search on a railway trestle and got caught near the middle of it with a train coming straight for us. We were closer to the side with the oncoming train, so I ordered him to sprint directly for it." She extended both arms to include herself and Hawk. "As you can see, we both made it. So if I think he's getting into trouble, I say 'Talon' "—Hawk jerked to attention and she laid her hand gently on his head in acknowledgment—"and he'll do whatever I say."

"Handy. I wish we could train our candidates at the house like that."

"Amen to that," Webb said with a grin.

Meg knelt down next to Hawk. "Hawk, something's got your attention. Find it."

Hawk's ears perked up and his head tilted at her.

"He's a little confused because he's not in his work vest," Meg explained to the men. "But he doesn't need it here. Come on, Hawk, we'll follow you. Find it."

Hawk turned and trotted through the open doorway melting into the darkness beyond.